A GIRL CALLED MARIA

RICK LEE

First published 2024

Copyright © Rick Lee 2024

The right of Rick Lee to be identified as the author of this work has been asserted by his accordance with the Copyright, Designs and Patents Act 1988.

All rights reserved. This book is sold subject to the condition that no part of this book is to be reproduced, in any shape or form. Or by way of trade, stored in a retrieval system or transmitted in any form or by any means, electronic, mechanical, photocopying, recording, be lent, resold, hired out, or be circulated in any form of binding or cover other than that in which it is published and without a similar condition, including this condition, being imposed on the subsequent purchaser, without prior permission of the copyright holder.

Author/publisher disclaimer:
This book is a work of fiction. Names, characters and incidents are the product of the author's imagination. Any resemblance to actual persons, living or dead, or events, are entirely accidental.

Many of the places are real, but are only used as backdrops.

The historical content is mostly real, but conjectures of unknown events and people are the author's.

ISBN: ?????

Also by Rick Lee

A MAN IN FLAMES
DAUGHTER OF THE ROSE
A RIPPLE OF LIES
SOME DANCE TO FORGET
THE RAIN IT NEVER STOPS
VOICES IN THE DARKNESS
THOSE WHO CANNOT DIE
BLACKTHORNS OF THEIR OWN
ONLY THE LIES WILL HAUNT US
A RAIN OF BLOOD
A PRICK OF CONSCIENCE

The author has his own website.

www.rickleewriter.co.uk

CAST LIST

As many of the characters in this story are regular 'suspects' in my books, I have included this 'cast list' with mini biographies.

You will see they're getting older like me!

Ex-DI Mick Fletcher – a Londoner who spent his detective days being moved from one northern force to another despite his clear up rate.

Louisa Cunninghame – arrogant rich Borders widow who eventually agreed to allow Fletcher to be her companion.

Tomasz Steil – ex-army long distance marksman now discharged.

Imelda – his tattooed Hebridean lover.

DI Magda Steil – his detective sister.

Helena Steil – their Polish mother.

Sigismund 'Ziggy' Hook – private detective/computer expert.

Ex-DS Janet Becket – Fletcher's DS now retired, but still angry.

Ursula Robinson – daughter of serial killer Fern in 'Daughter of the Rose'

Eleanora (Ellie) de Camville – Fletcher's 'adopted' granddaughter & amateur sleuth.

AND

A GAGGLE OF GHOSTS WHO WON'T LIE STILL

Serial killer Fern Robinson first introduced in 'Daughter of the Rose'.

is now reduced to the fading image of an inquisitive hare.

Carol Morgan first introduced in 'Some Dance to Forget' is still stalking about as a raven with a bejewelled badge over one eye.

Anna Kerr Fern's friend now a shadow of a small dog

SUNDAY FEBRUARY 24 2022

CHAPTER ONE

'Where are the kids?'

No reply.

Wilma puts the shopping onto the kitchen table and goes through to the front room.

Her mother is watching the TV. Sound deafening as usual.

She picks up the remote and brings it down to bearable, which gets her the Medusa glare, but long lost its power on her.

She asks again.

Her mother gives her a teenage pout.

'How should I know?'

'Didn't they say?'

Medusa gives her another glare.

Wilma sighs and goes back to sort the shopping.

Pete arrives carrying another box and adds it to the pile, then pulls out a beer, before heading for the verandah.

She follows him out.

He settles onto the couch with the paper.

She looks out at the 'view'.

This is what they were seduced by, although now they would admit it's the only good thing. The advert didn't tell them about the twenty steps uphill from the road or that the heating system must have been installed in the last century or that the TV only worked if you suspended it from the ceiling or that it could only get terrestrial.

'They'll be alright,' mutters Pete.

Wilma shrugs. As if he cared.

She goes back to the kitchen and has nearly finished putting things away when the door bursts open.

'Mum,' says Janey. 'We've found some bodies!'
Wilma shakes her head.
'Oh yeh, how many?'
'Seven!'
She turns to look at her daughter.
'What?'
But then she sees the cobweb dangling from her hair.

PC Holman and PC Robson arrive half an hour later by which time Pete is on his second whisky. He's still shaking and jabbering on about 'the eyes'.
'What do you mean, sir,' asks Holman.
Pete stares at him.
'You go and look for yourself.'
Holman looks at Robson, who pulls a face saying: 'it's your call'.
'Which is the house we're talking about?'
Pete shakes his head again.
'It's up the top of the lane, the last house, but the gates are locked so you'll have to go in through the hole in the fence.'
Holman now looks at the girl, who's stopped crying for a moment.
'You can't take her,' says the mother.

Outside, Holman calls Sergeant Kirk and tries to explain.
'I can't spare anyone else; you'll have to go and recce the site.'
Holman ends the call and shrugs at Robson.

The mother won't let the girl show them the way, so they drive up and park at the gate.
No chance of climbing over it with that roll of barbed wire along the top, so they scramble through the bushes to the hole in the fence the kids had found.
Even then it's not easy, as it's only kid sized.
'You'll have to climb over,' says Robson.
He gives her a shrug.

'You're the bloody climber.'

In the event he decides to give the fence a big shove and it collapses inwards. The two of them scramble over, struggle through the brambles and find their way to the house.

Again, they have trouble getting through the window, which the girl had told them about. Alright for skinny primary kids, but not good for cops living on petrol station sandwiches and too much chocolate.

Even with their torches it's difficult to see where they're going, given the amount of rubbish in the way, mainly stacks of newspapers, boxes and old furniture blocking every hallway and filling every room they pass.

The room they've been told about is on the first floor, which means clambering over everything on the staircase.

So, they're breathing hard when they get to the room, where the kids said they'd found the 'statues'.

Both of them have seen dead bodies before. Traffic accidents and drug deaths, but neither of them is prepared for what's in this room.

The light from the windows silhouettes the figures who are arranged as if for a photograph. Four of them seated and two standing behind.

As their eyes adjust, they can see that they're all dressed in white. Three girls, one boy in the middle, with two adults behind. One empty chair on the left.

The silence is deafening.

Robson is stunned. They're so real. If one of them had smiled and said 'hello', she wouldn't have been surprised.

Holman rubs his eyes.

Is this some horrible prank?

Neither of them has been to Madame Tussauds, but that's the connection they both make.

'This is sick,' mutters Holman.

'They must be dolls,' whispers Robson.

'More likely shop dummies,' says Holman, trying to show he's not scared.

Jane Robson can't believe afterwards what she did next, but she steps forward and reaches out to touch the face of the seated figure on the right.

She flinches.

Ken looks at her.

She starts the shake.

'It's not a dummy,' she says. 'She's cold . . . but . . . it feels like skin.'

The girl was right.

Seven bodies.

In one room.

All arranged like a photograph.

Or in a shop window.

It's only then that Ken clocks the body behind the chair over to the left. It's not another dummy, nor is it dressed in white, but it was alive not long ago before someone shot him, blood all over and the weapon on the floor.

*   *   *

URSULA

We didn't know anything about Freya's family.

She'd never talked about them, although that wasn't surprising as she never revealed anything about herself.

As it turns out there's quite a lot of them. A brother, two sisters and their partners, an elderly aunt and an assorted brood of teenagers.

I'm not good with children. The thought of having any of my own never even crossed my mind.

I suppose being the daughter of a serial killer makes you think you might pass on the genes, but actually I've never had the slightest temptation as far as a male partner is concerned. To be honest I prefer the company of women. Although, ironically, the most constant companion for the last three years has been a 'man' who has 'gender issues', which can be diagnosed by the weird feminine outfits he comes up with every single day.

Today, he's toned it down: black suit, white shirt and black tie, although the rouge on his cheeks is too much, so he looks a bit like one of those figures on a wedding cake.

We're a strange couple. For a long time, home was in Preston, but that was when I thought I was an accountant called Rachel Henderson, until it turned out my real name is Ursula White. My mother Fern is – or was – a Robinson … and she was suspected of killing at least five women and three men. She was known as the Snow White Killer.

I know…

Old news now, but back in the eighties she was famous.

We've been holed up in a cottage on the banks of Tweed throughout the lockdowns, where Ziggy, aka Sigismund Hook, has been monitoring the local criminal activities via a selection of computers and other wizardry. This has necessarily got us into contact with the local constabulary, including DI Magda Steil and her family. Her mother is a scary old Polish lady, called Helena, and her brother Tomasz is a highly decorated army sharpshooter. They're all standing together, although I then realise the woman who generally accompanies Tomasz is missing. Wouldn't be the best look at funerals, actually, as she's a bit of a nightmare, half her head shaved, the other half brassy yellow hair and then all the dragons and snakes crawling up her neck, down her arms and creeping out from under her skirts. I think she's called Imelda.

The only other person to mention is standing by herself looking down at the ground. Ex-DS Janet Becket. A closed book. Containing a long list of bad experiences, but far worse for the people who have crossed her. Most of them dead or in prison now.

Oh, I nearly forgot, because they're standing behind me. Ex-DI Mick Fletcher and, I think we can regard them as a couple now, Louisa Cunninghame, another scary lady, with the coldest blue eyes.

The family wanted to have the funeral back in Surrey, but Freya had made a will and it stated very clearly that she wanted her ashes to be thrown into the Tweed where she drowned herself.

So here we are.

And, embarrassingly, she's also said she wants me to do it.

Throw her ashes into the river.

The family have brought them in a large vase, or should I call it an urn?

I'm standing at the edge, holding it awkwardly, surprised by its weight and desperately trying not to drop it.

The priest they've arranged to do the ceremony is shouting the mawkish prayer they wanted to be said, trying to make himself heard above the torrent of water, which the river has this morning decided to contribute to the occasion.

I've got my eyes shut, hoping it's not much longer.

Is that him finished?

I squint my eyes open.

To see right across from me the hare on the far bank. Staring back at me with his amber eyes.

I swear he's smiling.

I realise people are tense around me, waiting for me to do the deed.

With one lunge I throw the whole thing into the water.

It hits a rock and smashes into a hundred pieces, the ashes disappearing instantly into the rushing waves.

I stare in shock at what I've done.

I daren't look at anyone.

But the hare is still there, his eyes blazing, smiling, grinning . . . disappearing, like the Cheshire cat, until only his eyes flash one last time and then she's gone.

Did that really just happen?

The only sound is the river.

There's a hand on my arm.

It's Janet.

She folds me in her arms.

I let her. Feeling the iron hard muscles holding me.

I don't remember going back to the cottage.

It's dark when I think I shouldn't be lying on my bed any longer.

So, I get up and wash my face at the sink.

It's quiet, but somehow, I know people are there.

I go out and make my way to the sitting room.

There's Janet and Ziggy, sitting like two old gimmers, glasses of wine and cake.

She gets up and comes and gives me a hug.

Now I'm sitting with a glass as well and we're all laughing, tears streaming down our faces.

'That's the best funeral I've ever been to,' says Janet, rubbing her eyes. 'Did you see their faces?'

I shake my head, but I'm thinking does it mean I'll never see that hare again.

* * *

Later that afternoon after the funeral Magda goes for a ride.

Three days into the first decent break she's had for nearly two years. There didn't seem to be any point taking leave when you couldn't go anywhere and, in any case, it had been quite eventful, considering people weren't supposed to be doing very much.

She encourages Hector up the slope. He's out of sorts for some reason. Probably feeling puzzled by this sudden need for urgency.

The day has been promising sunshine all morning but the mist in the valley still hasn't blown away, so she's decided to head up to the top farm and then onto the tops.

She didn't see the dogs until they were all around her, barking and jumping at Hector.

At first, he stops, probably bewildered, rather than frightened, because he's well used to Hengist making a fuss. But then one of dogs makes a lunge at his leg.

The next few seconds are a whirl of whinnying and kicking and then Magda is thrown off and falls under his flailing legs.

The shock kept her conscious for a few moments as she saw him rearing above her and then everything went black.

When she came round all she could hear was barking and whinnying in the distance.

The first movement she made caused her to blackout again.

The next time some voice in her head told her to be still.

She lay there looking up at the blue sky.

Where was she?

The last thing she remembers is a dog licking her hand.

*   *   *

DI Oswald Walker is standing on a beach.

DS Gill has gone back to Edinburgh on the train.

He declined accompanying her.

It isn't a beach he knows. He just needed to clear his head.

Why is it the sound and vision of waves pounding on an empty beach calms him?

There's only one other person in the distance throwing sticks for a collie dog.

The murder of the old man in that cluttered basement flat on Carlton Hill is resolved, in that they know the man who killed him, but he's dead as well now, in the most puzzling of ways. He didn't need an autopsy to confirm what had killed him. The burnt corpse was terrifyingly clear. His other victims' relatives wouldn't be shedding any tears.

The kidnapped girl has been restored to her family, although her father has received some strong words about taking the law into his own hands. Various other members of the gang have also died or disappeared in strange ways. One girl drowned, one man found half out of an old grave, like he was struggling to get out . . . or in . . . and two younger men nowhere to be found.

Stranger than fiction?

He shakes his head and looks along the beach. The woman and her dog have disappeared.

The waves seem to be retreating.

He stands watching the gulls swooping and floating in the wind.

His phone rumbles in his jacket.

He backs away from the wet sand and pulls it out.

Listens to the angry voice.

What?

She did what?

A long diatribe, to which he has no significant answer before he promises to 'get his arse back asap'.

The call ends and he looks out at the sea retreating away from him.

With a sigh, he sets off back to the car.

* * *

Fletcher is sitting in the car on Louisa's drive. She stayed with him for a while as they both contemplated the swathes of snowdrops now littering the borders. At her age she'd been to more and more funerals in the last few years, each one another nail in the coffin of her own life expectancy.

But then her natural resilience snaps her back to the present and she gathers her things, gives him a peck on the cheek and gets out of the car. Something told her to leave him there, rather than chivvy him out. It wasn't because he was older than her, in fact he's two years younger, but she knew he didn't want conversation or any homilies about getting older.

Still, looking back at him as she closed the door gave her heart a twitch.

She told herself to buckle up and sort something for dinner as they'd declined the cold meats. Something to do with the twitchiness of Freya's family, awkward southerners wishing they hadn't come to this cold and windy desolation.

It seems to have been the best decision, as here he comes looking a bit sheepish, probably feeling uncomfortable in one of John's old suits. Did he really not have any of his own?

'Sorry,' he mutters, 'getting mawkish in my old age.'

Louisa gives him her iciest stare.

'Don't you dare use that language in my presence . . . 'mawkish', indeed, I won't have any Dickensian tosh like that.'

He stares at her for a few seconds and then they both burst out laughing.

Later she deigns to accompany him on his walk along the river. Is that a first? He can't recall her ever doing it before.

'So, where's this heron you keep wittering on about?' she asks.

He stops and looks up and down the long stretch which he shares with the bird.

He rejects the first response, that Louisa might be responsible for its absence like a long-suffering wife not wanting to see the latest floozie he's taken up with, but then is saved by its appearance.

Not as if it seems bothered either way as it flaps twice, before gliding imperiously to its favourite spot by the beached log downstream of them.

They both stand watching. He as bewitched as ever by her grace and stillness, whilst Louisa's wondering whether she should tell him that it's her heron not his.

The moment lasts for ever.

Until the heron launches herself into the air, another two flaps and she's sailing off towards her next stop, finally disappearing round the bend.

The two figures remain still. A few feet apart.

Until he reaches out to her with his hand, and she takes it.

They embrace.

The river thunders on.

Other birds flutter hither and thither. Not yet gathering twigs, still just finding enough to stay alive.

The late afternoon sun falls behind the trees.

Back at the house, no words said, she's pottering about in the kitchen, absentmindedly preparing something to eat.

Fletcher is standing in the doorway of the library, now denuded of his granddaughter Ellie's overflowing detritus of books and scattered notes, no scrumpled throw-aways on the carpet, which makes him feel even more lost. Abandoned.

She and her friend, Mali, are now back at university in Edinburgh, managing to go to actual lectures again after the two years of online tuition.

He goes to the window and reflects on the latest adventures she's dragged him into. The terrible events at Dryburgh Abbey where she witnessed three horrible murders after being kidnapped and bundled into a car boot.

He turns away. Shuts the door. Walks back to the kitchen.

Louisa turns to look at him.

They embrace.

And . . . so to bed.

Later having found solace in their aging bodies, they're eating a meal, more ravenously than they should be doing for septuagenarians, when the phone rings . . . that is, the house phone.

There are a few seconds when neither of them can think where it lives anymore, as even they have now become used to black faced mobiles vibrating and chirruping wherever they've abandoned them.

Figuring it out, Louisa goes over to the side table and picks it up.

Fletcher listens to her end of the conversation.

After 'hellos' and 'how are you', she listens without interrupting, excepting to say 'oh, no,' and 'is she alright?' and 'thank goodness', before a long pause and then 'anything we can do, let us know' and 'goodbye'.

He waits, fearing the worst. Ellie? Her mother?

She comes back to the table.

'It's Magda. She's been thrown off her horse. Broken leg and rib injuries, but not life threatening.'

Fletcher has always been afraid of horses. As a young constable he was at the Grosvenor Square disaster and witnessed the terrible carnage wrecked by the mounted officers. An event that turned his heart against senior officers and their unwavering subservience to political leaders of whatever hue.

He shakes his head not wanting those images to return.

Louisa sighs.

The two of them sit there in silence.

The absence of the two young things making their solitude more unbearable.

Later in bed, lying quietly, neither of them wanting to read or talk, but each of them wishing the other would begin a conversation, they can hear the wind . . . and now the rain.

Until Fletcher can hear her steady breathing and realises, she's fallen asleep.

What was that homily his sister used to quote?

'You can sleep easy, if you've nothing on your conscience . . . or you've no conscience at all.'

Not a conundrum to get you to sleep in itself, but eventually he succumbs.

* * *

In a small fishing village like St Abbs, the arrival of the police and a SOCO squad is a once in a lifetime activity.

Along with a scattering of early season visitors the crowd grows at the end of the lane leading up to the old house on the cliff edge.

The locals have always given it a wide berth and only three or four people ever noticing the slight figure who occasionally visited or seen the series of vans that he had used over the last couple of years. The local kids frightened themselves with stories of a woman in white and savage dogs barking anytime they went near, although they're long gone, just their ghosts whispering in the undergrowth.

The scene they met on the first floor was something even none of these hard-bitten professionals have ever seen before. The many previous suicides or gang land shootings not a patch on this hospital morgue scene they'd only ever seen in laughable horror films. Every one of them relieved to realise they are waxwork figures, carefully composed into a photographer's pose.

Not immediately clear what's keeping them upright.

A family? Three girls. One boy. Mother and father behind? All dressed in white. The father in uniform. Medals and a silver star. One empty chair on the left.

It's one of the older guys who eventually announces that he knows who they are or meant to look like.

'It's the Russian Royal family,' he announces quietly.

The others stare at him.

The youngest frown, did the Russians even have a royal family?

'Nineteen nineteen, I think,' he offers, 'all killed during the Revolution . . . although I think one of them, Anastasia, might have survived.'

They are all still, silently trying to make sense of what is in front of them. One or two of them frowning at the empty chair.

'So, who's the more recent victim,' comes a voice.

They turn to look at who is speaking.

A black man, wearing a long coat like someone from a Sergio Leone western.

*   *   *

MARIA

Irena dumped her father's car in Edinburgh.

A shame, because it was very new and very fast, especially with her at the wheel.

Cams was sulking, didn't even get a chance to drive it.

Maria just stares out of the window.

Did that really happen?

Dr Kenneth McKinley 28/02/22

For the record I want to try to explain what caused me to fulfil the task I set myself.

Obsession? I know what it means, I'm a pathologist, but I looked it up.

'The control of one's thoughts by a continuous, powerful idea or feeling, or the idea or feeling itself.'

Sounds about right.

'People who are distressed by recurring, unwanted, and uncontrollable thoughts or who feel driven to repeat specific behaviours may have obsessive-compulsive disorder (OCD). The thoughts and behaviours that characterize OCD can interfere with daily life, but treatment can help people manage their symptoms.'

'Obsessive, compulsive disorder'?

Obsessive, perhaps, but only about one thing, which I think has ended now.

Compulsive? Well once I set about the task, it did become 'irresistibly interesting or exciting; compelling.' although I'm not so sure about 'exciting' – 'terrifying' would be more precise.

'Disorder'? Absolutely NOT! The task was the restoration of order.

So, when did this all start?

I'd always known my grandmother was an unusual person, but it was only when my mother died that I found the letters and the other documents. That was back in 2007.

I also knew that she was Russian and that she had escaped from the Bolsheviks because her family were rich aristocrats, although she arrived penniless in Edinburgh in the early twenties.

She always refused to talk about the war, or what she did before she met my grandfather, saying it was too distressing and miserable. I asked my mother, but she just told me to let the dead keep their secrets.

I do know that she met my grandfather John Wallace in Edinburgh and married him in nineteen thirty-three. He was a doctor, and she had a market stall. He died in the Second World War; his body never found. No grave. She never said much about him, even to my mother. The only thing she told me was that 'sometimes the truth should be kept hidden', which was a mystery to me.

I had to wait until my mother died to find out why she believed that.

CHAPTER TWO

Walker has become used to things like this happening to him.

His rather scary Tata told him it meant the ghosts of his ancestors were looking after him . . . wherever he went.

One minute he was walking to his car having been summoned back to Edinburgh to sort out what DS Gill had done to DS McAlister and then another call telling him to stay where he was and continue helping out in the Borders, as DS Steil would be out of the action for the foreseeable, following a horse-riding 'incident' and no-one ready to step into her shoes locally.

Gill herself is being sent back to be with him pending disciplinary procedures. No other explanations forthcoming.

And now the next morning he's standing looking at this bizarre exhibition.

'Exhibition', in that the only other 'display' he's seen anything like it is in photographs of Madame Tussauds.

The local DS is on the phone trying to find some relevant expert help before they start moving anything.

The SOCO team have got over the shock yesterday afternoon and are now investigating the rest of the rooms in this weird house. Half Madame Tussaud's and half hoarder's residence.

Their most significant other discovery so far is the room which looks like a cross between a backstage costume and make-up department kitted out with sewing machines, a washing machine and dryer, but most intriguingly a table with odd looking equipment, which turns out to be face modelling kit.

Another PC has found a stash of history books all about the Romanoffs and their terrible demise. Some of them in Russian. Walker has asked him to find someone who might be able to give them more information and confirm the historical 'identities' of the figures in the still life assembly.

But now they're struggling to find out anything about the author of all this nightmare.

No letters. No phone. No electricity.

A younger member of the SOCO team comes up to him.
'There's nothing on the dead man, sir.'
Walker stares at her.
She shrugs.
'No wallet, no cards, nothing, sir.'
Walker frowns.
'Is there a car?'
She nods.
'They're in the garage now, sir.'
He nods and makes his way outside.

It's still early and the sun hasn't got high enough to penetrate into the overgrown garden yet.

He follows a faint track, which the young woman indicated to him.

The garage is big enough for the two camper vans stashed inside it. The newer one is a more modern version of the other, suggesting someone who doesn't like change very much.

Here, at least, there might be some information about the owner.

He calls the local station and asks them to find the owner's details.

Why two vans?

He goes back inside the house.

Someone with initiative has called one of the big department stores in Edinburgh and asked for some information about shop window models, but it seems you can just buy them on the internet like anything else.

Walker looks at him wondering whether that's an expression of defeat, but the man is just staring at the bodies.

Before he can ask anything else he's aware that the others are looking beyond him, so he turns to see who else has arrived.

It's DS Kyne Gill, looking a bit white faced, although he doubts that's shock.

She nods at him and comes to stand beside him.
'You OK?' he asks.
'Better than these guys,' she murmurs.
Walker can't stop a smile.

He indicates they go elsewhere, so they go back downstairs and out into the sunshine.

'Do you want to tell me what happened?' he asks.

She shrugs and looks away.

He waits.

Without looking at him, she clears her throat.

'McAlister was waiting for me outside the loo, one of the other guys with him.'

Now she looks at him.

'He pushed me against the wall, puts his hand on my tit . . .'

Again, she waits till their eyes lock.

'I told him not to do that . . . he persisted . . . I stopped it.'

Walker waits, he was told about the injuries.

'Karate?'

She shrugs.

'This and that.'

He waits. Both full eye contact.

'Remind me of that if I forget . . .' he says, with a smile.

Her eyes are hard, but eventually she grins back.

She looks away.

'What's gone on here?' she asks.

He shrugs.

'What do you know about waxworks?'

'Enough to know you'd have to be well trained to do it like that . . . so we should check that out.'

He nods, but before he can say anything else the pathologist arrives.

'You got a minute,' he asks.

Walker nods.

They go back upstairs.

It takes quite some time, but eventually he summarises it by saying: 'What's certain is that this person is an expert in waxwork, someone who's done the training. But what's really interesting is that this didn't happen all at that same time, in fact the oldest one might be fifteen years ago, even longer, while the most recent was probably only a few weeks since.'

Walker stares at him.

'Fifteen years?'

'Yes, different techniques, different chemical mixes . . . it's like a masterclass in the recent history of the profession . . . and he must have had access to a freezer.'

The two detectives glance at each other.

'How many people could have done this?'

The man shrugs.

'Very few . . . it's not as if it's an evening class activity.'

Walker looks away.

'Could he be the dead body?'

'Possibly, but his face is a mess. There's no identification. Waiting for fingerprints.'

Walker shakes his head, having seen what had happened to the man's face. Whoever killed him didn't bother to ask him to take his glasses off before they shot him.

'It's possible he could have killed himself,' says the doctor, as he kneels down to the body again.

Walker frowns, thinking 'so where's the gun'?

'I know, there's no gun, so someone could have taken it afterwards.'

'But he didn't take his glasses off?' says Walker.

The doctor shakes his head.

'Look at his hand, definite powder smuts.'

Walker glances at the man's hand which seems to have been thrown carelessly away, but he can see the black marks now.

'Could he have . . ?'

A shrug.

The doctor starts to pack away his things.

'Where would we find a list of . . . 'wax-workers'?

The man shakes his head.

'I don't know of anywhere in Edinburgh . . . although now I think about it, I can remember going to one near St Giles when I was a kid.'

He fingers his phone and then shows Walker a newspaper article. It closed down in 1989.

Walker frowns at him again, but now he's wondering whether someone will be able to tell him what sort of gun.

The man gives him a sad smile.

'I don't think that made me more determined to be a pathologist. To be honest I find them scarier than real dead bodies.'

* * *

Tomasz hates hospitals.

On the two occasions he's been in one, he got out as soon as he could walk. Once when he was thrown from a horse himself when he was in his late teens and the other time in Iraq, which he didn't want to think about.

The horse wasn't Hengist, it was his friend Kenny's piebald, Domino. Mad as a hatter and as wild as the wind. He heard afterwards that they were thinking of destroying him and was outraged about that. It wasn't the horse's fault; it was Kenny taking him through the field with cattle in it. Anyway, he stopped the execution, only to find out he died a few months later when he was back in action.

The horse in Iraq belonged to a tribal chief. He'd never seen anything so beautiful and persuaded the man to let him ride her. The man had laughing eyes and said he could, but he only lasted a few minutes before waking up in the field hospital a few hours later. It was only a few weeks afterwards he heard both man and horse had been killed in a raid.

And then there is the business of having to sit in a waiting room. Another thing he doesn't do.

Eventually just when he thought he would go mad, a nurse beckoned him through.

He's never really thought about how his sister looked. Whether she was attractive? Even when she'd hooked up with Amelia, it hadn't shocked him or made him wonder how that happened. It just seemed right. They were good together.

But she didn't look good right now.

Bandaged head covering one eye, only a few dark hairs straying out on to the pillow.

The one eye opens, and the immediate frown is replaced by an embarrassed smile.

He holds her hand.

No words.

He'd let Amelia and his mother see her the first time, only two people allowed.

'How are you?' he asks, immediately feeling how trite that feels.

Magda grunts.

'Been *metter*,' is all she can manage.

Neither of them can say much more.

'Is he okay?' she asks.

He nods.

'A bit jittery this morning. He's in the garden field, keeps coming to the wall.'

She manages a smile, but then a tear creeps out from the bandage.

'You wouldn't . . .'

His eyes grow fierce.

'Never . . . you know that.'

He stays for the full half hour the nurse allows, but mostly she just dozes. They've said that's the concussion, but the scans are okay.

Eventually he squeezes her hand and stands to go.

It's only when he gets to the door, her voice follows him.

'I think it's a message,' she whispers.

He turns, but her eyes are shut.

He frowns but the nurse shakes her head.

'She needs to rest, she won't even remember what she means by that, so don't worry.'

But it does worry him.

*   *   *

URSULA

The thing about Sigismund Hook is that he has different antennae than most people.

This is partly because he's 'hooked' into the ethereal domains of the 'world wide web' most of the time, but also because he likes to have fingers in every pie.

So, it's no surprise that he's aware of the bizarre findings in St Abbs before its anywhere near the local news, never mind the national awareness, because he's constantly reviewing the local stuff, which he says is because the Scottish Borders have a particular historical susceptance to 'weird' goings on . . . and by the way, he says it's 'wyrd', not just the sanitised modern version . . . 'wyrd' being an old word to do with Druids and such like.

So, the first thing he tells Janet and me is when we're having breakfast.

'Listen to this,' he says. 'Six waxwork bodies positioned like for a family photograph, all dressed in old-fashioned clothes, found in a house in St Abbs yesterday.'

Janet and I exchange looks.

It's only yesterday that I 'dropped' Freya's ashes into the river. He can't be wanting to get us into another 'adventure' straightaway? But Janet is easily reeled in, even though she's always saying she's retired now, doesn't want to know, can't be bothered, etcetera.

'Where's that?' I ask.

She asks 'six?'

Ziggy points at the printer, which is burbling to itself as it produces a photo.

I know my place and go to collect it.

A quick glance confirms it's a family gathering, all in white, probably someone's birthday.

I hand it to Janet, who looks and then frowns.

'Where have I seen that before?' she murmurs.

Ziggy raises his eyebrows. Always something to get people staring, given that his make-up is often weird as well. Today's no exception. A bit clown like. Another version of what he wore at the funeral. White pasty background, dark red lips and rouge on his cheeks. This complemented by the old black suit, black bow tie and a rather grey-white shirt.

'Russian royal family, not long before they were all bumped off. Seventeenth of July, nineteen seventeen.'

I stare at them.

They don't look worried. The four girls are all smiling, dad and mum looking a bit clueless, which might be why they didn't survive.

'Waxworks?' asks Janet.

'Professionally, apparently, so they're looking for someone who would be able to do that.'

'You mean like Madame Tussauds?'

Ziggy pulls up another screen.

'This is the one which used to be in Edinburgh. It closed down years ago.'

I can't stop myself thinking of Mrs Henderson, my 'not-mother'. I didn't actually see her dead. It was offered, but I declined. She was scary enough alive.

'But, hey,' says Ziggy with a smirk on his face, 'look at this . . .'

It takes me some time to figure it out, because it's a wobbly handheld camera, which takes you across a cobbled farmyard to what looks like a cow shed. Inside it's suitably low lighting and this makes the figures really spooky.

The camera staggers here and there like the person is drunk, but then it focuses on a woman. White headdress, looking completely disinterested. Mary, Queen of Scots, Ziggy confirms.

But then he frowns.

'But there should be seven,' he mutters.

*   *   *

Louisa puts the phone down.

Fletcher gives her an enquiring look.

Louisa goes to the sideboard and finds the open bottle of wine.

Without asking she pours them both another large drink, before coming back to sit opposite him.

'She'll be alright, although a blow to the head is always worrying.'

Fletcher nods.

'What happened?'

'Dogs apparently.'

Fletcher winces. Never been fond of the creatures. What was the name of that fat bloke near Penrith? Bloody Alsatians? No, something bigger.

'So, still in hospital?'

Louisa nods.

'Aye, and only close family at the moment . . . so, you can relax.'

Fletcher looks away, to hide the relief.

And then the phone rings.

It's Ellie, the favourite granddaughter.

Louisa answers and brings her up to date, although, of course, she's done her own research.

After a few more questions about ongoing course work, Louisa passes the phone to Fletcher and sets off to the kitchen.

'Have you heard?' she asks.

'About Magda?'

'No, the bodies found at St Abbs?'

'What?'

'Ziggy told me.'

'Where's St Abbs?'

'A few miles north of Berwick, by the sea.'

Fletcher tries to think if he has ever been there.

'How many bodies?'

'Seven.'

'Seven?' he exclaims.

'Yeh, apparently six of them are waxworks arranged like in a photograph, while the other one was shot.'

Fletcher can hardly believe what she was saying.

'What do you mean 'arranged'?'

'You know, like a family photograph. Three sisters, one boy and parents standing behind.'

An image flashes through Fletcher's brain.

'Apparently, it's like the famous photograph of the Russian royal family before they were all killed.'

Again, something nags at him.

There's a pause.

'Are you there?' she asks.
'Yeh . . . just thinking.'
'Anyway, it's not my period . . . but I couldn't stop doing a bit of research.'
Fletcher laughs.
'I bet you did.'
'They were all brutally murdered in 1917.'

There's a long pause.

'Miss you,' she says.
'Hey, you, none of that.'
Silence.
'How's Mali?' he asks.
'Oh, she's fine, but she's gone to see her mother.'
'Is she ill?'
'She had a fall, but she's back at home now.'
'Oh dear, did you hear about Magda?'
'Yeh, that sounds terrifying.'

There's another pause.
Louisa comes back into the room with a tray of tea and toast.
'You want to come down tomorrow?'
There's a pause.
'Is that okay with Louisa.'
He looks at her, she nods.
'Of course, are you driving?'
'No, Mali's taken the car, I'll come on the train.'

After a few more words, Fletcher puts the phone down.

Louisa gives him an enquiring look.
'More trouble?'
He explains about Mali's mother and Ellie coming tomorrow, but she can see something else is bothering him.
'Is she alright?'
He shakes his head.

'Yeh . . . but . . . have you heard about these bodies found in somewhere called St Abbs?'

Louisa frowns.

'St Abbs?'

'You know it?'

'Of course, pretty little fishing village north of Eyemouth.'

Fletcher hasn't heard of that either, so he makes a face.

'It's only half an hour away,' she says, 'how many bodies?'

'Seven.'

'What?!'

He nods, but he's elsewhere.

A church? Yes, but abandoned, kids had got in and ransacked the place, although then there was a body. Just sitting there, like it was real, but it wasn't. A dummy like you saw in shop windows.

Louisa waits, fearing the worst. Another adventure?

'What did Ellie say?'

The Russian Royal family! That was it! The dummy was dressed like one of them. White dress. Hair long, back from her face, smiling.

He realises Louisa's staring at him, a frown across her face.

'Are you alright?'

'Yeh . . . blast from the past,' he murmurs.

Louisa shakes her head.

'Chorley,' he whispers.

Louisa frowns.

'No, not in Chorley, Preston?'

'What are you on about?'

'An old church, deconsecrated, ransacked by kids.'

She's staring at him.

'Someone gave us an anonymous tip off. Said there was a body, but when we got there, it was just this shop dummy, dressed up to look like a woman in white. It turned out it resembled one of the Russian family before they all got murdered.'

Louisa shakes her head.

'So, what happened?'

Fletcher shrugs.

'No idea, I got sent to Penrith.'

'Ah . . . to Snow White?'

'Exactly . . .' he breathes.

She waits, but he's miles away, lost in that old battle, which never seems to let him go.

'And Irene,' he murmurs.

Louisa doesn't want him going there, so she pours the tea and then realises it's gone cold . . . and then hears him sobbing.

MARIA

My full name is Elena Maria McKinley, although I've always only answered to Em. I didn't know my second Christian name till I was about fourteen when I needed a passport to go on school trip to Germany.

> **My grandmother was called Elena Mary McKinley.**
>
> **I only met her once when my father took me to see her.**
>
> **It was really scary. I was only six.**
>
> **All I remember was that it was like being in a haunted house. At first, I thought the walls were made of fur or feathers, because they rustled when you walked past them, but then one of the towers of newspapers fell down and you could see the real wallpaper and the big paintings behind them.**
>
> **She was sitting in a big chair in the one room that didn't have any newspapers.**
>
> **A huge white dog got slowly to its feet and growled. I could see it was very old and so I wasn't too frightened and in any case my grandmother reached down with a spindly hand and stroked his neck.**
>
> **My mother wouldn't come with us, but my father said I should meet her.**
>
> **I don't remember much else because we didn't stay very long.**
>
> **We didn't even get a drink or anything to eat.**

My father spent the time talking to her. I didn't really listen and in any case most of it was in a funny language, lots of shushing sounds.

The dog let me stroke him and I think he liked me.

Eventually my father said we had to go because my grandmother was tired.

I gave the dog one more stroke and he licked my hand. When I asked my father afterwards, he said it was called Abortzoy. It was only much later that I found out that was the kind of dog, not its name.

In the car, my father didn't set off immediately and then I realised he was crying.

DR KEN McKINLEY 31st August 2007

It was only when his mother died that he found out about the chateau in France where his mother took his grandmother to be buried. It was deliberate, I'm sure, because it's too much of a coincidence that she should die the same day as her family ninety years before her.

His father ridiculed the whole idea and this was yet another nail in the coffin of their marriage.

And when he did as he promised to take her there, despite having to leave Jennifer at home with Elena, which was the beginning of the end of their relationship.

The journey was uneventful, given that his mother's coffin was in the back of the hired transit van.

It was only when they were through the huge forest of trees between the entrance and the overgrown gardens, that the chateau was visible. He'd seen black and white photographs of it when there must have been an army of gardeners. But they were long gone.

The house was musty and cold.

Going from one room to another felt like more and more deathly.

Not even creepy, just dead.

The funeral director showed him where he proposed to bury his mother, but it was by then no consequence to him. He had thought there might be a grave somewhere, but none they could see.

In the event, it was mercifully done the next day.

No-one came.

He'd tried to sleep in one of the bedrooms, but only managed a couple of hours, finding himself wandering about with a candle, until it got light.

No ghosts.

He just wanted to get back home.

The next afternoon he was driving back. Doesn't remember the journey . . . just the frosty welcome he got back home.

CHAPTER THREE

Walker is puzzled.

Despite their efforts they are struggling to find out anything about the ownership of the house or who was paying the bills. The two vans had deleted plates, probably taken from a scrapyard.

The locals all said that the house had been abandoned for as long as they could remember, but eventually they found a woman in an old people's home in Eyemouth, who had cleaned at the house until the old lady died in 2007.

When she was asked who that was, she just mumbled something about Miss Haversham, which didn't make any sense until one of the older doctors wondered whether that was a Dickensian reference.

This still wasn't much help to any of the other younger investigators, but then he showed them a synopsis of Great Expectations and it did.

So as far as they can gather the house was abandoned fourteen years ago, when the 'old lady' died.

'Big house like that, you'd think someone would want it,' says Gill, fingering her mobile and then shakes her head.

'Look at this.'

Walker peers at the images she's showing him. A large house with extensive lawns and trees.

She flips through the pictures of lots of rooms and then back to the first page which tells you the price is £2.4 million.

'That's just down the road,' she adds and there's plenty more in that bracket.'

Walker frowns.

'So why wasn't this house up for sale?'

Gill shrugs.

'Better to ask the council, I think.'

A quick call isn't much help, because believe it or not the council offices for this seaside outpost are located in Newton St Boswells, forty miles away, not far from the scene of their previous investigations.

Neither Walker nor Gill have much patience with council officers, all intent on covering their backs, rather than being helpful.

But anyway, the initial response is 'no idea – we'll look into it.'

'C'mon' says Walker, 'let's do some old-fashioned policing.'

Gill smirks at the thought of this, but then realises he really means they're going to go house to house!

Which doesn't get them anywhere.

Most of the houses are either holiday homes or people who work elsewhere, many of them in Berwick and a sizeable number in Edinburgh.

Very few can remember ever seeing anyone at the house and those with children have warned them not to go as it's not safe.

'In what way 'not safe'?' asks Gill of the fifth person she meets.

The woman shrugs.

'Well . . . no-one's lived there for years . . . as far as I know. The garden's a jungle.'

Gill waits, something telling her this older woman might remember something else.

She makes a face.

'I wasn't born here, my mum and dad moved here in the nineties. But when I was growing up it was always a scary place. Once or twice, we saw the old lady. She was tall and thin with long white hair. She had dogs. Like huskies, but bigger. If you even walked past the fence, they'd come running to get you. Jumping, barking and throwing themselves at the wire'

She shivers.

'So, the idea of doing a trick or treat was a no-no?' says Gill.

The woman grins and shakes her head.

Gill waits.

'But what happened after the old lady died?'

The woman frowns and shakes her head again.

'I can't remember when that was.'

Gill waits to see if there's anything else.

'But, as far as you know, it's been abandoned for years?'

The woman nods.

Gill looks back along the street to see Walker coming towards her.

She thanks the woman and waits for him.

'Anything?' she asks.

'Nada. Zilch. The haunted house. Etcetera.'

They cross the road and stand looking out at the sea. It looks calm today. Just a few rollers lazily flopping the last few yards to the beach.

'So how can you get electricity and water without paying the bills?'

Walker grins, but then he realises he knows nothing about Gill's background or upbringing.

'Where I grew up in Manchester,' he offers, 'lots of people bypassed the boxes to get electricity, gas and water, what about you?'

She stares at him.

'We had our own generator, water supply and plenty of wood,' she countered, 'I was brought up in an estate cottage.'

'By 'estate' you mean a huge piece of land?'

She nods.

'We didn't own it; my father was a gamekeeper.'

He looks out at the sea.

There's a long pause.

'I can't imagine that,' he says eventually.

Gill looks away.

'I loved it,' she murmurs.

Walker frowns.

'Did you just say 'generator'.

She looks back at him, making the same connection.

'Aye, but back then they were big heavy things . . . now, I think they're the size of a handbag.'

He nods and they set off back.

*   *   *

Tomasz didn't respond to the man, when he'd rung to apologise for what had happened to Magda, he'd just slammed the phone down.

He's known him since they were kids together at Fettes.

Never liked him. An arrogant bully.

Now of course he was a fat, ugly, but very rich, even bigger bully.

Tomasz has driven over to the house with Imelda. She'd insisted on accompanying him when she realised what he was up to. He wasn't happy with that but realised she'd probably stop him from going too far.

Lawrence Kershaw had inherited an estate twice the size of the Steil's and only abutted it for about a mile or so way up on the tops above Walkerburn. The big house was even further away.

Tomasz pulls up outside the main gate, which isn't closed. He sits staring at the ridiculous great coat of arms welded to gold tipped iron gates.

Imelda peers down the drive at the gothic monstrosity, which had been built over two generations ago.

'Nice,' she murmurs.

Tomasz growls.

'Aye, if you're into Harry Potter fantasies. Apparently, he offered it up as a possible site for filming, although they turned him down. Apparently, the woman who went to check it out didn't take kindly to his Victorian attitude towards her.'

Then he turns the landrover in a savage swirl of gravel and charges up the driveway.

By the time they'd gone the quarter of a mile or so up the house, he'd gone cold eyed, which she knew was to be feared.

Inevitably, they were met by dogs. Four of them. Two wolfhounds, a rottweiler and a very excitable Scotch terrier, who, unable to rip their way into the vehicle, ran round and round in circles barking and jumping up at the doors.

Tomasz just sat there, engine still running, eyes blazing straight ahead. Imelda wishes she really hadn't come – just about the worst nightmare she could imagine.

Eventually the dogs give up and revert to attacking each other, before a loud voice tells them to 'come by'. Surprisingly for Imelda, it turns out to be a woman. A big woman, tall and broad chested, dressed for gardening rather than hunting, carrying a pair of large garden shears.

As the dogs quieten down, she comes over to the landrover, with a big smile on her face.

Tomasz's face changes slightly, more smirk than angry.

He winds the window down.

'Clarissa, how lovely to see you,' he sneers.

She comes up close and puts her hand on the window ledge.

'Long time, no see,' she announces, her gravelly voice redolent with cigarette smoke.

Tomasz sighs.

Looking beyond him, she stares at Imelda.

'Ah, and you've brought your dragon lady as well, how charming!'

Imelda stares back at her, unable to avoid the comparison to the rottweilers she so resembles, with the thick rubbery lips and wiry orange hair going white at the roots.

Tomasz gives her another look.

'Where is the fat bastard?'

'Er, you mean my darling husband?'

Tomasz continues to stare.

'Well, I'm sorry to say, you've just missed him. Gone off to the big city, claiming he has to visit the lawyers, but we all know he means the bordellos.'

Tomasz shakes his head.

'Why on earth do you stay with him?' he asks.

She laughs, but it immediately breaks into a hacking cough.

Tomasz looks away, but as she just about composes herself, turns to stare at her again.

'Well . . . tell him to get his dogs to the vets, because I don't think they're looking very well, maybe they've eaten something that doesn't agree with them . . . maybe they'll have to be put down.'

She gathers her breath to reply, but he revs the engine and pulls away in another swirl of gravel, before pulling up in a savage brake sending a wave of stones over the nearest bank of daffodils.

'And you can add that I suggest he doesn't go walking or riding in the open, there's plenty of high hills around here from which a man with the right sort of gun could easily pick him off.'

With that he revs up again and spreads a lot more gravel this way and that as he slaloms down to the gates.

It's nearly two miles down the road before he slows down and pulls up in a lay by. Rests his head on his hands on the wheel and tries to catch his breath.

Imelda waits until his breathing slows before she reaches out to stroke his hair.

Although he flinches at first, he then rests his head on her shoulder and cries like a baby.

*　*　*

URSULA

So as usual Becket and I get sent out on a recce.

I suspect she doesn't mind too much, no matter how much she grumbles about still having to do what's she's told and not even getting any remuneration for it, although the recently acquired brand new Range Rover suggests otherwise.

I'm thinking her friend John might have left her a tidy sum as well as the cottage down by Hadrian's Wall, and his dog, Cuff, although I wouldn't dare ask her . . . and in any case, Ziggy never seems short of cash for the latest gadgetry etcetera. Just me who's the church mouse, not yet taking my pitiful retirement pot or selling up my little terrace house back in Preston. It seems we're still not thinking of going back to our past lives before the pandemic.

So, we're soon roaring our way along the lanes eastwards to the sea.

I guess I'm bit of a landlubber, having hated the compulsory holidays at Southport, not Blackpool obviously, as my mother's *pride would never have allowed us to even think of mixing with the 'hoi-polloi'. And in any case, this is the North Sea not the Irish one. I've no idea what it will be like.*

Nothing like Southport.

No promenade, no 'entertainments', the sea up front and personal, not a thin line in the distance which occasionally limped up with a few tired, lazy waves. Here, it's crashing up over the sea wall.

Having survived Janet's joyful testing of the new vehicle's ability to sweep round the lanes all the way, we slow down through a close walled village called Coldingham and then up and over to St Abbs, where we arrive at the scene of the crime, easily identified by the clogging of police vehicles, a small crowd of gogglers and a couple of TV vans. Instead of joining them, Becket continues on and pulls up in a school yard, except it's now a jolly little café, surprisingly empty of customers apart from a couple with two spaniels sitting outside in the sunshine.

I can't stop myself from giving them both a bit of ear wiggling, whilst Cuff gives them a quick sniff and then ignores them.

Inside we order our lunch and then Becket gets onto her mobile, presumably thinking she'll get more info from Ziggy back at base than trying to get through the scrum outside the house.

*   *   *

Ellie arrives late afternoon.

She puts her bags into what she now considers 'their' room, although that only makes her feel a bit lost as Mali's not here.

Telling herself to 'woman up' she goes to find Fletch.

He's sitting in the conservatory, staring into space. No glass of something to hand. Just alone.

He hasn't heard her coming so she just stands and looks at him.

The hair is grey now, but still all there. The face is lined with wrinkles, and she knows there are those funny marks like freckles on his hands. The way he gets up occasionally makes him wince, but he never complains, always says he'll never go to the doctor's, so she can't help worrying about him.

As if he's aware of this concentration he turns to look.

He smiles and gets up out of the chair.

'You've always been light on your feet, young lady, you'd make a good murderer.'

She laughs.

'No,' she says, laughing, but then thinks that's probably true, so she sighs.

They embrace 'a la francaise', even though Fletcher always finds it awkward.

'So, what d'you know?' he asks.

She shrugs and curls up in the armchair opposite him.

'Nothing much . . . except this strange business at St Abbs.'

'Ah, yes, I might have something to tell you about that.'

'Really?' she demands, her eyes shining.

He tells her about the dummy he found back in Preston.

She frowns.

'Do you think they could be connected?'

He shrugs.

She pulls out her phone and calls Ziggy.

He listens.

'Um, that is weird. Let me check that out.'

He cuts the connection.

Louisa appears at the door, sees the mobile and Fletcher's intent as Ellie puts it down.

'Oh, no, what are you two up to? You've only been together for five minutes.'

The guilty couple can only grin and then both try to look innocent.

An impossibility for either of them.

*   *   *

Back at the house, one of the local team gestures to them.

'Sir, guess what we've found?'

'A portable generator,' says Walker.

The young woman frowns and looks away feeling silly.

'Go on then, where is it?'

She indicates the garage, but then takes them round the back to a smaller shed, where sure enough there's a small green machine next to a stack of empty gasoline containers.

'Um,' says Walker, 'so that's that mystery solved . . . any ideas about where he got the gas from?'

She shrugs.

'Could have been anywhere, sir, there's nothing on them to indicate where he bought them.'

Walker continues to stare at her, as though she's keeping something from him, but then she realises he's looking a long way past her.

'So . . .' he says, not really speaking to her or Gill who's leaning on the door jamb staring out at the overgrown garden.

Whatever it was, he changes his mind and stalks away towards the main gate.

Gill looks at the young policewoman, shrugs her shoulders and follows him.

When she catches up with him, he's standing next to her car.

'Where to?' she asks, wondering where his car is.

'Back to that bigger place over the hill.'

She assumes he means Coldingham, so they both get in and she drives the few minutes to the narrow street.

He points at the entrance to the caravan park, and she pulls in.

He gets out and goes into the shop.

She waits. Not her scene. She was taken once to one north of Dundee. The wind never stopped. The other kids were stupid, and her parents argued all the time. It's then, she makes the connection, where would you get a portable generator from?

Walker reappears, blank look on his face, then shakes his head and walks back to the car.

Driving back over the hill, he tells her to pull into a layby, where you can look out at the sea.

He gets out and stands looking over the hedge.

She waits.

Why here she wonders? There's no evidence that even way back that the family ever made friends or were known by any local folk. So maybe they had something to hide? Who was the white lady with the 'big' huskies? What was the 'Russian' connection?

She pulls out her phone and asks it about the murder of the last Russian Royal family. She's vaguely heard about one of them surviving. Yeh, here it is. Anastasia . . . but then it says the many women who claimed to be her were all fakes, even the one called Anna Anderson. Her body was found much later with her brother. DNA proved it was them. But then it goes on to say that it wasn't her, but her elder sister Maria and that Anastasia's body must have been with the rest of the family.

She shakes her head, then looks again.

'Hang on,' she breathes, 'there's one missing.'

A shadow crosses her and she looks up to see Walker staring at her.

He's been on his phone as well.

'Guess what,' he says.

She frowns, why is he shaking his head?

'I've met him, you have as well.'

She shakes her head, trying to make sense of that, out here?

'It's Doctor McKinley.'

Again, she doesn't make the connection.

'That old guy battered to death in Carlton Hill, he was the pathologist.'

She recalls the dreadful scene. The old man with another unrecognisable head. How weird is that?

'But . . .' is all she can manage.

'Ay,' says Walker, 'but it can't be the same murderer, can it?'

She stares at him.

'Well . . . no . . . but?'
He looks away.
'But there's another thing,' she rasps.
He doesn't seem to hear her.
'There's one missing.'
He turns to her frowning.
'What do you mean? One missing?'
'The girl on the left, she's not there.'
'What?'
She shows him the old photograph again and then flicks it across to the photo she took in the room.
Zooms in to the empty chair.
They both stare at it.
How can they have missed that?
Walker looks at her, his eyes big, 'like the wolf'.
Without another word he sets off.

They go back into the house and up to the room.
The local forensic team is still there, although they're only concentrating on the recent dead body for now, thinking someone more knowledgeable will be required to investigate the waxworks.
But, yes, they'd checked the fingerprints and as his were obviously on record, they were confirmed pretty quickly.
'So . . . what was he doing here?'
She frowns.
'You mean you think he did this?'
He frowns back and then shakes his head.
'Someone else?'
Walker's phone bleeps.
He takes the call, nods at her, walks to the window.
She waits.
Stares at the bodies.
Why would someone, especially a doctor, want to do this?
She shakes her head. She's never understood the idea of waxworks. Why would anyone want to do that? Although a doctor would have a lot of knowledge about bodies.
Walker finishes the call and stares out of the window.

She waits.

'Unbelievable,' he mutters.

'Apparently, he could have retired five years ago, but he persuaded them to let him stay on until he was sixty-five . . . his birthday was yesterday.'

She shakes her head.

Seriously?

And why is one of them missing?

She checks the old photograph again and reads the names on the bottom.

'It's Maria who's missing,' she murmurs.

.

MARIA

Mallaig was what it sounded like: 'Smelly water'. Fortunately, they were just in time for the ferry, although it was a frantic run from the station to the terminal.

'Terminal' as in end of the world.

The sea was rougher than it looked from the start, so we sat down in the passenger cabin, with a noisy crowd of mainly men dressed in full climbing gear like they might have to climb out of the boat.

Apparently, they were set on doing the Cuillin ridge, which has four 'VS climbs', whatever that means.

Anyway, she managed to find a corner and got some sleep.

But it didn't get any better when they got there.

Raining . . . bucketing down.

And then Irena did something she'd never expected from her.

She came over all girly and persuaded a couple of the climbers to give them a lift.

Nauseating.

She just stared out of the window all the time, ignoring any conversation, while Irena wittered on about going to a self-sufficiency camp, which didn't seem to impress the two guys at all.

So eventually they were put down at a junction and had to wait in the rain, until another guy, a local, who knew the camp and said he'd take them to the end of the track . . . which he did, mercifully with hardly a word.

And then they had to walk the last two miles, lugging the rucksacks and bags . . . in the rain.

Irena kept having to stop to wait for her to catch up but didn't say anything.

And when they got there, it was just a huddle of tents and a few sheds.

Not exactly a kibbutz in the sunshine.

The next few hours were a blur of handshakes and hugs and mugs of coffee and spliffs.

So, getting into a tent and lying down was heaven.

DR KEN McKINLEY 17 JULY 2007

My mother died yesterday.

She lived in the house alone for nineteen years, ever since my father died, although she'd stopped having anything to do with him long before that.

I used to visit her, but sadly less and less often.

It became increasingly difficult to talk to her. She'd no interest in talking about what was going on in the world, even though it was obvious she knew very well what was happening, probably more than most people. She didn't only read the English papers, but the French, German and of course the Russian ones as well.

Every time I tried to talk about recent events, she would just shake her head and tell me that I didn't understand and that things would always get worse.

It was a couple of days afterwards I found the photographs and realised who she thought she was . . . and who her mother might have been . . . ?

That's when I decided I had to find out.

CHAPTER FOUR

Gill brings up the articles she's found about the Romanoffs.
'The remains of the last two children were found in 2007. Alexei and Anastasia . . . but then there's some disagreement whether the girl might be Maria. The DNA is degraded'.'
'Degraded?'
Gill shrugs.
'I suppose if they've the same parents, it's like . . . well, it must be similar . . .' she tails off thinking 'what does she know'?
Walker is looking at her, a smile coming onto his face.
He looks away.
The wind is getting stronger. Big clouds gathering behind them, whilst the sea is a dark blue. One ship far out.
'Why did he start doing this after his mother died?'
Gill thinks about when her mother died. She wasn't there, not even in the country. On holiday in Vietnam, didn't get the message until three days later. Her dad told her not to come back, but she still feels bad about it. It changed him. The happy guy now an angry man with a drink problem.
Thinking of this she doesn't realise Walker's set off back. He's nearly at the gate.
She follows on, telling herself she needs to go and see her father when she has some leave.

Inside the house she finds him in the big room looking at the portraits. Are they Russians? Difficult to tell. There's a man with a military costume with a woman in a long white dress. A marriage? They don't look Russian. He's wearing what looks like a British uniform. Who is it?
'Have we even got a name?' he asks.
'Well, yes, McKinley,' she murmurs, thinking that's not much help.
'Yeh, so he'll have a birth certificate and the rest.'
She nods and fingers her phone.

It doesn't take long, but it's easier on her laptop.
He went out of the room while she did this, no idea where he went, although she did think she heard him upstairs, but then he appears at the doorway.
She shows him.

Elena Maria Markovich d1966 m (1931) John Wallace 1900-1944
/
Elena Mary Wallace 1933 - 2007 m (195) Kenneth McKinley 1924 -1988)
/
Kenneth Alexei McKinley 1958-2022 m (m1990) Jennifer Leyton b1964
/
Elena Maria McKinley b 2004 (18)

He stares at it.
'So, the scary old lady with the big dogs was 'Elena Mary Wallace'?'
She nods.
He frowns.
She taps away. Highlights the two 'Elenas' and the 'Maria' and changes 'Mary' to 'Maria'.

'There's no birth date for the first one?' she murmurs.
He shakes his head.
'And we've no idea where the last one is?'

They're both quiet.
Walker gets up and walks round the room, looking at every painting, not knowing what he's looking for. Are the scenes all Scottish? Or is there any hint of Russia? His mind his whirling. Is this something to do with what she said about the mystery around one of the Romanoff's daughters? What was she called? 'Anastasia'?
He goes back to Gill, whose fingers are a blur.
'What have you found?' he asks.
She shrugs.
'There's loads of stuff about the Romanoffs.'
He goes round to look at what she's showing him.

She flicks through the many photos of the family, including the one that's closest to the horror upstairs, which includes the girl who is missing from the waxworks, who she has confirmed was Maria.
'Are you thinking what I'm thinking?' he asks.
She stops and looks up at him.
He points at the family tree.
'Bear with me.'
She nods.
'Would it make sense if McKinley thought that his grandmother was a surviving member of the Russian royal family, that's why he might create what's upstairs.'
She pauses.
'It seems that it's what he's done, but 'makes sense' aren't the right words for him doing it.'
He nods.
'But to be fair, he didn't kill anyone to do it,' she adds.
Walker turns away.
'But why do it?'
She looks back at the laptop.
'And why leave Maria out of the frame?'
The room nestles around them.
They both become aware of a clock ticking.
Walker goes over to it.
It's stuck, somehow, the minute finger trying to get past the hour, whilst the hour hand is at eleven.
    'Hey,' she says.
    He turns to look.
    She holds up her phone.
    He goes to look at it.
    Images of war.
    Is she showing him something that happened back then?
    No, because it's interrupted by a newsreader.
    The Russians have invaded Ukraine.

*　*　*

URSULA

If anyone would be the first to know about the Russian invasion, I'd have put money on Ziggy Hook. I've never really read newspapers or even watched the news on TV, so I'm always the last to hear what's going on.

Except, of course, since I signed up to be his dogsbody.

I didn't know I was going to do that, when I was trying to find my mother. It was just potluck. And in the event, it wasn't the best outcome . . . to find out that she was a serial killer . . . of other women. She became known as the Snow-White Killer. The only time I saw her she was on the top of a burning tower, way up north, but her body's never been found, so . . . she'd be ninety something by now.

It was early morning when I woke up to the sound of explosions.

Disconcerting to say the least, in this sleepy hollow by the river, where we've been consigned since the beginning of the pandemic. Ziggy, Freya, Janet and me.
A more diverse, unlikely quartet you could not imagine.

Although we're now only a trio.

I try to put my head under the pillows, but it's no use. Sounds like he's left the TV on and fallen asleep. Except, of course, there isn't a TV in this cottage, and I doubt you'd get a signal anyway, unless it was way up the hillside next to 'my castle'.

I tumble out of bed and wash my face in the little sink, put my dressing gown on and make my way to the kitchen. Tea a necessity, before facing the next adventure.

I didn't get there.

He's standing in the room he's made his HQ, watching flashing images on a screen. Only in his short Japanese dressing gown, skinny legs and trainers, hair standing up.

I go to look.
It's a war film?
No . . . it's for real.
The Russians have invaded Ukraine.

*   *   *

Imelda has always been an early riser, never needed much sleep anyway. She was born and raised by the sea, which was never quiet.

But this morning she knows she's not the first up.

She can hear the television, which in itself is unusual in this household. Amelia's kids are under strict instructions not to put it on, although she knows they sometimes do without the sound and in any case, they prefer their phones.

She slips away from Tomasz's body, gathers his dressing gown from the floor and tiptoes out onto the landing.

She isn't that surprised to find Helena is the early riser, she generally is the first person up most days. But not watching the television, in fact not someone who watches it at any time.

She's in the 'small' sitting room, which of course in this house is larger than most ordinary house's front room .

She's standing up, an empty cup dangling from her fingers.

Imelda goes to stand beside her.

She's watching a war movie.

No, it's interrupted by a newscaster, who says these images are in eastern Ukraine and that the Russians have advanced on three fronts with airstrikes attacking military targets.

She can't believe it.

She glances at Helena.

Tears streaming down her face.

Without thinking she puts her arm round her, as they stand there staring at the screen.

This is where Tomasz finds them five minutes later.

Now sitting together on the settee.

It takes him another few moments to realise what they're watching and then he gasps.

Unusually the swearwords are in Polish, which make his mother frown, but then she reaches out her hand for him to hold.

Imelda goes to make some coffee.

Tomasz sits with his mother, knowing this will be bringing back the horrors of her childhood, running the streets of Warsaw in the war and then from the Ubeki. No-one knows better the ruthless inhumanity that Russians show to the rest of the world.

The three of them are still there when the first of Amelia's children come running down the stairs, bursting into the room containing the silent grown-ups, one standing white faced, the other two with tears streaming down their faces.

* * *

Ellie comes awake from a dream.

In some ways it's a relief, because it wasn't the usual nightmare with the man charging towards her with his sword in the air.

She quickly figures out where she is.

Louisa's.

Mali? No, that's okay, she's gone to look after her mother.

She listens.

The house is quiet, although it's so big that people could be having a rave at the other end of the building, and she wouldn't be able to hear them.

But then she realises her phone is vibrating.

She picks it up.

Inevitably it's Mali.

But this early?

She reads the message.

What?

She sits up and calls her back.

Five minutes later she goes downstairs to find Louisa in the conservatory standing at the doorway with a cup of coffee in her hand.

She turns to look at her and smiles.

Ellie shakes her head and goes to show her the images on her phone.

Louisa gasps and then they go through to the living room and put on the television.

Which is where Fletcher finds them.

Like the rest of the world, they can't believe that this is happening.

*   *   *

Walker and Gill have gone back to the café, which is now quite busy. The owner has put a TV up in the corner and everyone is watching the images of people trying to escape or army vehicles charging about and explosions in the distance.

There's a huge cry when suddenly a tank just rolls over a car! And then disbelief as the next pictures show the person wasn't killed.

But now Walker takes his coffee outside. Gill follows him.

They sit in the surprisingly warm sunshine, shielded from the breeze, which is a far cry from the battering and rain there's been the last fortnight.

'Show me that family tree again,' he murmurs.

She gets her laptop out and fires it up. Finds the file and turns it so he can see it.

'So . . .' he says. 'Let's just imagine that this is true.'

She frowns.

'You mean that he thinks he's descended from the Russian royal family?'

'Yeh . . . he's dead . . . but he has a daughter.'

She shakes her head.

'You're thinking she's the only surviving descendant?'

They can both hear the sound from the TV inside.

'Does she even know? We don't even know if she's still alive herself?'

Walker looks away.

'What did the pathologist say?'

Gill shrugs.

'He said he couldn't be certain whether the man shot himself or that someone else did it, although the absence of the gun would suggest that it wasn't him.'

Walker shrugs and looks away again, thinking a murderer would have taken the gun anyway.

'But she might not even know her father's dead, might not know what's happened here, or even ever been here.'

Gill shakes her head.

'Where did he live?'

He shrugs, gets out his own phone and calls the Chief.

He gets up and walks to the gateway.

The conversation is long, and he doesn't say a lot to start with, but then gestures to Gill for pen and paper and writes down an address.

He finishes the call and sighs.

Gill waits till he comes back to the table, wondering whether her recent altercation was part of the chat.

He grins at her.

'Not to worry, the daft bastard's fessed up and you're in the clear . . . sort of.'

She frowns.

He shrugs.

'Anyway, we've got McKinley's home address, somewhere called Dunbar, do you know it?'

She nods.

'Half an hour up the coast.'

She was right.

They find the house, not as big as his mother's, but still pretty grand for a pathologist.

No-one in, so Walker effects an entrance, which amuses Gill. Not that she couldn't or wouldn't do the same, but that he didn't hesitate for a second.

Interestingly the house is not unlike the one in St Abbs, although no mountains of newspapers and no statues.

He sends Gill to check out the garage, but it's empty. No evidence of any of the equipment or chemicals that he had at the other house.

The only relevant evidence is the bookcase full of Russian history.

Walker stands looking out of the window at the sea.

'So why do all that?' he whispers, again.

Gill goes to stand next to him.

'Here, I found a phone book. It's got his daughter's number, although there's lots of previous ones crossed out, mainly in London and also one at a university.'

He makes a face.

'Let's try them.'

He rings the latest. Goes straight to messenger. He hesitates, then cuts the call.

Gill nods that she's through to the university, holding as someone tries to connect her. She gets a response. She explains who she is and that they need to contact the young woman.

She listens, frowning, ends the call.

'They haven't seen her for the last two weeks, no explanation given and they were getting worried about her.'

They're stumped.

Walker flops down onto a settee.

*   *   *

Ellie has persuaded Louisa and Fletcher to go to St Abbs.

It's a sunny day for once after all the wind and storms.

Fletcher's driving, Louisa next to him doing the navigating. She always knows the uncrowded routes that inevitably go past lots of huge houses with long perimeter fences and trees hiding the rich owners, who she gives them chapter and verse about.

After the fourth such passage, Fletcher can't stop himself from issuing an outburst of revolutionary expletives.

'Bloody rich, what on earth do they need all this land for. You never see the buggers out in it anyway.'

Louisa shakes her head.

'That's precisely why they need all the land, so that they don't have to see or come in to contact with riff raff like you.'

Fletcher laughs.

'Fair enough.'

He stops the car as they reach the A1, where they have to wait until there's a gap in the army of lorries and fast cars zooming along.

Back on a small lane again they're soon able to catch glimpses of the sea. A blue hazy line with one apparently stationary tanker sitting there like a thin white slug.

It's still there when they come up again the other side of Coldingham.

Five minutes later they're following the signs to a café.

They'd past the big house they'd seen on the television, seeing a much smaller crowd than there was earlier.

Ellie has spent most of the journey researching the Romanoffs and their terrible ending. The irony of an upstart peasant like Putin now behaving like a mad Tsar making her shake her head. But what's the connection with this tiny out of the way place to the Romanoffs? And how can she find out anymore?

Of course, she realises, and sends a text to Ziggy.

The answer is swift. In the form of a family tree.

She shows it to Fletcher and Louisa.

'My, my,' says Louisa, smiling at Fletcher, 'fancy that. I can imagine some of the people you were just ranting about, finding out belatedly they had such exotic royal connections in their own backyard.'

Fletcher shrugs.

'From what we've heard, they were not too keen to be exposed to that.'

Ellie is still puzzled.

'But why here?'

Louisa looks around the half-empty café, at the high windows giving it away that it was a former school room.

'Back of beyond?' she suggests.

'Aye, it used to be,' mutters a voice from the next table.

The three of them turn to look.

A rather thin old lady, a similarly scraggy old sheepdog at her feet.

'Well, it was when I was a kid.'

Ellie smiles at her, which Fletcher knows is a strong part of her interrogation technique, something he had never cultivated or could manage himself, but knowing how effectively she uses it.

'So did you come to this school?' she asks.

The woman grins.

'Aye, this was Ma McGregor's room.'

Ellie waits, the encouraging smile widening.

'Ye'd not be about to ever even try to look oot of the winder if you didn't want to get yerself a thrashing from her stick.'

Ellie laughs, but then her eyes are bright with interest.

'So did you know the people in the big house?'

The woman's eyes narrowed.

'Aye, I ken the old lady and her dogs when I were young. Not even the Cormack boys would dare try to climb the fence. Them hounds were reet scary, especially at night. Sometimes if you walked past, you could nay hear them but then they'd be throwing themselves at the wire and you'd run fer yer life.'

Ellie gives her big eyes to show how scary that sounds.

'So, what about her family?'

The woman frowns.

'We never met them . . . she lived on her own . . . although, I think I saw her son once. Tall and thin like her. I think he was a doctor.'

Ellie waits to see if there's anymore.

The woman is staring into the past.

'Strange, isn't it, now with all this trouble kicking off in Russia . . . makes you wonder why she ended up here . . . maybe to get away from all that?'

Ellie nods, seeing if she makes any other connections.

'Mind you, she wasn't like this weaselly looking man, Pootin, or whatever he's called, she was an old-style aristocrat . . . elegant, tall, always dressed in white . . .'

Ellie waits again.

The woman looks down at the dog, who is lying patiently at her feet.

'C'mon, Tag, time we went home.'

With that, the woman gathers her things and stands up.

Ellie smiles at her.

'Nice to meet you,' she says and bends down to stroke the dog.

The woman smiles back.

'Aye, yer've got the touch alright, he disna let many folk touch him.'

The dog is now licking Ellie's hand.

Louisa and Fletcher glance at each other.

The woman gives them all another smile, but then she frowns.

'Mind you, there was another young lady here the other day, had the same way with her. Blonde hair like you and the same eyes. Could have been your sister.'

Ellie frowns thinking of her own sister, who's nothing like her.

'But that was before all this upheaval. I don't think they should be interfering with the past, all this talk about dead bodies and all that.'

Ellie nods her agreement, but the woman turns away and slowly walks out of the café.

They all realise that the café has gone quiet. Maybe six pairs of eyes all staring them. For a moment it's awkward and then the eyes are averted and conversations restart.

'Amazing,' breathes Fletcher.

'What?' frowns Ellie, but then has to grin.

But that's not the end of her investigation.

She's straight on her phone and finds the Cormacks. Fishermen, although now they seem to have turned one of their quayside buildings into a café. She hustles the two oldies back out into the car and Fletcher drives carefully down the steep winding hill to the little harbour.

As they've just had coffee and cakes, she leaves them to wander out along the sea wall which guards the dock, while she goes into the café.

As usual with her, her luck holds out. There's a grizzled old 'gimmer', as her grandmother would have called him, sitting on a bench in the sunshine. The girl behind the counter says he's her grandfather and for a cake he'll tell her tales all day long.

He turns out he is a Cormack and when she asks him about the house, his eyes light up.

'Ay, lassie, I member well the 'lady in white'. She was well scary! And then there were the dogs. Great shaggy beasts, twice the size of sheepdogs. Their barks were awfie loud and deep.'

He gazes out to sea.

'So, you never climbed over?' she asks.

'Nay, niver. We'd seen what they did to any daft cat that tried it.'

She waits again.

'But have you heard there's been dead bodies found there just now.'

She nods.

'Yes.'

'Aye, well . . . there were allus a scent of death about the place.'

Ellie is intrigued by this odd phrase.

'A scent?'

He stared out at the sea for a few moments as if looking for the explanation written on the horizon. She couldn't see the ship anymore so it must have woken up and slithered away.

'Aye . . . mebbe her perfume. Like you get in church.'

This really puzzles her. She's never been a churchgoer, both her parents being strong atheists.

It's then she realises his eyes are shut, so she stealthily slips away.

Shading her eyes, she can make out the distant figures of Louisa and Fletch and is then astonished to see them come together into a close embrace.

She frowns, having never seen that before, their relationship always seeming to be fractious and argumentative. But surely, it's far too late for them to get married, they're both in their seventies?

Shaking her head, she sets off slowly to tell them what she knows.

* * *

MARIA

Where is she?

Sun coming through the tent.

Is that the sea?

Where's Irena?

She gets half out of the sleeping bag and pulls down the zip.

Skye?

Yeh, there's the Cuillins. The tooth of Am Basteir biting a chunk out of the blue sky.

Irena's sleeping bag wrapped up neatly, but no Irena.

She crawls out of the tent and stands up.

Hummocks of grass everywhere. Not a house in sight.

She can hear the sea, which reminds her of the house and the nightmare.

She goes back in and finds her bag, extracts her phone.

No messages, so she goes online, which she wasn't expecting to get.

At first the images don't make sense, but then she realises it's actual war footage. The Russians have invaded Ukraine.

She's vaguely aware of the previous few weeks build-up, but then she wonders what's happened to her father has any connection to this. If what his research seems to imply, then maybe it might.

But she can't believe she's descended from the Russian royal family. What would . . . how would? She shakes her head. It's unbelievable.

She reads some more.

The Russian President, Putin, seems to be regarded as being deranged, but given the weapons at his disposal that's incredibly scary. Although now his army is getting bogged down by brave resistance. Lots of photos of fires burning and damaged buildings, people fighting to get onto trains, long queues of cars on motorways.

    But then she realises Irena's coming towards her.

    'Are you okay?' she asks.

    'Have you seen what's happened?'

    Irena sighs.

    'Yeh, so it's best you're here.'

Then she comes towards her, puts her arms round her and kisses her.

ELENA MARY
October 1992

It took me some time to get help to read her diaries. I didn't know anyone who I could really trust and although I bought some Russian to English dictionaries, it was still too hard and her handwriting was very old fashioned.

But by chance Maggie told me there was an old sailor who had been injured during a storm and was brought ashore to recuperate while the ship continued on to the Atlantic.

So, she invited him to come and help me.

Fortunately, he was an educated man, who'd travelled the world.

At first, he also struggled with the handwriting which was very small and spidery. He told me that they were written by someone who was well educated and pointed out that some of the later entries were in French, which I can read, but hadn't realised.

In the event they weren't that interesting or tell me what I wanted to know about her.

She seemed to be more interested in recording wildlife than people. Geese flying north or south, deer in the woods and lots of memories of the sea. The only place mentioned was Odessa, which she found very frightening. Lots of fighting in the streets and continuous bombing.

There were few lines here and there about a long train journey, but no mention of where it started or ended.

The last entries were in French and talked about another train journey, but no indication where from or to. Just one sentence about Paris, saying that it was very noisy.

CHAPTER FIVE

Walker stands in the room where the old lady must have lived, because it is the only room where there was enough space not suffocated with newspapers.

They'd spent a couple of days getting a small army of uniforms to see if there were any clues in the walls of news, but it became pretty obvious she was only interested in Russian news, as indeed everyone else was just now. It also became clear, from the heavy highlighting she'd done, that she was way ahead in fearing what was happening right now, even though she died sixteen years ago, as the most recent things she cut out and stored with the rest of her enormous catalogue all focussed on Putin, who was already in power when she died. Who remembered that?

But it is Gill who comes up with the bizarre suggestion.

She is looking at the clock. The one that's stuck at five minutes before eleven.

'What was the cause of death?'

Walker is standing looking at the view yet again, which he often ends up staring at, as though it might tell him something.

'Whose?'

'Hers. The old lady.'

Walker frowns.

'Old age? She was in her seventies I think?"

Gill glances at him.

'Did we check?'

He shrugs.

'I think so.'

'Who did it?'

He pulls out his phone and checks.

'Here it is,' he says.

She goes to look.

She was found on the floor. Estimated three days after death. The post-mortem was done locally meaning at the Borders General near Melrose.

Gill contacts the hospital.

It takes some time, but she's nothing but persistent, her hunch getting more determined the longer it took. Some of this accompanied by sighs of frustration.

'Aha,' she breathes eventually.

Walker is putting his coat on after seeing the rain outside.

'What you got?' he asks.

'McKinley didn't actually do it, obviously, but he was asked for his opinion.'

'Why?'

'Possible suffocation.'

'What?'

'The BGH pathologist was unsure of a bruise on her face, although he suspected it was a result of the fall. She was found lying on the floor near her chair. So, he asked for a second opinion.'

She shows him the report and draws his attention to the signature at the bottom.

Walker stares at her.

'Is that even permissible?'

Gill points him back to the top of the page where the deceased's name was printed. 'Elena Mary Wallace'.

Walker is stunned.

'How can that have happened?'

Gill shrugs.

'Well, we can hardly ask him.'

'No, but we can damn well ask the BGH guy.'

Ten minutes later Walker has contacted the BGH. It takes some time, but it turns out the doctor there was new back then and didn't know the connection.

'So, is it possible that the old lady could have been pushed over and fallen face down . . . or even a hand over her mouth?'

The doctor pauses.

'Yes, that's why I asked for a second opinion.'

'So now you know he was her son, would you have asked him?'

'Certainly not.'

There's a frosty pause.

'Well, we must have another post-mortem.'

But a quick check blows that out of the water because her body was taken by her son to somewhere in France to be buried.

Walker is pacing up and down, which is difficult in the small space available.

He stops.

'So, let's assume he didn't do it. Who else could have been responsible? And why didn't he do anything about it?'

Gill is staring at the piles of newspapers.

'Maybe he did . . .'

Walker frowns.

'You mean he killed her?'

'No, but he knew who did.'

'You mean the Russians?'

Walker stares at her.

'You mean Putin?'

She shrugs.

'I'm not sure producing a surviving Romanoff would have been his number one publicity event. Especially given she was here in the UK.'

They both stand thinking.

Walker's wondering if he was even in power then, but Gill is ahead of him.

'I'd forgotten this, although I can't say I paid much attention to what was happening In Russia back then . . . he was President from 1999 to 2008 and then from 2012 to today.'

Walker rolls his eyes, thinking where did all that time go?

He was only an angry young black guy living in squats and running the streets at night, looking for cars to steal and girls to share his rampant sex life.

Coming back to the present, he feels slightly uncomfortable in his new suit, which he'd said he'd get himself for his new job.

And then he looks at Gill, who's still flicking pages on her phone.

'So, what were you doing in 2007?'

She looks at him and then away.

'Skiving off college I expect,' she murmurs, but then laughs.

He waits for more information, but her face has hardened, and he thinks he won't go there just now.

'That means he was president when she died, so he would have had the power to do that.'

She nods.

'And he was a KGB officer for fifteen years before that during the Cold War, so he'd know all about the ways they used to silence people.'

Again, they're both silent, then realising they're standing in an empty room in a hospital.

Back in the car, he's staring out of the window, while she's eating a sandwich. He's declined, not that he isn't hungry, but he can't abide petrol station food.

He wants to go back to the house, thinking there might be some other clues, although he can't think what they might be.

His phone stutters.

He answers and listens.

'You sure?' he asks.

He listens for good few minutes, hardly saying anything, and then closes the phone.

Gill waits.

Looks at him.

He shrugs.

'The gun . . . is an antique. A Nagant M1895 'officer's revolver'.'

Gill frowns.

'1895, because that's when they started making them,' he adds, thinking 'as if he knows anything about guns, especially old ones'.

She stares out of the window, thinking the phone conversation was longer than that.

'He also said that given that the bullet was found in the floorboard, that he must have been already on the floor . . . and that in his opinion it wasn't self-inflicted, even though the gun must have been very close to his face.'

Gill's thinking about where the body was found to one side of the 'tableau'.

This gets them both thinking about how and then what this might tell them.

Eventually, Walker makes a decision.

'Let's go back to the house, I need to make some sense of this.'

It takes a good hour to get back to St Abbs, but as it's a sunny day now, the little village is crowded with early spring visitors, but Gill makes her way through them and up the short lane to the house.

There's a couple of bored officers, who are pretty tired of moving the nosy parkers on, and unfortunately neither of them has met this couple, neither of whom look remotely like Scottish police officers. One of them is black and the other might be one of his 'workers'.

So, embarrassments over, the two of them make their way into the house.

It feels truly abandoned now, even though the broken fence has been hastily repaired with brand new panels and they are able to use the front gate as the keys were eventually found.

It feels even more cold and creepy without the quiet bustle of the SOCO officers. The stairs creak as they ascend in the gloom as the lights no longer illuminate the way because the generator has been turned off.

However, the curtains in the room are still pulled back and one window is left ajar to help clear the space of the smell.

Walker stands looking at the outline on the floor.

Without saying anything he lies down inside the outline.

'If he killed himself, how would he have fallen?' he murmurs, but can't imagine how that would play out. Who would be able to tell him about that?

*   *   *

Ellie is a bit lost.

It's a short break in classes this week. The university don't like to call it 'half-term', but that's what it is. Her parents have swanned off to Madeira claiming they deserve a holiday on their own. And so have her siblings and her cousins, all to different other places. Mali still at her mother's.

Apart from going back to the Dordogne, she's never been keen on any other holiday destination, so she is stuck here with these two oldies, tinkering with a new investigation, like she's turning into a private detective?

Is that true?

On cue Fletcher puts his head round the corner of the library or what Louisa has called 'Ellie's office' some time ago.

'We're going into town; do you want to come?'

She blinks.

Does she?

Fletcher comes towards her.

'Are you okay?' he asks.

She gives him a wry smile. This level of empathy from an older person generally arouses suspicion in her, but not with him.

'Yeh, just deep into recent Russian history instead of writing my essay on 'the origins of the Hundred Years War'.'

'Ah,' he says with a smile, 'the classic butterfly mind's excuse.'

She pulls a face at that, but then realises he's right and laughs.

He shakes his head.

'Mind you, it's essential for a detective.'

'How do you mean?' she asks.

'Well, it's not taught as such as opposed to procedural thinking, but second guessing the criminal mind doesn't easily fit into simple boxes.'

'Are you suggesting I should become a detective?'

He sits down next to her.

'I'm not sure you'd last very long, you're even more stubborn than I ever was.'

She can't help another smile.

He smiles back and then his eyes gleam. Always a scary thing. One green, one blue.

'Maybe you could team up with Ziggy and Becket,' he murmurs, thinking if her mother could hear him saying this, she'd be giving him her own mother's stare, which makes him look away.

'I didn't say that . . .' he mutters.

Ellie smiles.

'It's okay . . . but I think I'll just stay here and do some proper work.'

When he's gone, after giving her a kiss on her forehead, she looks at the notes she was making for her essay, but then she stops.

She grins to herself, picks up her phone and texts Ziggy.

'What do you know about the Romanoffs?' he asks, not wasting any time on small talk, as though he was expecting her to call him.

'A bit more than I did a few hours ago,' she says, feeling less guilty when confessing to him.

He ignores this as though of course she's being doing the same research as him.

'So, you know all about Anna Anderson claiming she was the Duchess Anastasia?'

'Yeh, but didn't they do a blood test and found she couldn't have been.'

'Yes, yes, but that's just the side show, the cover story, obviously.'

She frowns.

She can hear him tapping away.
'You think there's a real connection?'
'I'm sending you the family tree the police are investigating.'
She realises he's cut the call.
She sits there astounded. Is he serious?
But then she thinks what Fletcher was saying. Could she really do what Ziggy does?
Her laptop pings. She opens the message.
Just a family tree. That's something she's very used to looking at.

Elena Maria Markovich d1966 m (1931) John Wallace 1900-1944
/
Elena Mary Wallace 1933 - 2007 m (195) Kenneth McKinley 1924 -1988)
/
Kenneth Alexei McKinley 1958-2022 m (m1990) Jennifer Leyton b1964
/
Elena Maria McKinley b 2004 (18)

She notes the underlining.
'Alexie and 'Maria' both stand out as Romanoff names, but she's not so sure about Elena. Maybe if this was the true Maria heritage, then the earlier ones might have disguised themselves to avoid capture or investigation.
But then she's struck by the age of the youngest, nearly the same age as her.
She texts Ziggy.
'Any idea about the current Maria?'
'Gone awol.'
She frowns.
'Since when?'
'Not at Uni for last 2 wks.'

She sits there thinking.

Could this girl, her age, be a descendant of the murdered Russian royal family?

She flicks her phone onto the latest news about Ukraine.

It's getting worse, thousands of people trying to get out and a long trail of tanks slowly making their way to Kyiv.

She can't imagine what it must be like to be there, but then thinks about the little she knows about what happened back in the revolution.

Much the same, if not worse. The Russians had been at war with the Germans, then the revolution happened, and the royal family were hustled out of Moscow and taken to a place called Yekaterinburg, where they were all murdered in 1917. But then she sees that it wasn't just UK versus Germany, there was fighting everywhere all over Europe and the Middle East.

Which meant Maria would have been only eighteen.

She checks the family tree. No birth date for the first Elena, but if she was born in 1899, she would have been 67 when she died. Which isn't that old. Fletch is already 73 and he's still got all his marbles and doesn't seem to have any physical disability . . . although she can't remember him running anywhere and that he hates bikes.

*　　*　　*

The last person Tomasz expected to see arriving at their door is Magda's DS Gatti looking very sheepish.

Tomasz assumes he's come to see how Magda is getting on and initially that's the first conversation.

He agrees that disturbing her isn't a good idea, but then hesitates.

Tomasz frowns, then it dawns on him.

He laughs first and then gives him a glare.

'So, you're the stooge sent round to give me the warning?'

Gatti looks away, his fine Italian features silhouetted against the bright sky.

He looks back at Tomasz and nods.

'We received a complaint from Sir Lawrence Kershaw that you threatened his wife . . . sir,' mutters Gatti, who is obviously squirming inside.

Tomasz glares at him, but then bursts out laughing, before gesturing to him to come inside.

Five minutes later Gatti is sitting at the breakfast table drinking a coffee he has to admit is far better than the usual insipid efforts he's had to endure from Scottish people.

'Bloody hell,' says Tomasz, 'when did the conniving bastard become a 'sir'?'

Gatti shrugs, having never been able to understand the Scottish, indeed the UK, system of handing out honours to dubious people, although he was well aware of the corruption in his own country.

'Have you met the 'lady' in question?' asks Tomasz and then bursts out laughing.

Gatti can't help but grin, recalling his brief encounter with the 'lady' who was extremely drunk and embarrassingly half-dressed.

He nods.

Tomasz shakes his head, but then looks away.

Gatti senses that there's going to be another shift in mood and he's right.

Tomasz looks back him, his eyes hard.

'To be exact, sergeant, I did not threaten his 'lady' wife at all . . . but I did threaten him.'

Gatti is as still as he can be.

'His dogs are out of control and probably not looked after properly.'

Gatti nods, he can't disagree with that, recalling the terrifying moment when they came bounding towards him and only just managing to get back into the car before they reached him.

'And secondly, it wouldn't take me very long to find several young ladies who would testify to his grotesque and violent misogyny.'

Gatti hasn't been expecting the latter accusation and frowns.

'Do you have evidence of this?'

Tomasz laughs.

'You give me half an hour I can get you no end of evidence.'

Gatti isn't sure this is what his superiors would like to hear, but he can hardly go back without reporting it.

Tomasz is staring at him and then stands up.

'I tell you what, sergeant, leave it with me and I'll see what I can do. You go back to your Inspector and tell him I promise to be a 'good boy' and then in a couple of days I'll bring you some incriminating information about his lordship.'

Gatti doesn't know whether to be relieved or more worried, but he stands up as well and allows himself to be summarily ushered out to his car.

Imelda is standing at the inner door as Tomasz waves the policeman away, and watches as he stands frozen on the steps.

Realising she's there, he turns, his face a mask of anger.

She continues to look at him.

He relaxes and comes up the steps to embrace her.

Back in the kitchen, he sits at the table, head in hands.

She goes to him and strokes his neck.

His hand comes up to hold hers.

His blue eyes burning into hers.

'There are far worse things that fat bastard's up to and I know a man who'll give me chapter and verse in short order.'

Imelda is at least relieved that this sounds like a less violent approach and so offers to make him some breakfast.

He grins and goes to find his phone.

The 'man' he calls listens and agrees to investigate.

Tomasz isn't sure about the whispers that he's heard about some of Kershaw's weekend parties, but given the current situation, the presence of both UK politicians, businessmen and Russian 'entrepreneurs' might not be something he would like to be made public.

Ziggy Hook on the other hand is very intrigued and his mascaraed eyes are soon going big as he quickly undercovers a vast web of connections stretching all the way to the Kremlin.

* * *

URSULA

Like many folks, I imagine, Becket and I are glued to the news reports the last few evenings.

Just when you think everything is going to go back to 'normal', this madman who we've all forgotten about has now decided to start World War Three as soon as the Paralympics have finished.

It's distressing and what on earth can we do about it. Lots of Tory MPs declaring they'll sort him out etcetera, as though they'll be going over there themselves and give him a 'right good hiding', as my 'not-mother' used to say. Except, of course, Mrs Henderson carried out her threats swiftly and comprehensively, leaving you in no doubt she meant it. This bunch of liars are more excited by dressing up in battle gear than actually doing anything.

Ziggy gave up assembling a list of Russian autocrats, who live on super yachts avoiding paying taxes anywhere, saying it was a waste of time, because no-one is serious about doing anything about it as they're all slavering over their handouts and backhanders.

But now he's making a different list, which is nearer to home, that is, up the Tweed a few miles away. A Mr Kershaw he says with a sneer. Now, where have I heard that name before.

He had been keeping an eye on what's happening in St Abbs, but that seems to have gone quiet for the moment, no obvious leads beyond that the man who was found dead was a pathologist. Nothing else to report.

* * *

MARIA

It's difficult to comprehend what's happening.
How can anyone do that?
Irena just shakes her head and frowns.
Cams is more interested in one of the other girls and is out of it most of the time anyway.
Most of the other people here, in this 'commune', are just getting on with the gardening, although at this time of the year she doesn't know what they're doing, nothing's growing this far north yet as far as she can see. A lot of them have been collecting seaweed that was left after a big storm a few days ago. Apparently, this is really good for the crops.
There's only one TV and so she's getting most of the news on her phone.
What's happened to her father seems to have been forgotten. Not even on the local Borders news.
She's standing staring out at sea.
They weren't close, she and her father . . . and her relationship with her mother had deteriorated after she changed her course two years ago.

She remembers when her mother decided to leave her father just before that.
First, they were living in her other grandmother's house, but that didn't last very long, she remembers the rows. Then her mother got the job in Newcastle, and they went to live in a little flat in Whitley Bay, which was where she was at school with all those Geordies who couldn't even speak English.
They moved from one flat to another two or three times, before her mother was able to buy the little house, it's just a blur of different rooms, other teenagers, but not many people she could call friends.
Occasionally she would go to stay with her father for a couple of days and sometimes he'd take her to the big house, but it still frightened her. All those towers of newspapers.

He could have retired at sixty, but he insisted on carrying on, saying he'd be bored if he stopped. Didn't want to play golf.

He's not said anything recently about that house. Her mother said once that something really bad had happened there and it wouldn't surprise her if he did something terrible.

When she asked what she meant she just shook her head and walked away. Sometimes she heard her crying in her bedroom, but she wouldn't talk about it.

She still has nightmares about the house, the newspapers rustling and talking to themselves and then like they realise that she's listening and coming to get her, flying down endless stairs, grabbing at her clothes, and pulling her hair.

But that isn't going to stop her from going back to find out what she can.

She hasn't said anything to Irena, although she goes through her things and finds the gun under her bed. The gun they found in that room with the bodies and her father. There are no bullets so she can't 'use' it, but something tells her that it might be important.

ELENA MARY
July 17th, 1990

People probably think I'm lonely.

It's true that I don't get many visitors.

George left me a long time ago. Not long after Kenneth was born. He couldn't be doing with staying in all the time. He missed the night life. The restaurants, the gossip, other women to flirt with.

So, I was quite happy to come and live in this old house by the sea.

He had liked th idea of having a seaside house, especially as compared to Edinburgh prices it was a bargain.

For a while we used to come down lots of weekends, inviting a crowd or just a chosen few.

But it soon became clear that he sometimes used to come with other women. He thought I didn't know, but a woman always knows when other women have been in their bed. My mother taught me that, although I don't think my father ever did it to her.

He died in the war. No-one knew where or how. No body. No grave.

It broke my mother's heart.

Although it wasn't until much later when I realised that, when she came to live with me in the house.

When she was really old, if there was someone at the door, she'd ask if it was him.

Sometimes in the last years, she'd talk about being 'on the train'. She'd never said anything about it when I was younger. She was really busy in the shop and went to bed early. I had to look after myself and as soon as I was old enough, I'd be behind the counter as well or on the bike taking people their orders.

My dad was a doctor and when he went off to war in 1940, she had to take over the business like a lot of other wives.

Towards the end she kept seeing people who weren't there, talking to them in Russian or sometimes in French. Like the Duchessa as she called her. I asked who she was talking about, but she'd just smile and look away.

So now I'm becoming like her.

Not 'doolally' as we used to say, I've 'got all my marbles'.

But I miss her, even though it's over twenty years ago since she died.

I don't miss George . . . although I don't hate him. He was spoilt as a child, I think. His mother and father were what the Scots call 'auld rich'. Huge estates in the Highlands, although they only went in the spring, before the 'midgies', then in September for the hunting and at Christmas when they would invite a huge crowd to their enormous castle by the loch.

I went for the first few years, but then there was that time when I caught him with someone's daughter, a young woman half his age. So since then, I've lived here.

I don't go out much. I can't understand what they're saying, so Maggie does the shopping locally or we go into Berwick.

Kenneth is doing well and is working all hours in the hospital, so he's got himself a little flat in Edinburgh and can only get down occasionally.

And then I found her diaries.

CHAPTER SIX

As it happens the Edinburgh firearms expert isn't busy and has said he can be with them in an hour or so.

Walker suggests they go back to the school café and get some lunch.

As it's unexpectedly warm and sunny they decide to sit outside, which means Gill ends up talking to the old couple with the spaniels.

Walker is definitely not a dog person even if they're fluffy little squirmers who are just after a tickle. He's using the time to find out more about the Romanoffs and particularly Maria. The more he reads the more intriguing and puzzling it gets, as experts seem to be at odds about whether she could have survived.

But the family tree which Gill composed includes the dead guy's grandmother, called Elena Maria Markovich, who died in 1966, so she could be her. She would have been only 68 and many of the newspapers were Russian, although there were plenty of other language papers.

So, looking down the list he stops at the youngest.

Maria.

Eighteen years old, skiving off Uni for the last two weeks.

He decides to contact the college.

It takes for ever, but eventually he gets to speak to one of her lecturers. Introductions over and explanations given, he asks her what the young woman is like.

There's a short pause.

'What do you mean?' comes the cagey response.

'Well . . . is she a good student?'

Again, a pause.

'Does she attend the lectures, is she up to date with her work?'

Another pause.

'If you'd asked me this two weeks ago, I would have said yes, but . . . she's . . . she seemed to be a bit distracted and now she's gone missing.'

'Have you heard what's happened to her father?'

'Yes, and that's awful, but she'd gone missing before that.'

'How long ago?

'Ten days or so.'

Walker's thinking.

'There's another thing.'

'What?'

'She was seen recently in the company of . . . well, frankly . . . another older student, whose politics are rather, shall we say, aggressive.'

'How do you mean aggressive?'

There's another pause.

'She's been involved in clashes with police on marches and protests.'

'Do you know if she's ever been arrested?'

'Yes, I think so, but I don't know any details, just 'hearsay'.'

Walker smiles to himself at the use of such an old-fashioned term.

'Okay, what's this woman's name?'

'Irena xxxxx, I think.'

'And is she missing too?'

'I've no idea.'

Walker hesitates.

'Do you have any contact details for her?'

There's another pause.

'Well, no, she's not one of our students, but someone will know, you'll have to contact her department. She's doing politics, I think.'

After a few more exchanges Walker ends the call.

He's been aware that Gill has been in a prolonged conversation with the dog owners, while he's been on the phone. But, before he recontacts the college, Gill turns to him and says that the couple have some information that could be useful.

Without moving any nearer to the dogs, he smiles and introduces himself.

It turns out that this couple live quite near to the big house and have had a few brief conversations with McKinley.

'Nothing really,' the man says. 'Just 'hello', 'nice day', etcetera.'

'Was there ever anyone with him?' Walker asks, glancing at Gill, who's looking serious.

'No, but then we've only lived here for five years or so.'

He glances at Gill who nods him back to them.

'Well, yes, as we told your colleague, his car was here, but it disappeared a couple of days before you arrived. We just assumed he'd gone away again.'

'But you didn't see anyone else driving it away?'

They both frown and shake their heads, realising that he couldn't have done that, someone else must have done it . . . probably the person who killed him.

They look a bit worried now, as though they ought to have been more observant.

Then the woman looks at him and frowns.

'There was a girl,' she murmurs.

Walker waits.

'I only noticed her because of her hair.'

He smiles.

'You know they have such funny styles and colours nowadays . . . she was tall, but her hair was cropped in a short bob with a fringe . . . and red. I mean crimson.'

He's already on the phone calling the contact he'd spoken to at the university.

It doesn't take long.

'Have you tried contacting her?'

'Yes, but she's not responding to our calls.'

He ends the call and frowns. How and why is McKinley's daughter involved with this older student?

Then he calls back again.

'Sorry to bother you again, but do you have a photograph of the young woman.'

'What?' comes the reply.

Walker waits, listening to the woman having a muffled conversation with a colleague presumably.

'Well, we'd have to ask his parents.'

'This is a murder case.'

There's another pause.

'I can give you the mother's details.'

Walker thanks her and finishes the call.

Bloody rules.

He indicates to Gill that they should go and sets off.

Gill follows him, after saying goodbye to the couple and their dogs and paying for their coffees.

She finds him back at the house, eventually, upstairs.

He's standing looking at a painting, which is hanging above the fireplace in the room where the old lady died.

'Where's that do you think?' he asks, thinking he's seen it before.

Gill photographs it, gets an immediate recognition.

'Odesa – the church of the Transfiguration.'

He shakes his head.

'This is crazy! Here we are in sleepy old Scotland finding connections to what's going on right now thousands of miles away in a war zone.'

'Actually, the Russians pulled it down in 1936,' she murmurs with a frown.

'What?'

'And they've attacked the new one recently.'

Walker shakes his head and puts his foot down.

Ten minutes later, they're sitting in the car, the sun shining through the window. People are strolling along: a couple eating ice creams, a woman with a pram and a big dog, two fishermen fiddling with their equipment. She sits waiting to hear what else he's thinking, but he seems to have gone into a trance.

'So where does a daughter go when she finds her father murdered and doesn't contact the police?'

Gill hesitates.

'Could she have done it?'

Walker looks at her.

Gill shrugs.

'Maybe they found him with his waxworks and were so disgusted, angry, that she or her older friend killed him?'

He looks away.

'But then, why did her father do it anyway?'

He realises he keeps coming back to that. Why on earth would someone want to recreate a famous photograph taken over a hundred years ago?

He reaches into his pocket and finds the piece of paper with the family tree scribbled on it and stares at it.

Gill is frowning at him thinking why he needs to have it handwritten on a piece of tattered paper, whilst she brings it up on her screen. She then wonders whether like her he's got the names Elena and Maria highlighted.

He stuffs the paper back in his pocket and stares out the window.

Gill waits.

Thinking about that upstairs room she recalls that it was the only one completely devoid of newspapers. The chair by the window seemed to have been where the old lady used to sit. They'd found a pair of glasses and a hairbrush there, beside an empty cup and saucer.

So, had McKinley left it like it was when she died?

Was she actually sitting there dead when he went to see her?

When was that?

She looks back at the family tree.

17th July 2007.

She checks the others.

The older Elena died on the same day and so did Dr McKinley.

That can't be a coincidence.

Some kind of weird chance. She shakes her head. Two maybe, but not all three. No, if you count the massacre of the royal family back in 1917, that makes four!

She looks at Walker.

Has he realised this?

He turns to look at her with a weird smile on his face.

'Well, if I was the daughter, I might think I was safe for another year at least.'

*   *   *

Tomasz is watching Imelda.

The first time he saw her shaving the left side of her head, she'd stopped and glared at him before whispering to him to go away.

But then the next time he asked if he could watch and since then she'd tell him when she was going to do it. The sex afterwards was exceptionally erotic for both of them and neither of them quite knew why.

Today is no exception.

Afterwards, lying on the cooling bedclothes he sighs.

'Is your name Russian?'

She's staring at the curtains fumbling in the breeze.

'No, I don't think so, maybe Spanish?'

He sits up on one elbow.

'But your father was a Scot, a Hebridean?'

She nods.

'So, who was your mother?'

She looks at him and frowns.

'She left us when I was seven.'

He stares at her.

'Why?'

Imelda shrugs.

Tomasz can't imagine not having a mother.

A long silence settles on them.

'Do you miss her?' he eventually murmurs.

She turns her face to look at him.

'Not really . . . she was very quiet, didn't say very much, spent a lot of the time on the beach, even when the weather was terrible.'

Tomasz waits, trying to imagine what that would be like.

'So didn't they get on, your parents, lots of arguments?'

She sits up, gathering the bedclothes around her.

'No, not really, they were both very quiet. The house was quiet. No TV. Just a radio for the weather forecasts.'

Tomasz looks away.

When he was young the house was always bustling. People coming and going. Lots of laughter and sometimes arguments. Kenny, the gamekeeper and his horde of kids all coming in and out. How much did his mother love all that!

But Kenny's wife put a stop to it, just disappearing one day and never seen again. The poor man couldn't cope, the kids were taken into care and he's now down the lane fiddling with a thousand jobs, none of which he'll ever finish, whilst the ducks and geese argue and waddle about amongst the broken-down vehicles, assorted half dead machines and half-finished outhouses he leaves in his wake.

He realises that whilst he'd been musing, Imelda has got off the bed and is now in the shower.

He goes to join her.

Downstairs later, his phone burbles.

It's Ziggy telling him he's 'dug up plenty of dirt' on Lawrence Kershaw and suggests he comes to look, rather than him sending such sensitive information to Tomasz's 'unguarded equipment'.

This makes Tomasz grin, knowing that even Amelia's youngest child is more computer savvy than him.

He relays this to Imelda and suggests they go on horseback which is fine with her.

The day is blustery, but sunny, which is better than the ravaging storms they've suffered for what seems the whole of spring this year. They take the route over the bridge and past the remains of Amelia's burnt-out cottage. Her husband had left her nothing and the building only holds bad memories for her. The only thing she did do with help from Magda is to upgrade the horses' barn.

Her four horses are as usual very excited to see his and Imelda's and there's a lot of galloping about and whinnying as they pass up to the lane.

It's only another mile or so to the White Cottage, where they find Ursula pegging out some washing and Becket sat watching with a mug of coffee in her hand.

They both smile at the visitors and Becket offers to make them a drink which they accept and then Tomasz goes in to see what Ziggy has to show him.

There's never anywhere to sit in Ziggy's room, so he stands watching the flickering images and news reports, which are all about or in Ukraine. Far more than Tomasz has seen on the television back at home. They're also in a wide range of languages, including, he assumes, both Russian and Ukrainian.

But now Ziggy's pointing to another screen where he recognises Lawrence Kershaw. He's talking earnestly to some other guy in a suit.

'He's one of Putin's best buddies,' says Ziggy and then flicks through a few more different similar meetings with other men in suits.

'Most of them have property and financial interests in the UK and I can show you the same guys meeting up with Johnson and his cronies.'

A lot of these photos show the men - all men - in a variety of costumes like they're trying to show they can play many different roles. Soldier, businessman, yacht owner, horse owner, conference attendee, but also partygoer, film star companion, golfer, family man.

Tomasz can feel his hackles rising. These are the people who rule the world and also seem intent on destroying it.

'So . . .' he growls, 'who do you suggest we take out first?'

Ziggy shakes his head.

'I'm afraid it would only make it worse and Putin would be really difficult anyway, even for you. Have you seen the distance he puts between himself and other people? You couldn't call that face to face. Apparently, he rarely leaves his bunker.'

Tomasz nods his head, recalling the ridiculous big table scenarios.

He shrugs.

'So, Lozzer Kershaw is up to his neck in all this? Maybe I could just do him for starters?'

Ziggy shakes his head again.

'They'd suspect you straight away.'

They both stand there watching the flickering images.

'But then I did have one idea.'

Tomasz watches as Ziggy shows him different images.

This time it's bodies of Russian soldiers, destroyed tanks and other vehicles, even captured soldiers looking miserable and broken.

'Yeh, I've seen some of this on TV, there are lots of young guys, teenagers even.'

Ziggy nods.

'These aren't the veterans from Syria or Afghanistan. They are what used to be called 'cannon fodder'. Young guys who have no idea where they are going and have very limited or no battle experience.'

Tomasz nods again, thinking of some the younger British guys he'd seen in Iraq and Afghanistan, facing tribal warriors who'd been fighting all their lives, as had their fathers and grandfathers before them, men and young men who'd played with real guns when they were babies.

'But their commanders aren't novices,' whispers Ziggy, 'so someone taking out those guys would render them helpless.'

Tomasz doesn't look at him, just keeps watching the flickering images. Then turns round and walks out.

* * *

Ellie has frequently been getting links from Ziggy ever since her terrible experiences last year. He was one of the few people who seemed to completely believe what happened to her at the Abbey and has subsequently showed her a lot more about other unexplained, unbelievable experiences other people have had for centuries.

He's now being sending her all sorts of stuff about the links UK government people have with Russian oligarchs, which whilst not that surprising, is so blatantly not even that well-hidden, that she wonders why more people don't know about it. But then when she thinks about oldies like Fletcher and Louisa, who don't even have sad Facebook accounts, and then on the other hand, her generation who can't breathe without permanent contact with numerous online gossip pedlars spreading disinformation and lies, but only about sports stars and other performers, she can only sigh.

But now he's getting more interested in the Romanoffs, which is definitely not her period.

'Do you think Walker and Gromit know about this,' she texts him.

The reply is instant.

'Probably . . . I've been investigating the family tree, the one I sent you.'

Ellie brings it up on her screen, reminding herself of the obvious connection between the repeated name and her own. She shakes her head. Bloody 'coincidences' or what that weird companion of Tomasz Steil calls 'wyrd'.

'Okay, so what do you think?'

'That's it possible that he's Maria Romanoff's great grandson?'

'Uhuh . . .'

Ellie waits to see if there's anymore.

'BTW drop the NDPs'

Ziggy switches to voice mode, which she knows is encoded.

'NDPs?' she asks, but then gets it. 'Nommes de plumes'.

'Yeh, Walker grew up on one of the roughest estates in south Manchester and Gill is an E3 Krag Mara.'

'A what?'

'Probably the hardest martial art in the world.'

Ellie can't imagine what the 'hardest' might be.

'Do you mean the most lethal or the most difficult to achieve?'

'Both . . . but then she started when she was eight years old. Her mother is one of the highest rank practitioners.'

Again, Ellie can't imagine what that might look like . . . apart from the man in the real-life nightmare she survived . . . and he had a sword.

She waits to see what else he's going to tell her.

'The girl, who is younger than you, is a friend of someone else who is a bit scary. Take a look.'

Her screen produces a stern looking woman staring resolutely at the camera. No smile. Just hard dark eyes.

This then reduced into one corner to allow her to see her police record. Numerous arrests and court appearances related to marches, protests and break-ins of public property and some private houses.

'The private houses are all Tory donors or supporters,' Ziggy points out.

Ellie shudders.

'I wouldn't like to meet her in a dark alley,' she mutters.

'Oh, you'd be OK, you're female and not a Tory,' he laughs.

She's not convinced by that, but then waits to see whatever else he's unearthed.

But he's gone silent, although the image is still there.

'Are you there?' she eventually asks.

Silence.

She's thinking this means she should cut the connection, but then suddenly there's another photo. A bit blurry? A high street? It's a video moving down the street and then opening out into a large space. The camera scans the people walking around and then focusses in quickly on a young girl getting out of a car.

'Banjo!' says Ziggy.

'Who's that?' asks Ellie, wondering whether he meant 'Bingo'?

'A ghost from the past,' he murmurs and does some magic with the screen which puts the girl next to an old black and white image.'

Ellie gasps. She's seen the photographs of the Romanoff family.

The hair is not that different, probably light brown like her sisters seem to be.

'Are you sure?' she whispers.

He reverts the screen to the video which shows the young woman walking quickly off camera.

Ziggy sighs.

'That's the only time I've spotted her.'

'When was this?'

'Five days ago.'

Ellie dismisses asking how he could do that, knowing he won't tell her.

'The day after the bodies were found,' he adds.

'Where is that?'

'Portree, Isle of Skye.'

Ellie has no idea where that is, but then Ziggy's putting up a map of Scotland and then zooms into the north-west. A large island with lots of inlets.

'Skye is Norse for winged,' Ziggy tells her.

She can see why.

'So why there?' she asks.

'Ah,' he murmurs, 'this is the good bit.'

He changes back to an 'eye in the sky' view and then zooms in again to an inlet in the north and then down to a collection of old cottages and a gaggle of tents.

Ellie is momentarily confused but then recognises that it's some sort of encampment like you see at festivals.

'What's that?' she murmurs.

Ziggy laughs.

'It's about as remote as you can get, end of the road, but then this hippie community is another mile or so on a rough track.'

So, they've gone into hiding thinks Ellie.

'Good place to hide,' he confirms.

'How did you . . .?'

Ziggy laughs again.

'I'd have to kill you,' he murmurs, 'but you could go there.'

'Me?'

'And Becket, maybe.'

She can't believe he's even suggesting this.

'But . . .?' is all she can manage.

He's silent, but the image sits there.

'Have you even asked her?'

'You won't be missing any lectures, will you,' he whispers, ignoring that question.

She instinctively looks over her shoulder wondering where Louisa and Fletcher have gone and then remembers she's dragged him off to do some shopping in Kelso.

Five minutes later it's all agreed. Becket not difficult to persuade as she's already been complaining that she'll go mad if she doesn't do something to someone. Ellie ignores that despite she is still scared of the fierce ex-detective, who has always seemed to be a woman on a mission to punish errant men.

She goes to assemble some clothes wondering whether Becket has done 'krag mary' or whatever it's called.

* * *

URSULA

I know that something's up because Janet's packing a rucksack.

She gives me a shake of the head.

'Why do I do this?' she asks me wearily, but the twinkle in her eye gives her away.

'Where is he sending you now?' I ask.

'Some hippie community on the Isle of Skye.'

I've only a vague idea where that may be, the far north, mountains, sea etcetera.

'Has he said why?'

She shrugs.

'Something to do with the bodies found in a haunted house down near Berwick,' she mutters.

I've heard about this, but the information is very limited, although I'm sure Ziggy's well up on it.

'Some young girl connected with it somehow. He thinks she's in danger. Now you know as much as I do.'

Half an hour later Ellie arrives, trying hard to stop the gleam in her eyes. I worry about her, but then she's faced up to more horrors than the average young lady.

It doesn't take long and then I'm waving them off.

I'm not looking forward to just being here with Ziggy, especially if he's on a case. I won't get much conversation and will return to my dogsbody duties. How did all this happen? Oh, yes, I was looking for information about my mother. The serial killer aka the 'Snow White Murderer.' But that was years ago now. Never found.

She'd be in nineties by now . . . I think.

* * *

MARIA

I'm going to go mad staying here.

It's not as if these 'hippies' are having any parties or playing guitars all night.

They've even got TVs and laptops.

They also have 'meetings' all the time, like they're businesspeople. The ones that I've 'attended' are all about 'forward planning': what they're going to grow, produce and budgets, who's going where to sell stuff . . . I could scream.

My main problem is that I can't drive yet, still struggling with lessons, which my dad was paying for without ever complaining and in any case most of the cars here aren't automatic. Who can be bothered with that?

I've checked the local bus timetables, although when I say local that doesn't mean from here. It's at least two miles to the castle we passed and then an hour on a bus to get to Portree and then it's a good four hours back to St Abbs.

Irena seems to be okay with all this 'business' stuff, which I hadn't expected. Not sure how that fits in with her hatred of 'businesspeople', who are 'the main cause of all the problems in the world'.

She's now standing on the edge of the beach looking towards some mountains covered in cloud. The 'Coollins' and are revered by climbers. A more introverted bunch of folks you could ever have to spend time with, in her limited opinion, having once gone on a field trip with a couple of beardy guys who just wittered on about 'A-fives' and 'E-sixes 'all the time.

So, how's she going to get back to civilisation?

Looking round she can see one of the younger guys, who has smiled at her a few times. Not her type obvs, but 'needs must' as her mother would never say.

She smiles back at him and wanders over to where he's fiddling with a net.

A few hours later she's on a bus going south towards the bridge, back to the mainland.

What she had to do to get this far isn't something she ought to be proud of, but the ease of the seduction makes her shake her head. She didn't even have to let him fuck her, as the thought of it seemed to be enough and a few tugs of his surprisingly big cock sufficed.

The last sight of him standing forlornly at the bus stop makes her sigh, but then she started to think about Irena and whether she'll follow her.

KENNY (1970)

I rarely see my dad anymore.

My mum says he doesn't want to be with us.

Sometimes I hear her crying.

Once when I was passing her bedroom, I saw her kneeling by her bed with her hands together, praying.

Once a month or so, but not every month recently, he comes to take me out.

We go in his big car.

To the zoo or the castle.

Then a big restaurant, where he knows lots of people, who come to talk to him or he goes over to them, or stands at the bar, leaving me alone, which I don't like.

Sometimes there are other kids there, but they make fun of me, asking where I got my clothes from and when I shrug that I don't know, they laugh and say things like the 'Sally army' or 'charity shops', which aren't true.

I love my mum, but she's not happy and I don't know what to do.

CHAPTER SEVEN

Imelda is worried.

Yesterday got scarier as the day progressed.

They'd ridden back from Ziggy's in silence, except she could almost hear Tomasz's brain working in overdrive.

Back at the house, he was straight onto Magda's laptop, which rarely happened. When she asked him what he was looking for, he just shook his head and didn't even look at her.

This continued until dinnertime, where he was monosyllabic and twitchy, after which he went straight back to the laptop.

Helena wanted to know what was eating him, but Imelda could only shrug her shoulders. Magda was still in hospital, so she couldn't object, although normally she was very wary of anyone touching her machine.

Imelda was resolutely computer illiterate, saying she'd rather spend the time watching the tide come in, which this far up the Tweed was not possible, so she would go down to the river and watch that.

The following morning, she wakes to an empty bed. Not even a warm place beside her.

Worried, she gets up quickly and goes downstairs to find him.

More worryingly he's packing a rucksack.

She stands watching him.

'Where are you going? she asks softly.

He turns, startled, and stares at her, then looks away.

'I've got to go,' he says.

She comes into the room and goes to stand in front of him.

'You mean Ukraine?'

He looks at her with his fierce blue eyes and nods.

She waits.

He looks away.

'I've contacted Kasper.'

She frowns.

Tomasz can't help but smile.

'He's my cousin, my mother's nephew.'

She waits, in that still way that always makes him uneasy.

'He lives in Krakov, it's about two hundred miles from the border.'

'Ukraine?'

He nods.

'Not far from Lviv,' he adds.

These are names she's only just heard on the TV or read about.

She stares at him.

Time passes.

Neither of them looks away.

'Okay, when are we setting off?'

He frowns and shakes his head.

'You can't come. It's too dangerous.'

She continues to stare.

'Yes, who would take a woman into a war zone?'

This startles him and he can't help but grin.

She continues to stare and then opens the shirt that she had commandeered from his wardrobe as a dressing gown a long time ago. The snakes and dragons are as a bright and scary as always.

'You think I can't hide this?' she asks.

Tomasz stares back at her. The grin morphs into a frown and then she turns on her heels and leaves the room.

He stands there staring after her, before deciding he'd better follow her.

Upstairs he finds her in front of the huge mirror, which they like to watch themselves in when having one of their more excessive sexual pursuits.

In her hand she has the shaver.

She turns and offers it to him.

Frowning, he takes it, although they've only just done it two days ago, but then realises what she means.

'All of it,' she whispers.

There's no excessive sex afterwards. They just lie there on the bed.

'I'm not frightened to die,' she says.

He turns to look at her.

'If they capture you, they'll do terrible things before they kill you.'

'Worse than you do?' she murmurs.

He can't help but laugh.

'I bet you haven't even got a passport.'

She smiles.

'Oh yes, I have. Roper made me get one in case he had to leave the country. In fact, he got me three different ones, different names . . . and one of them is male.'

Tomasz stares at her . . . shocked into remembering how they met.

She stares back.

Then . . . there was some gentle sex.

* * *

Gill has a thought.

The two of them have spent the night in a hotel in Kelso. Different rooms obviously.

He's not shown the slightest interest or acknowledgment in her sexually, which makes her throw the bedclothes off with a snort. At herself.

Standing in the shower, she looks at the slight bruise going yellow on her shoulder. She knows her mother would be proud of her not inflicting any more damage than she did and sticking to the severe rules of her training, but she knows well that the look McAlister gave her means he won't be able to let it lie. The damage to his reputation now in tatters, he'll be making plans.

She arrives at the breakfast room to find Walker staring out the window, the remains of a full breakfast in front of him.

She smiles and goes to sit opposite him.

'Not eating your egg?' she asks, with a grin.

He shakes his head.

'I don't eat babies,' he says, solemnly, looking at it with a shudder.

She frowns.

'But piglets?' she asks nodding at the abandoned bacon rinds.

He looks away.

An older woman appears at the door.

'Full breakfast, madam?'

Gill shakes her head and asks for cereal and brown toast. The woman frowns and disappears.

There's no-one else in the room, so the silence gathers. No radio mumbling elsewhere, no sound of traffic outside.

The silence gathers some more.

'If it were true?' he murmurs, pushing a paper with the handwritten version of the family tree towards her.

She glances at it. The two Elenas have been changed to Maria.

She looks up at him and shakes her head.

'You can't be sure of that.'

He nods.

'I know, but there's one other person we haven't questioned yet.'

'The mother, Jennifer?'

'Yeh, we couldn't find any address or contact for her . . . she just seems to have disappeared.'

Gill frowns.

'Divorced, died?'

He shakes his head.

'Nothing legally.'

Gill thinks again.

'What about the house in Dunbar?'

'No evidence she was ever there. No clothes. No real sign of a woman ever living there.'

'Did you check back?'

He shakes his head.

'He bought the Dunbar house in 2008, after his mother died.'

'Driving licence?'

He shakes his head.

'Maiden name?'

'Nothing so far.'

'Marriage licence?'

He grins.

'Bingo.'

Gill shakes her head again. Bloody gameplayers.

On cue her breakfast arrives.

'Where is she?'

'Newcastle. She's a nurse.'

Half an hour later they're on their way.

'Have you spoken to her?' she asks.

He shakes his head.

'I think it's better face to face, don't you?'

She shrugs.

They're both silent for a few miles.

'Do we know when she left him?'

'Well, she didn't start working in Newcastle until 2017, so maybe not immediately.'

'Do you think she knows?'

He shrugs.

'What would you do if your husband started fashioning shop window models to represent his ancestors?'

She shakes her head.

'I doubt he showed her.'

He sighs.

'Love and marriage?'

An hour later they're sitting in the hospital staff canteen with Jennifer McKinley. It's nearly empty apart from the canteen staff, who are out of earshot.

She's staring at the photograph Walker's just given her, which doesn't include her husband'.

As a nurse she's certainly seen a fair number of dead bodies, many of them looking a lot worse than these.

She hands the photo back and looks away.

The two detectives wait, not sure of this reaction.

She looks back at Walker.

'I didn't know, but I'm not surprised.'

Walker waits. Gill frowns at her.

The woman leans forwards and looks at her hands.

'He changed . . . he wasn't always like that.'

They wait.

She leans back, looks away, a stray tear creeping down her cheek.

She wipes it away.

'It was good for a while . . . but then his mother died.'

Gill stares at her.

'When did that happen, can you remember?'

The woman nods.

'Her birthday, 17th July 2007.'

The two detectives can't avoid a mutual frown.

'Why are you so sure it was then?' ask Gill, trying not to look disbelievingly at her.

The woman shakes her head again.

The room echoes to the sound of cutlery being clattered into drawers.

'We had a big row, because he'd wanted to take Maria to see her on her birthday.'

The penny drops for Walker.

'They had the same birthday, didn't they?'

The woman glares at him.

'Of course, and previously we did get together for it . . . but on another visit Maria got really frightened because one of those piles of newspapers fell down on us as we were going up to her room.'

The two detectives stare at her.

'It was the same day he found her dead . . . imagine what that would have been like for Maria.'

The two detectives don't look at each other and wait again.

'Maria's fourteenth birthday,' she murmurs.

She grimaces.

'He'd become obsessive, spending all his spare time researching the Russian royal family, trying to prove to himself there was a connection.'

'Did you believe in it?' asks Walker.

She sighs and stares at him.

'I assume you know what happened to them. They were all murdered on that date in 1917.'

He nods and waits.

'And that women later who claimed she was Anastasia, the youngest daughter, that she'd escaped.'

He nods again.

'Did he show you any evidence of this?'

She nearly laughs.

'This was back when the internet wasn't as all-pervading as it is now. He even went to Russia to see the place where they were all killed. It's become a shrine to them now, although the original building was pulled done in the 1980s.'

'Did anyone else know he was doing all this?' asks Walker.

She laughs.

'No, of course not, he didn't even tell me. When he went to see the church, he told me he was going to a conference in Germany.'

She gets up from the table and goes to stand looking out of the window.

'I got tired of the rows. I worried he was going mad. Begged him to go to a doctor, but then one day he got violent, shouted at me, and pushed me away.'

She reaches for a serviette on the table next to her and blows her nose.

'I packed our bags and left him.'

Then she got up and walked to the nearest window.

She eventually comes back and sits down.

'It's been really hard. At first, he wouldn't support us, I had to get a job again before I really wanted to.'

Gill is thinking whether the man's superiors knew about all this.

'I had to give in to letting Maria go to stay with him now and then, but I found it really difficult.'

She gathers herself and looks hard at them.

'And now what has he done?'

Walker doesn't look at Gill.

'He's dead.'

She stares at him.

'Dead?'

Walker nods.

'He was found at his mother's house two days ago, lying beside the bodies I just showed you.'

She looks back at the photo, puts her hand to her mouth.

'You mean they are real dead bodies?!'

Walker shakes his head.

'It's sort of worse than that, but on the other hand not so bad.'

She shudders and stares at him.

'He fashioned waxwork faces onto shop models.'

She shakes her head again.

Gill can't stop herself.

'Do you know where your daughter is?'

The woman's hands go to her face.

'No, don't tell me.'

'It's OK,' says Walker, 'as far as we know she's alright, but she's not at her digs or been to any lectures for the last two weeks.'

The woman fumbles for her phone, scrolls down and presses call.

It takes an agonisingly long few moments but then the call is answered.

'Hi, darling,' she says, and then listens.

'So, where are you now?'

She looks at the two detectives.

'I'm on my way.'

She ends the call and stands up, her eyes blazing.

'Why didn't you tell me?'

'Where is she?' asks Gill.

'On a train going to Edinburgh, I'm off to fetch her.'

The two detectives stand up.

'We can take you.'

The woman glares at them again, but then relents and gives in.

* * *

Louisa reads the note that Fletcher has found.

He's just handed it to her with a shake of his head and a mumbled 'it's not my fault.'

Louisa gives him a stern look, but decides not to contradict him, even though she knows it is mainly his influence that makes Ellie take such risks.

'One of my favourite places,' she murmurs.

Fletcher stares at her.

'I went there once,' he says.

Louisa waits, not sure which one of his 'adventures' he's referring to.

'Or was it some other island? Harris? That's it? That bunch of child rapists!'

She shakes her head.

'I'd rather not think about them.'

Fletcher looks away.

'Me neither . . . but I'm pretty sure it still goes on, they just got better at hiding it.'

They're both silent, not liking the images slipping though their memories.

'So, what's she doing going up there?' she asks.

'It's Sigismund Hook, I'm afraid, training her up to be his hunting dog.'

'I thought that was Janet's job,' she sighs.

Fletcher frowns.

'I'll contact her.'

He goes to find his phone, which is still always an ongoing problem. He comes back to find Louisa reading the paper.

'I can't find the damn thing, can you call it?'

Louisa shakes her head and reaches for her own phone on the side table beside her.

They listen.

Can't hear it.

Fletcher goes out into the corridor.

Is that it?

He follows the sound and finds it in Ellie's 'study' as Louisa's husband's library used to be called.

He calls her.

'Where are you?'

'On the way to Skye,' she says.

'Just you?'

'No, Janet's driving.'

Fletcher laughs.

'Braver than me.'

He hears the shouted verbals from Janet.

'So, what's the plan?'

'We're hoping to catch up with the daughter, Ziggy thinks she could be in great danger.'

'You do know there are police officers who are supposed to be dealing with this?'

'Yeh, but you know Ziggy thinks they're too slow.'

'Okay but take care.'

The call is cut.

He glances at Louisa.

'She's not my granddaughter,' she murmurs.

He shakes his head. That may be strictly correct, but he knows that she'd move heaven and earth to protect her.

* * *

Ellie answers the call.

They're just getting to the outskirts of Edinburgh.

She listens to Ziggy and then indicates to Janet to pull over, which she does in her usual abrupt manner, disconcerting the traffic behind.

Ellie finishes the call, shakes her head.

'Apparently she's on her way back on the train.'

Becket frowns.

'Just her?'

Ellie shrugs.

'He thinks so.'

Becket waits, looking out the window, figuring in her mind's eye the best way to the station.

'So, what does that mean?' murmurs Ellie.

Becket shrugs.

'Change of mind, falling out?'

A silence gathers.

Ellie glances at Becket who's staring out of the windscreen. The gaunt face, the hard eyes, the ghost of a sneer.

How did it come to this, she thinks, spending her time chasing people, alongside this scary woman?

As if Becket's in her head, she sighs.

'You mustn't end up like me, you know,' she says, her voice hoarse.

Ellie instinctively reaches out to touch her arm, which flinches.

They look at each other.

Ellie is disconcerted to see her eyes are brown. Were they always like that? But then, given how scary she is, she's maybe never dared to look before.

'You've got brown eyes' she whispers.

Becket grins and twitches her nose, before looking at her directly.

'Well, someone has to be normal, unlike you and Fletcher . . . green eyed dragons.'

Ellie grins back and makes her eyes go big.

Becket pretends to be scared and puts her hand over her eyes.

'No, don't stare at me, I'll wither and die!' she cries.

They both fall about giggling, until Ellie's phone burbles.

It's Ziggy, telling them to get a move on, saying the traffic between them and the station is terrible and is sending Janet an alternative route on her phone.

Ellie's relays this and Becket snaps back into 'chase and contact' mode, revs the engine and bursts out into the traffic, causing lots of hooting and tyre screeching.

The next fifteen minutes is the sort of hyper rollercoaster ride Ellie knows is one of the exhilarating things about being with Becket, although she can't imagine ever doing it herself, as she's already failed her test twice, ironically for 'not keeping up with the traffic'.

They arrive at the station and Becket pulls up in a reserved parking place and slaps her old police sticker on the dashboard.

Then Ellie is trying desperately to keep up as she charges into the station and with a quick glance at the arrivals board she sets off to the designated platform, which is up and over a crowded gantry.

They're just in time as the train comes to a screeching halt and people start tumbling out of the doors.

They stand looking for the girl, who they've only seen in photographs.

Becket puts her phone to her ear as she knows Ziggy will be scanning the crowd via the stations system.

Sure, enough his voice comes calmly.

'Fourth carriage, second door,' he tells her.

Becket spots her and finds her old police card.

Ellie watches as she stops the girl and ushers her to one side. She goes to join them.

'It's okay,' Becket is saying, although the girl's looking scared. 'We've been asked to meet you from the train, your mother is very concerned about you.'

The young girl frowns but allows herself to be taken to a quiet corner out of the milling crowd.

Five minutes later they're in the station café, Ellie is getting the coffees.

When she gets back to the table, she can see the girl has relaxed and is speaking on the phone to someone.

The call ends and she stares at her.

'Hi,' she says, 'I'm Ellie.'

There's a faint smile, but then another frown.

Before anything else is said, Becket receives another message from Ziggy.

She looks away and tells him where they are, listens briefly and then cuts the call.

'Apparently your mother is on her way and so we'll wait here for her.'

The young girl frowns.

'My mother?'

Becket shrugs.

'She's being brought here by a couple of police officers who are looking for you.'

Now she looks scared.

'Why?' she mumbles. 'I haven't done anything wrong.'

Becket gives her a stern look and then frowns.

'I expect it's to do with what's happened to your father.'

She stares at her, looking like she might burst into tears.

Ellie is thinking Becket's being a bit harsh, so she puts out a hand and touches her arm.

She flinches and gives her a terrified look.

Becket is stony-faced but is also scanning the crowds.

Ellie frowns at her. What or who is she looking for?

'We need to get you safe,' Becket rasps.

Ellie nods at her and Becket leads them back over the gantry and onwards to the car.

It's then she says she needs the loo.

Becket doesn't like it, but she relents.

It only takes seconds.

Two police officers appear and go into the toilets. Becket frowns and follows them in.

The next thing is the disappearing police uniforms coming out and the back of the girl's head.

Ellie chases them out, trying to make sense of what's going on.

Where's Janet?

She looks this way and that.

Her phone beeps.

It's Ziggy.

'Janet's hurt, lying in a corner in one of the loos.'

She follows his directions and finds her.

Her eyes are shut, Ellie fears the worst but bends down and touches her arm. She flinches and her eyes open, gives her a weak smile.

'Two of them, bastard stabbed me.'

Ellie realises her hand is clutching her side and that blood is seeping through her fingers.

She backs away and screams.

The next half hour will always be a blur.

People arriving. Police whistles. Shouting. Hands helping her away. Startled faces and very stern ones. Uniforms. Not knowing what's happened to Janet.

Darkness.

MARIA

Maria can hardly breathe. Sticky tape over her mouth, the taste making her want to gag. She tries to be calm.

She's lying on something soft like a coat, she can feel a button biting into her arm.

The sound of an engine. Angry gear changes. Other traffic noises. No windows. Must be in a van. There's no seats.

A hand touches her.

She flinches.

A face looms up in front of him.

It's a young woman.

Dark eyes. Fearful.

'Shush' the woman whispers. Some thick strands of blonde hair escaping the scarf over her head and covering her mouth.

The woman realises Maria's hands are tied with sticky tape in front of her.

She struggles to sit up. The woman helps her. She's not tied up, but her eyes are frightened.

They stare at each other.

Maria tries to smile, but an angry voice from the behind the partition terrifies her.

She doesn't know what the voice is saying.

It sounds like a man, but not English.

The woman puts her fingers to her lips.

It takes a few minutes, but the woman manages to help her sit up with her back to the shuddering metal.

They're constantly rocked back and forth as the driver seems to be following a very tortuous route, other traffic noises seeming to indicate they're still in the city.

She's been to Edinburgh a lot of times when she was younger, although she's no idea of the layout, because her father always drove them places like he knew all the short cuts and traffic avoiding routes. She remembers the zoo and the castle and the big street with that tower they climbed every time they went.

The van screeches to a halt. Lots of other vehicles honking.

It does a rapid noisy reverse and then the whole thing swings round knocking her and the other girl over, so they fall into the middle.

Now accelerating really hard, but still swinging back and forth.

The two of them hang on to each other.

But then the van slows and turns left, gathers speed, but now more calmly.

The road isn't straight, although there's no more screeching and whirling.

She looks at the girl who is shivering. Her eyes tight shut.

Without thinking she reaches out and touches her arm.

She shudders.

Opens her eyes.

Maria tries to smile, although it's not easy. She thinks of what her mother says that eyes smile more truthfully than mouths.

The girl manages to smile back.

But only with her eyes as well.

*   *   *

ELENA MARY
August 1966

My mother's funeral was bit of a nightmare.

Kenneth and I had an almighty row about me wanting to take her to be buried in France. It was her final wish.

In the end I had to arrange it all myself and then there was another row when I said I wanted to take Kenny with me.

He was shouting and yelling about taking his son all that way, when he was too young to go to a funeral anyway.

But somehow, I managed to stick to my promise and we went.

I told Kenny what we were going to do and he was very excited.

The journey was long and I did feel a bit bad about taking him.

In the end he gave up asking 'are we there yet?'

The other thing that stopped the tantrums was finding out that I can speak French, which really puzzled him, but then he started to remember some words and tried them out on waiters and people in shops.

So, by the time we got to the chateau, he was quite looking forward to it.

But it was a big disappointment.
No-one had lived in it for a long time.
The gardens were untended and had gone wild.
The house was all boarded up and there were holes in the roof.
Still, she had arranged for the funeral from home and they dealt with it the next day.
Her mother was buried where she wanted to be, although there were no other graves that they could see.
Afterwards, she was standing by the grave, crying.
But Kenny put his hand in hers and squeezed.
'It's alright, mama,' he said. 'She's gone to the angels now.'

CHAPTER EIGHT

Tomasz is relieved.

The difficult conversation with his mother is done. In fact, he's surprised she wasn't more resistant, but then realised the worst thing for her was that she couldn't go with them . . . because she isn't going to abandon Magda.

As it happens one of the three passports Roper had made for Imelda was also EU Polish. Was that just a premonition? She just shrugs.

'Maybe from the gang you got that gun from,' she suggests.

Tomasz nods.

'Perhaps . . .' he murmurs, not wanting to think of what his mother had to do with that. Best she wasn't coming. Wouldn't be fair on the Russians.

He smiled to himself. The thought of her running from one battle to another back in the sixties.

As it happens, Magda is being let out today. On condition she doesn't go anywhere near a horse or drive a car.

Tomasz goes to get her.

It's only fifteen-minute drive back, but it's long enough for her to inform him she's going to take early retirement. A quick glance at her pursed lips tells him it's not worth arguing about at the moment, so he just nods. The rest of the journey is her looking out at the sunshine dancing off the Tweed.

He knows she's no idea what he's planning and has decided to wait until they're back at home.

He pulls up next to the stables.

She gets out slowly and goes straight to the gate.

And there's the culprit, Hector, whinnying his greeting. She reaches over and strokes his neck. Tomasz gets out and comes round to stand with her.

'He's missed you,' he whispers.

She nods.

'And I've missed him,' she says, tears streaming down her face.

Tomasz manages to find a handkerchief and offers her it. This makes her laugh.

'If any of those nurses saw the state of this 'rag', they'd be giving you a right telling off.'

But she wipes her tears away and gives it him back.

Then it's Hengist's moment to turn up, not as rollicking as he used to be, but his tail is wagging hard to make up for the arthritic legs.

She turns to look for her mother.

A figure at the door.

Thinner than she remembers.

How can that have happened in only a few days?

Ensconced in the kitchen the three of them are quiet.

'I'm not going back,' says Magda, quietly.

Helena just smiles.

'As long as you're not thinking you're just going to look after me,' she says sternly.

Magda laughs.

'Actually, I was hoping you were going to look after me, that was the deal the doctor agreed to let me out.'

Now they're all laughing.

Which presages the arrival of Amelia's children, who have been told they can't hug or cuddle her; but the armfuls of flowers and hand-made presents takes a good half hour to deal with and then a lingering gentle hug from their mother.

So, it's much later that day before Tomasz manages to tell Magda about his plan.

They've come out onto the terrace with a glass of Talisker each. The sun is still up but sinking fast. The wind has dropped, and the air is full of the distant cries of new-born lambs and the hurried chirruping and bustling of blackbirds and sparrows.

Helena and Imelda are doing the washing up. Something has made them laugh.

'We're going to go to Ukraine,' he murmurs.

Instead of a look of shock or outrage, she doesn't look at him at all, just continues to stare out across the valley.

He waits.

'I know it's no use telling you not to go and I'm assuming you've told her.'

Then she looks at him, with that stern face that he knows has produced a lot of confessions.

'Of course . . . although I know she wants to go with us, as well.'

She shakes her head and smiles.

They sit in silence.

'Imelda?'

He nods.

There's another pause.

She stands up.

'God help them,' she says, and reaches for her glass.

* * *

Ellie is sitting in a corridor.

It's now nearly an hour since she got to the hospital.

Janet was rushed away from the station, the ambulance crew not letting her accompany her.

She's been on to everyone on her phone and knows that Fletcher and Louisa are on their way.

Ziggy is keeping her up to date with what's happening, although he's very nervous about hacking into hospital systems, saying they're prone to lots of faults and system failures.

It seems to be positive, although she's still in surgery.

He's also said he's completely lost the girl.

She can't help thinking about her.

Could someone really think she's a descendant of the Romanoffs? It seems that her father had convinced himself they both were.

But in any case, what would happen if it's true?

The little she knows about the Russian Revolution is that it was total war and that the idea of somehow declaring that she survived in the current situation would just be . . . what?

It's over a hundred years ago!

What she does think is that the UK is the only major country left in the world that still has a 'royal family' in anything like a position of power.

What would Putin do?

Wouldn't he just dismiss it as a Western pack of lies.

So, why now? Who has kidnapped her?

She didn't even see them.

She texts Ziggy.

'No idea,' he says. 'Even though there are loads of cameras at the station, all I saw was a few seconds of her being bundled out. Two men in balaclavas. I say 'men', but I can't be certain.'

There's a pause.

'I think they're on one of the cameras outside, but then nothing else. A lot of the cameras are temporarily blocked anyway, which I think will be the police. Lots of abrupt voices on radio mikes. Incident moved up to terrorist status, which makes it hard to intercept.'

Another long pause.

A nurse comes out of the room and hurries away.

Two more come running, go quickly inside.

Ellie is thinking the worst.

She calls Fletch, knowing Louisa will be driving.

'What d'you know?' he asks.

'Nothing really, lots of nurses rushing about.'

There's a pause.

'Don't worry,' he says quietly, 'I don't know anyone harder to kill than Janet.'

Ellie can't speak. Cuts the call. Realises she's shaking. Now crying.

She wipes her face with a sleeve and grits her teeth.

The door opens and a man in a white coat comes out and spots her.

She glares at him.
He frowns.

    * * *

URSULA

Ziggy tells me what's happened to Janet.

At first, I can't take it in.

I've always thought she was indestructible. What people call 'a force of nature'? What does that mean? No-one's indestructible . . . although Janet . . .

I don't know what to do with myself, so I wash up, put some clothes in the washing machine, take the wet ones out to put on the line, brush the hall, clean the toilet, make a shopping list . . .

But then, Ziggy's standing watching me, a strange look on his face.

'You're weird,' he whispers.

This coming from a man who's wearing a long Victorian dress, a bright red wig and purple boots is, as always, a bit rich, but on this occasion, I can't stop myself bursting into tears.

The next shock is finding his arms round me, muttering to me in what I now know is Czech.

I pull away. He's never even touched me before.

Tears are dribbling down his face now, the mascara taking the chance to follow them.

I push him away, but gently.

'She's going to be okay,' he says.

I stare at him, rubbing my eyes.

'The blade missed any vital organs. She's already conscious . . . probably giving them a hard time.'

I have to sit down.

He kneels on the floor in front of me.

I don't know how long we were in that awkward pose, but we both knew something had changed between us. Not that we wanted to face it then, but it was in that moment.

Eventually, although it's a bit of a blank, we are back in the house. Me making coffee, him back in the ether.

No more updates on Janet for some time, but now he's in multi-connection with Fletcher, Ellie, and the police conversations.

As far as he can tell, the young woman, Maria, has been kidnapped, by whom, he's not sure. He's not able to find the actual event on any cameras and then realises they've been blocked.

He's stumped. Never been locked out like that before . . . which he decides means it's really top secret. This doesn't stop him from trying, but it does mean we don't get to talk about what just happened between us.

I decide to do what I always do when things get tough . . . go for a walk.

I don't remember the ascent to my 'castle', but the heavy breathing is a clue to the pace I must have tackled it.

I sit down on one of the fallen stones and try to catch my breath.

And there he is.

My hare.
His amber eyes shining at me.
I shake my head.
'I thought you'd abandoned me,' I whisper.
He just stares.
A tear snakes its way down my face. I rub it away.
The hare starts to clean itself. Bending one ear down and licking it and then the other. Changes to his chest and then eventually his paws.
What happens next is . . .
First, a very large black crow, that I later decide must have been a raven, lands on one of the big chunks of castle wall that has fallen from the ruin only five or six yards away. I've seen them circling high above and think they have nests up there, but never this close.

It ruffles its glossy blue-black feathers and then gives me a very loud squawk like it's about to give me a message. As it turns its head, I can see it's left eye is damaged somehow or like some of its feathers have covered it up.

Then, as I'm puzzling about that, I'm aware of some other creature off to the left. I turn slowly. At first, I think it might be Cuff, he often shadows me, as if I need looking after, which I do, but then I realise although it's the same 'make', as it were, it's not him. This one is leaner, almost skeletal, and 'she' has the same colour eyes as the hare.

I look back at the hare.

She's stopped cleaning and now just staring at me.

It begins to feel like I'm under interrogation.

They're all very still, so I can look from one to the other.

I'm just about to say something . . . I can't imagine what, when the raven ruffles her feathers again and just floats away with one flap of her broad wings.

The dog just disappears. I mean fades away.

I've no idea how long this takes, but then with a shake of her head the hare wanders off, checking out the odd leaf, but not partaking.

She disappears past the wall.

It's only then I realise that I've decided they're all female. Why, I don't know. But there's also an inkling at the back of my brain that I know all these creatures.

Somehow this calms me and so I set off back down to the cottage.

But the nearer I get the more fearful I become.
Something has changed and I'm not sure I'm ready for it.

What hasn't changed is seeing Ziggy's back and his hands flickering this way and that over the range of buttons and keys.

Nothing said.

So, I make him a coffee and take it in to him.

As always, he doesn't acknowledge my presence. Back to normal?

But then I go into the front room to drink mine, there's that thin vase that I've never used, standing on the table. Three fresh daffodils, proudly blaring their golden trumpets.

A business card lying next to it.

I pick it up.

'Hook, Becket & White Detective Agency'.

*   *   *

Walker has always hated using the police siren. It reminds him of his father's death.

Not wanting to go there, he shakes his head.

Gill is puzzled but says nothing.

She couldn't go much faster on the A1 and reaching the outskirts of Edinburgh makes it impossible.

They're there in an hour anyway.

By which time the woman is out of surgery and out of danger.

The little she's learnt about DS Janet Becket, supposedly retired, tells her she's one 'tough cookie', a phrase she overheard someone calling her.

Walker shows his card, they get access.

Ten minutes later he's sitting next to her bed, while Gill waits outside.

He's not long.

He nods and they walk out. Back to the car.

The frown seems to be stuck on his face, so she thinks she'll wait till he's figured out what's bothering him and what line of thought he's pursuing.

The young woman's mother is distraught, but there's nothing they can do and in any case another couple of officers and a social worker have taken her away, which is a relief for them. Dealing with hysterical women is in neither of their skill sets.

The hospital carpark is huge and there are constantly people moving about heading to one of the many buildings or coming back to their cars.

Gill hates hospitals with a passion and has been known to refuse to go to them after been injured more than once.

It's then they see DI Fletcher getting out of a car, followed by a tall woman with long silver-grey hair.

The two of them make their way to the main door and disappear.

'What are they doing here?' he murmurs.

Gill frowns.

'Aren't they the couple who have some relationship with that girl. The one who was kidnapped.'

Walker frowns.

'No, the girl, Ellie, I think she's called, she and her friend were in the bar when another girl was kidnapped.'

Gill shakes her head. She's always suspicious of recurring connections.

'Yeh, but why are they here now?'

'More worryingly how did they know to come here?' he murmurs.

They're now both frowning.

Without either saying anymore they both get out and go back into the hospital.

They eventually find the old couple in the canteen with the young girl. Fletcher is in the queue for coffees, so Walker nods Gill to him, whilst he goes over to the old woman and the girl.

A few minutes later the interrogations have stalled.

Walker is still trying to get his head round how this trio of interfering busybodies can have found out so much.

He's not sure he believes a word any of them is saying. Or not saying would be more accurate.

So, deciding that an ex-DI might appreciate this, he turns to the old man again, although the smiling face is not convincing.

'Okay, but how did you know the young woman would be here in Edinburgh?'

Fletcher smiles and taps the side of his nose.

'Old dog,' he murmurs.

Walker glares at him.

'No, you must have had some connection to her to know she was coming back here.'

'Well, it's Ellie, they're friends.'

Ellie stares at him, but then clocks the wink.

She pulls a face and then shrugs.

'Yeh, well, not exactly friends - we met at a party.'

Walker waits.

'But you're not even at the same University?'

Ellie nods.

'Yeh, I know, after . . . a 'carol' concert.'

Walker frowns. He's never heard of the band.

He looks at Fletcher again, who just gives him another shrug.

He glances at the older woman.

The response is chilling, like she's channelling Cruella. Pretty convincing actually. He looks back at the girl.

'So, who's the woman who got stabbed?'

The old woman and the girl both look at the old detective, whose eyes go wide.

'Er . . . yeh, Janet Becket.'

Walker waits.

Fletcher rolls his eyes. Always a scary sight.

'She was my DS for a while . . . but that's ages ago.'

Walker turns back to the girl.

'So, when did the girl contact you?'

Ellie shrugs.

'She was already on the train, said that she was scared that someone was after her.'

He stares at her again. Somehow, he knows she's lying, but why?

'Why you? If you hardly know her?'

Ellie shrugs again.

'Yeh, I was surprised, but she did tell me about her mother being a bit of a worrier and I'd told her about Fletcher being a detective.'

'So instead of informing the police, you thought you'd meet her on the station?'

Ellie shrugs.

'I didn't think it was that serious.'

Walker looks back at Fletcher, who just makes a face.

'She didn't tell me, otherwise I would have told her to call the police.'

Walker shakes his head, not believing that for one second.

Gill has been on her phone.

'Colourful history, DI Fletcher,' she murmurs, then looks up at him with a hard smile.

Fletcher can't help a grin, which he fails to hide.

'I prefer to say: 'an exemplary results list',' he mutters trying to sound offended.

'Ay, and numerous disciplinaries . . . and I thought I was a bad girl,' she adds.

Walker looks from one to the other.

Fletcher shrugs again.

'To be honest it's so long ago, it's all a blur.'

Walker glances at Gill who gives him the 'your call' look.

'Well,' he says, trying to sound severe, 'I think you now know it is very serious. Ms Becket has suffered a dangerous stab wound and could have died.'

The three 'suspects' put on a good show of serious faces, but he can tell their eyes aren't on the same page.

Back in the car he gets a call from DCI Culshaw.

'Where are you?' he asks.

Walker glances at Gill who's staring out the window.

'Still 'by the seaside',' he lies.

Culshaw sighs.

'Have you heard about the stabbing here?'

'No.'

'Another sigh.

'Well, there may be a connection with your case, the injured woman, who's a retired detective, was with the daughter of the man you found dead.'

'McKinley?'

Now Gill is frowning at him, wondering why he's lying.

'Anyway, we're dealing with this here, although I've already had a call telling me someone is coming to take charge as it's been regarded as a 'sensitive matter'.'

Walker waits, assuming he's going to be told to do something else, but realises Culshaw's having another conversation, and must have put his phone down . . . so he waits.

Gill gives him another frown. He puts his fingers to his lips.

It takes some time, but then Culshaw's talking to him again.

'Okay, you better tidy up down there and get yourself back here. There's plenty of other things you could be dealing with.'

The call is abruptly ended.

He stares out the window.

The old detective, Fletcher, with the girl and the posh woman come out of the hospital and make their way to their car. An old Merc, so hers probably

For some reason he thinks they might know things which might be relevant, so he nods to Gill to follow them.

She makes a face, but he knows the last thing she wants is to go back and face the music.

It's soon clear that they're making their way back south, but not to where the rich woman lives, because they're sticking to the Al.

Back to that house on the cliff?

MARIA

She comes awake.
>Where is she?
>Then it all comes tumbling back.
>The men in the station toilets.
>That girl.
>Blonde hair, strange eyes, were they green?

>It's very quiet.
>No traffic noises.
>No-one talking.
>Are the men still in the front?

No movement she can detect.

The back windows are painted over, but there's some light getting through.

She's never worn a watch; they don't work on her.

She feels for her phone but knows it's not there.

Her mother's face. She'll be worrying, which normally makes her angry, but not just now.

But, of course, then, where's her bag.

She looks around her and to her relief sees the bag beside her.

Tears run down her face. He wipes them away.

It's only then he sees the girl's eyes.

She's forgotten she was there.

She frowns and reaches out to her.

She cowers away.

What can she say?

'My name's Maria,' she whispers.

The girl just stares at her.

She now realises she's older than her, maybe thirty. Difficult to tell in the darkness.

She hutches herself up against the side of the van, which is difficult with her hands and ankles tied together.

She figures that although there's some light, they must be inside somewhere, because it can't be night-time yet.

It's then she realises she's hungry. Starving in fact. When did she last eat?

An image of sitting at a communal table with all those hippies, eating home-made muesli, which was horribly thick, and dry, sticking in her throat, she'd only managed a couple of mouthfuls.

Only a bar of chocolate and can of coke on the train.

She looks back at the woman.

She's still watching her.

'Olga', she whispers.

KENNY McKINLEY 1965 age 7

My grandmother was really scary.

Her room was on the second floor, where she would sit for hours looking out over the trees and bushes at the sea.

She was tall and very thin. She had long white hair brushed back from her face. Her hands were like bird's claws, with long hooky nails.

She had pale blue eyes, which didn't move, I don't think she could see very well.

The rest of the house was scary as well. Each room had lots of furniture, which was never used, because she never had any visitors.

The walls and paintings in the corridors were covered by the piles of newspapers. Once I went up to the top floor and bumped into one of the walls of papers and they fell on top of me. I tried to put them back up again, but they were so old they just fell into bits. I didn't tell anyone.

When I dared to look at some of them, I realised they were in different languages: a few in English, but also French, German, Italian and other languages I couldn't read, but mainly in Russian, which I'd heard she and my father talking to each other.

One time I asked why she read so many newspapers.

She just looked at me as though I was stupid and ought to know, but then she whispered so softly I could hardly hear.

And it was in Russian anyway.

But then she said it again in English.

'We need to know if they're coming to find us.'

She didn't say who 'they' were, but in my nightmares, they were like huge paper birds . . . their wings flapping like the noise of the papers falling on top of me.

She died on my eighth birthday.

CHAPTER NINE

'I know. . .' says Tomasz, trying to be calm.

He listens as Kasper goes on and on about what bastards the Russians are and what he'd do to them, if only his lungs would allow him.

He's always been a loudmouth and a bully, since he was a young kid.

He's just two years older than Tomasz, but always big for his age and takes after his father, who drank himself to death a long time ago.

'So have you been to the border?' he asks, interrupting the stream of Polish invective.

There's a pause.

'Nie,' he says, when he stops coughing.

'Do you know anyone who has been?'

'Tak, some of the guys from the bar went out there, but all they saw were people queuing at the gates, lots of cars and trucks. Mainly women and kids.'

Tomasz tries to picture that; he's been through one of the border posts some years ago. Hardly anyone there, the guards bone idle and rude. He can't imagine them being more helpful now.

'But not many people going the other way?'

Another bout of coughing, he sounded like he was dying.

'Yeh, there were some. Going to help their relatives I suppose and some of them daft enough to join in.'

Tomasz knows they've reached the difficult bit but doesn't want to tell him what he's planning as he doesn't trust him to keep his mouth shut.

'I'm bringing a friend; she has relatives in Lvov. Never met them or even seen them before, but she's been in touch and they want her to come and bring one of her cousins back to the UK, she's not well.'

Another bout of coughing.

'Good luck with that,' he manages to say.

Tomasz finishes the call after telling him he'll let him know when he's booked the flights.

He sighs and then realises his mother is standing at the doorway.

'Was he drunk?' she says through gritted teeth.

Tomasz shakes his head.

'No idea, but he's not long for this world, I think, coughing his guts out.'

She only nods and turns away.

He decides it's no use pursuing that and goes to find Imelda.

She's packing her rucksack.

Just like a young soldier, he has to admit. From the back she just looks like any young squaddie with the recently shaven head.

She turns, realising he's there.

He sighs.

'You almost convince me to turn gay,' he murmurs.

She stares at him and then gives him a lascivious glare.

'Which of the two humps do want to try first?' she growls.

But as usual with them, they have to do both.

Later, after dinner, Tomasz tells Amelia's children the story his mother used to tell him, first in Polish, then in English, about the two sons who killed a dragon by offering it sheep skins filled with sulphur.

Amelia pulled a face, but the kids loved it and could be heard re-enacting it with gleeful joy, for many days afterwards.

So now they're all ready to go, flight booked in a couple of days' time.

* * *

Louisa isn't exactly pleased to be going back to St Abbs, although missing out on her weekly cards afternoon is hardly that important. They're getting to be a bit of trial anyway as most of the older folk are gradually all losing their marbles and can't count the cards anymore.

So only managing a few glares at Fletcher, which is hardly anything he isn't used to by now, she drives in her usual manner back down the AI.

Occasionally she glances back at Eleanor and is pleased to see she's got her investigative face on, rather than worrying about Janet.

It's raining by the time they get there, although she thinks that's not a bad thing as it'll mean there'll be less nosey parkers at the house.

Anyway, she thinks a cup of coffee and a cake or two would be best before they make yet another illegal entry into a crime scene.

She shakes her head. What has this old 'detective' turned her into?

As if he's in her head, he laughs.

'We're turning into something out of an Agatha Christie series.'

She gives him her sternest look, but can't hold it and in any case, Eleanor isn't laughing, she's miles away. In her case, probably centuries ago?

Coffee and cakes done, they head for the house, where they find a miserable looking couple of uniforms, feeling left abandoned in this dreary 'haunted' house, stopping absolutely no-one trying to gain access.

Perking up, the young male officer tells them 'There's nothing to see, please move on' in his best hard-faced voice.

Fletcher merely flashes an old card and informs them they've come to do an inventory of the paintings and introduces

Ms Hetherridge, from the Arts and Antiques Unit and her secretary Miss Parker.

This doesn't convince the young man and he says he needs to contact HQ, but this is forestalled by the arrival of two real police officers who vouch for their authenticity.

So now the five of them are standing in the room where the old lady used to sit.

'So . . . what do you think?' asks Walker, thinking he'd better make use of these three busybodies, before he and Gill get another call back.

Fletcher's a bit doubtful of this couple's motives, they're not exactly sticking to the rules, but then he recalls that's what he always never did.

Before he can offer any suggestions, Louisa clears here throat.

'Well, actually it reminds me of that scary moment when Pip first meets Miss Haversham . . .'

The four of them stare at her, only two of them making the connection.

Louisa shrugs and half smiles at Fletcher who is one of them.

But surprisingly the other one is Gill, who frowns at her.

'Do you think the woman was 'jilted' by someone?' she asks.

Louisa smiles and shrugs.

'No not necessarily, it's just the atmosphere.'

They all wait.

'An old lady abandoned, just sitting here day after day, watching the sea, even though you can't see the beach or the waves crashing against the cliffs.'

The others glance at the window, to check out the truth of what she's saying.

'How do you know she did that?' ask Walker.

Louisa indicates the chair and the way the rest of the room is arranged.

'She's not sitting at a table. So not eating or writing here . . . there's not even somewhere to rest a book or a cup.'

'Maybe someone else removed other pieces of furniture . . . a table?' Walker thinks out loud.

Louisa shrugs, looking round.

'Completely?'

The others simultaneously come to the same conclusion, but that just leaves them all the more confused.

'Maybe . . .' muses Fletcher, 'but they might still be in the house.'

They all consider this, wondering what those objects might have been and where they might be now.

But now Fletcher's bending down, kneeling on the polished floor beside the chair, feeling the patina.

'Look,' he murmurs, 'there are faint marks, polished over, but they're still there.'

The others bend down to look.

Sure enough, they eventually identify four round marks, no not round, oval with dimples on one side.

Fletcher gets to his feet, with a sigh and a grin.

'So, we're looking for a table about three and a half feet long by two foot and half wide – with, I think, actual feet and toes.'

'What's that in new money?' asks Gill, then realising she's in the minority here, so grins at Ellie, who rolls her eyes back at her.

Either way they set off to hunt the table down.

Inevitably it is Ellie who finds it. Whilst the others go into rooms on the same floor, Ellie goes upstairs.

First door on the left, a table standing by itself in the middle of the floor, looking awkward in what was at one point a child's room, given the small bed, teddy bears and other toys tidied into a big box.

She shouts down.

'Found it!'

The others appear on the landings and make their way up to her.

Gill and Walker carry it down, she wondering when they agreed to be the willing servants for these people.

Back in the room they carefully carry it to where Fletcher had found the 'footprints' and gently place it onto the marks.

Then it made sense the way it was angled away from the window, so that the person sitting at it could write or read at it whilst only having to turn their head to the left to see the sea.

'You should sit there, Louisa,' says Ellie, softly.

Louisa frowns at her, but can't help smiling, before easing herself on to the chair and sitting in her customary upright manner.

As they've not put any lights on, they then realise that the afternoon sun is coming through the window from the other side of the room silhouetting her against the front window.

With her long silvery hair and slim figure, she looks all the world like a Russian émigré Duchess. Even her pale blue jacket and pearl necklace seem a perfect choice.

The others are just astonished by the image, which they just arranged without considering where the light would be coming from.

Walker is the first to speak.

'What's in the drawers?' he asks softly.

Louisa stares at him and frowns, but then opens one and then another.

She shakes her head sadly, even trying to feel at the back to see if there's anything trapped there.

'Nichivo,' she whispers, making them all frown. 'Nothing,' she translates.

Walker shakes his head.

But then she reaches underneath and feels this way and that, until she stops, and her eyes go big.

There's a soft click and a thin drawer comes out of the left-hand side.

She reaches over to it and fingers out a white envelope.

Bigger than an A4, and not modern.

She puts it onto the table and then looks at the four pairs of eyes staring at her like hungry owls.

Walker stands up.

Taking a step towards her, he pulls out some plastic gloves and offers her a couple.

She makes a face, she hates them, but in this instance, she thinks it's necessary. The flacking noise she makes putting them on seems totally inappropriate and makes her frown again.

Carefully she opens the envelope and pulls out a stash of photographs, glances at the first one and her other hand goes to her mouth.

She puts them on the table and sits back staring at them. The others go to look, as she then carefully separates them one after another until there are eight of them lying in two rows.

They look at each other, knowing they all recognise who these people are, except the rather fierce looking man, long unwashed hair, top right in two of them, who, unlike the others is dressed in a long black robe, with a huge ornate cross hanging on his chest.

'It's them, isn't it? whispers Ellie.

Louisa nods.

'And I'm pretty sure that's Ras-Putin,' she whispers, as she and then everyone else realises the connection, which no-one's yet pointed out, since the recent trouble began.

'And these photos are different from the arrangement McKinley composed with the dummies,' he says softly, 'which I think means he probably hadn't seen them.'

Without anybody saying anything they find themselves all backing away.

Gill looks at Walker.

He frowns back. This is going to be difficult to explain to Culshaw.

As if he's in his head, Fletcher sighs.

'Oops,' he says. 'I think I recognise this situation . . . out on a limb, not telling people where I am or what I'm doing.'

Walker can't help but give him a wry smile.

* * *

URSULA

I hate hospitals.

I always have.

I'm also not a fan of driving anymore. Well, certainly not in big cities. Ironically, it's been Janet who drives us to do the shopping, but even that's only a few miles away to Galashiels or Peebles, depending how she's feeling. They are after all, very different places. The former the biggest place in the Borders with all the major supermarkets, whilst the latter only home to Sainsburys, obviously, given the high self-esteem of the royal burghers.

Fortunately, Edinburgh Royal Hospital is on one of the main routes into the city, so I don't have to tangle with the town centre and the parking is enormous.

A nice lady on the reception tells me where to go and then a young black man points me to her bed.

I'm lucky because a doctor is just finishing his check-up.

Ziggy has thoughtfully given me various papers and documents to show that although I'm not a relative, Janet having nobody else extant, I qualify as next of kin.

He reads them and frowns, but then shrugs. Not as if he hasn't met anyone else with no 'next of kin'.

By this time Janet has realised it's me and is managing a wan smile, which is something I never thought to see on her face.

The doctor says I can have half an hour, but not to get her upset. I roll my eyes at him, as if she were ever capable of that.

I sit down and put my hand in hers.

It's as cool as usual.

She manages a weak smile.

'Not the first time,' she murmurs, 'bastards.'

I can only smile, thinking these particular 'poor bastards' have no idea the lengths she's already promised herself she'll go to exact retribution.

'So . . .' she rasps. 'Anyone on their trail yet?'

I shrug. I don't know about the local police here, but Ziggy is obviously on the job, which doesn't need saying.

'I think Fletcher and his team are on their way to the scene of the other crime.'

'You mean in the big house on the cliff?'

I nod, not really knowing much more than seeing a few photos on one of Ziggy's screens.

So now we're sitting not speaking.

Janet's eyes have closed.

I become aware of the hustle and bustle around me, although I can't see any of it.

'Sooka . . .'

I stare at her.

Her eyes flutter open, struggle to focus and then she grins.

'I don't think it was a compliment . . . he'll have a bruise on his cheek.'

The grin fades to a smile and then her eyes close again.

I wait for a few minutes to see if there's another resurrection, but then she starts to snore, so I think that's not going to happen.

I pull out my phone and call Ziggy. I don't do texting. Too many fingers and thumbs and life's too short.

I tell him what she's just said.

As expected, it only takes a few seconds.

'It must have hurt, it means 'bitch' in Russian . . . and Ukrainian.'

I wait.

What does that mean?

It's then I can hear Ziggy talking to himself . . . as usual.

'Either way would be a problem . . .' he mutters and then the call is cut.

I decide I'll go for a coffee.

I can't help but think what either the Russians or the Ukrainians would do with someone descended from the Russian Royal family?

Just sitting there in a crowded canteen, I remember how much I hate hospitals.

And then I realise a woman is staring at me. Who is she? And now she's coming towards me.

'I'm sorry,' she says, 'one of the nurses pointed you out to me.'

I'm still giving her my puzzled look, no idea who she might me, but I can see she's upset.

I grew up with a 'mother' whose first response to any upset or injury was to tell the person to 'get a grip' or 'what doesn't kill you makes you stronger' along with a whole host of other puritan homilies, so I resolved a long time ago to be the opposite of that.

So, I pull out a chair and ask her to sit down.

Would she like a cup of tea? She shakes her head, but now tears are rolling down her face.

Again, unlike my mother who thought handkerchiefs were for decoration only, I always have a couple in my bag.

The woman accepts my offer and blows her nose.

'Is your friend going to be alright?' she asks.

I frown again.

'How do you know about her?'

She bites back a sob.

'She was trying to help my daughter.'

It's at this point I wish I could have Ziggy here, but then I realise I can do that.

'It might be better if you talk to my. . .' I stutter, then couldn't for the life of me think of a word that would describe Ziggy.

The woman frowns.

I look at the phone he's given me. Nothing like the things he has, because it had to be simple enough for me to use, but cleverly organised so that I only have to press a limited number of buttons to get him on screen.

'. . . friend . . .' was all I could come up with.

I press the three buttons in the correct order and then abracadabra there he is!

I pass it over to the woman, who is puzzled, but easily adjusts to a person on a screen.

They then have a conversation as though I'm not there, although as expected, Ziggy cuts straight to the chase.

The upshot of this, which I have no idea how even he managed to do it, is that two hours later, the two of us are following a private ambulance carrying Janet back home. Well, we're going to the private hospital he's having her transferred to and then back to the cottage.

Ziggy has convinced the woman that he's the best person to help her find and rescue her daughter. This despite he's wearing ridiculous make-up and that unconvincing glossy black wig.

Two hours later she's sitting in the front room and looking dazed.

Well, you would be, wouldn't you?

*   *   *

MARIA

She comes awake with a jolt.

No, not her, the van.

The driver is grinding the gears or there's something wrong with them.

It's dark, but she's no idea how long she's been asleep.

The van is going slowly, the driver having to keep changing gear, as it seems to be navigating a tortuous route. Occasionally there are lights, but not white light, more orange or dimmed.

It stops, but the engine's still running, a noticeable cough interrupting the motor.

Is that a voice?

And a different one. Much deeper. What language is that? Not English . . . or French. Lots of shushes. Incomprehensible. Not even any clue to how the person is feeling. Annoyed? Disinterested? Impossible to say. Well, they're not shouting. The engine is turned off. The van sways and creaks and then rests. The man has got out. It feels like he must be a big man, heavy.

Now they're moving away, still talking, but soon they've gone.

She feels for her bag. It's still there.
What's that smell?
And now she can hear something else. Something swishing, lunging.
The sea?
Which one?
There's no sound of a wind, maybe they're in a big shed.
It's only then she remembers the girl.
Where is she?
She feels this way and that but can only find empty plastic bags and a tyre.
She gets on her knees and tries to crawl towards what she thinks is the back.
But then she touches something warm. A leg?
There's a sound.
An intake of breath?
Two eyes glimmering at her.
She backs away.
'Sorry,' she mutters.
The eyes keep watching her.
'Do you know where we're going?'
The girl adjusts her position, and a shaft of the orange light illuminates her face. She puts up her hand to block it, but not before she sees she has long hair, all tangled, dropping onto her shoulders. She's wearing some sort of coat, although it looks too big for her, might even be a man's.
Her face is pale, and her cheeks are streaked with dirty marks.
'What's your name?''
The eyes harden.
'I'm Maria.'
This makes her frown.
'Are you okay?' she asks.

She looks down.
'Do you speak English?'
A slight nod.

A hundred questions crowd into her brain, but the same one jumps to the front of the queue.

'Do you know where they're taking us?'
She looks up.
A ghost of a smile, then a flash of anger and then fear.
'Adyessa.'

KENNY MCKINLEY AGED 7, 1965

My mother used to take me to see my grandmother.

She has two really big dogs.

They are 'Bortzoys' – which is Russian for wolf hound.

The older one is called 'Nikolaev', but he only responds to Kola and sleeps a lot and when he walks or tries to run, he's a bit stiff. The bigger one is Lexy and he's really playful, although he's never hurt me. The one thing I don't like is that he likes to lick me and his tongue is really wet and rough.

Grandma Elena tells me strange stories about her sisters and her little brother, who wasn't very well . . . but it made her cry, so I put my arm round her . . . she has a strange smell.

CHAPTER TEN

The two police detectives and the threesome who aren't, decide to go back to the old school café, although when they arrive, they realise it's nearly closing time.

The good thing about this as far as Fletcher and Ellie are concerned is that they're selling off the cakes at half-price!

While they tuck into a huge plateful, watched with disdain by Louisa, Walker is on the phone trying to speak to Culshaw, which he's finding difficult. Too busy apparently.

So, when Ellie gets another message from Ziggy, she hands her phone to him.

He listens.

His eyes go wide.

'Are you sure?'

The others are all now frowning at each other.

'Where?'

He shakes his head at the crowd.

'Well . . . I can't really do . . .'

He listens . . . for some time. Nodding and occasionally giving them a roll of his eyes.

'Okay, we're on our way.'

He puts the phone on the table and then looks at Gill.

He frowns and looks away.

'What?' she asks, thinking maybe she's going to have to face up to what she did to DS McAlister . . . although how would Ellie get that news?

He shakes his head and then looks at the other three with a frown.

They all give him their versions of 'not me, guv?', which in Ellie's case is a faux innocent smile, Fletcher giving a wider smile meaning 'maybe' and the Cruella version of 'I think you might have the wrong person' from Louisa.

'Apparently, your friend ex-DS Becket has been hi-jacked from her hospital bed and taken to a private establishment by that weird guy with the eighties fetish.'

Ellie assumes this means Ziggy, but it's lost on Fletcher and Louisa.

'You mean Ziggy?' she says.

Walker nods.

This just makes the other two frown.

And then he looks at Gill.

'I think that means the 'bollocking' is on hold for now, as we have to go and question Ms Becket . . . oh, and the missing girl's mother is also conveniently included in the hi-jack, so 'two birds' etcetera.'

This cheers Fletcher up no end, but Louisa is getting tired of all this gadding about, so she says she's to be dropped off at home, while the rest of them can go play detectives.

*   *   *

Two hours later they're all crowded into the White Cottage's small front room, apart from Ziggy, whose room is flashing with all sorts of things going on, including continuous footage of the war zone, although now mainly focussed on the southeast region where the war crimes are being committed.

No-one can think of what to say or do about that, so not talking about it.

Walker and Gill have been to see Becket in a rather austere, but very expensive nursing home, but she's in late seventies 'some dance to forget' land, so no sense of what's going on.

The strange woman, Ursula, is busy doling out tea, coffee, and snacks as if they're just living in café land for the day.

The girl's mother, 'Jen', she's said to call her, is in a bit of daze, surrounded by all these odd people and wondering how she has managed to end up here, when suddenly she feels the buzzer on her phone which means Maria's alarm function is calling.

She fumbles in her bag to find it and texts her.

Her eyes go big.

But then the connection is cut.

The only other person who knows about modern health alert systems is Gill because her school friend had one.

She turns to look at the woman and frowns.

'Is that a problem?' she asks.

Gill stares at her, but the tears well up.

'She's a haemophiliac,' she blurts out.

Gill's eyes go big.

'A or B?'

Jen takes a deep breath.

'B, but very mild and the message was to say she's okay.'

The phone stutters again. Incoming mail sound.

Jen reads it and stifles a cry.

By now all the others have realised something's up and are all looking at her.

She looks up at the three pairs of eyes staring at her. She slowly translates the abbreviated message.

'She says she's been kidnapped. Now travelling south. Back of a van. With another girl, who is also very frightened.'

Ziggy seems to have always had highly sensitive antenna for things like this and is now standing in the doorway, his eyes bright with anticipation, although Jen just stares at him . . . which is understandable, given the cockeyed makeup and the cloak of many colours, which doesn't quite hide the stripey shorts and naked chest covered with weird symbols.

'May I,' he asks, holding out his hand.

Jen wouldn't normally give her phone to someone she doesn't know, especially when it concerns Maria's welfare, but she meekly hands it over.

No 'thankyou' or 'I'll be careful' with it, he turns quickly and disappears into his room.

The others all glance at each other, but it's Fletcher who tries to be helpful.

'He's the weirdest person I've ever met, but he is good at this . . . I mean tracking people down . . . so . . .'

He grinds to a halt, aware of the big eyes all looking at him.

He shrugs.

Gill and Walker exchange glances. He gives her a nod towards the girl's mother.

Gill gets up and goes to sit next to her.

'How is she normally?' she asks.

The woman frowns.

'You mean with the condition?' she asks.

Gill nods.

The woman looks away.

'Nothing for ages . . . although I doubt she'd tell me, anyway. . . we've. . . sort of fallen out. . .'

Gill just waits.

'It's the girl she's shacked up with . . . except she's not a girl . . . she's twenty-three.'

Gill knows Walker's letting her continue – 'woman to woman', which always irritates her. She can't stand most women. Always letting men get away with everything. And this woman's a good example, not far off whining.

'So how is your daughter, I mean, how well does she deal with it?'

As she expected the woman gives her a sharp look as though she's implying that she hasn't taught her properly.

'She's good. She knows the risks . . . but . . . it's rare in females and not as severe.'

Gill waits.

The woman looks away, angrily wiping a tear from her cheek. She gets up and goes to stand at the window.

Gill glances back at Walker, who gives her a slight shake of the head.

But it's Ellie who goes to the woman and suggests a walk in the air would be a good idea.

When they've gone, Gill gives Walker another frown, but he says nothing.

The strange woman, Ursula, who Gill is now puzzling where she's met her before, looks uncomfortable and gathers up the cups and goes to the kitchen without a word.

'We can't deal with this,' Walker eventually murmurs. 'If she's been kidnapped and taken down south somewhere it'll be an English problem.'

Gill shrugs again. Not her call.

Walker looks at his phone.

Nothing from Culshaw.

Despite what he's just said, he's intrigued by this development. What's this got to do with the staged photograph and the family connections. If it's for real, then the girl is . . . what? A descendant of the Romanovs? What would that mean to the Russians? Is she a threat or something else? He doesn't even know who the people are who've kidnapped her.

Ziggy reappears at the doorway.

'They've just left the A1 north of Newcastle . . . I think they're heading for the airport.'

Walker frowns at him.

How are they going to stop this?

Standing up he goes to Ziggy's doorway.

And stands there in disbelief.

He's not seen anything like it before. He's been in the comms room in Manchester and although he's not been to the one in Edinburgh yet, he assumes there's a similar set up there, but nothing like this.

Apart from the assemblage of computer gadgetry, one on top another and wires everywhere, there's the incongruous paper lists hanging from washing lines, pictures and messages and articles all mixed up, looking like handmade Christmas decorations.

Ziggy's hands are flickering from one keyboard to another, whilst he's oblivious to Walker's entrance as he has headphones on and another two around his neck.

He's also talking to what sounds like two or three different people, one of them in a harsh language Walker doesn't recognise.

He just stands there. How can he interrupt this? And, then he realises Gill is standing behind him.

He glances back at her.

Her eyes are big and it's only then he realises they're a very pale shade of green, in fact almost yellow, like a cat.

She shakes her head.

Ziggy turns with a frown on his face, which reminds Gill of a clown, which makes her shiver.

'I suspect they've got a private plane, because all of the afternoon flights are going to Spain.'

Walker has only had one dealing with airport police and security at Manchester, which was not a successful operation. A more unhelpful and arrogant group of guys you wouldn't want to work with.

'Still,' says Ziggy, 'if they don't take the meds tracker off her, we'll be able to follow her.'

Walker and Gill exchange glances.

'But they must know about that?'

Ziggy shrugs.

'Not necessarily, they don't look like a phone. They might not know she's got the condition . . . it's very rare in females. And now they're often incorporated into a watch or a bracelet. You'd better ask her mother.'

Gill pulls a face at him, so Walker goes to look for her outside.

They're nowhere in sight but there's an obvious track going towards the river which he can hear.

Sure enough, he finds them on the riverbank.

The woman is sitting on a bench whilst Ellie is throwing stones into the water.

He smiles at the woman, but only gets a stony face back.

He asks her.

She nods.

'It's part of her bracelet. Her father bought it for her not long ago.'

Walker nods.

'So can you contact her?'

She looks away.

'Since we had the row, she told me not to,' she almost whispers and then tears flow down her cheeks.

Ellie puts her arm round her and makes a face at Walker, which he interprets as 'give her some space'. He walks to the edge of the river and stares at the scenery without really seeing it.

* * *

Tomasz is watching the news.

Whilst he's pleased that the Russians have decided to give up on Kyiv for now and are focusing on the southeast, that's a long way from Warsaw. The only place he's been in that area is Odessa and only for one very long drunken, girl excessive week.

What was her name?

Yana!

He almost blushes at how much he was 'smitten' by her? Is that the right word? Sounds like being stoned . . . which they were a lot of the time . . .

But then they'd go walking along the front or swimming in the sea which is strangely very dark.

So how do you get there now?

It's only recently he's had anything to do with computers or searching the web, which he's still very suspicious about, knowing there's plenty of people out there who would want to harm him.

Normally he'd ask Magda or Amelia, but recently her eldest son Davy, who's only just fourteen, has become a bit of 'whizz' at the keyboard, like a young Ziggy, although thankfully without the bewildering taste in cross dressing and clown make-up.

As usual he finds him in what was once his father's office, which Magda decided should be the 'communications hub' with an array of three laptops and various other communications devices. Davy is the only one who uses it, as the others prefer to communicate or play on their phones wherever they happen to be. He's not above playing games still but seems to have moved on to more sophisticated activities way beyond Tomasz's knowledge.

'Hey, Davy, what do you know about Odessa?' he asks, knowing any other opening is likely to be ignored or answered with a brief shrug of his thin shoulders.

Without a pause the answer comes like he's just pressed a button or two.

'Ukraine's main port, on the Black Sea not far from the Russian invasion forces. It's likely to be their most important target now as they've given up on Kyiv.'

Should a boy his age know all this, thinks Tomasz, and then shrugs. Dead right he should.

'So, how do I get there?'

This takes a bit longer.

'No direct flights at the moment, I'll try somewhere else.'

Another few minutes.

Where's Imelda?

'OK, Saturday three pm Heathrow, arriving in Bucharest at six, four hundred pounds first class for two,' comes the laconic answer, although still no eye contact yet.

Tomasz stares at the back of his head.

Not just finding the bookings but assuming he'll be taking Imelda with him and that four hundred pounds is not a problem.

'No hurry,' the boy continues, 'there's plenty of seats left.'

Tomasz is for once in his life uncertain.

'You can reserve them for twenty-four hours,' adds Davy, still not yet turning to make eye contact.

'Okay.'

Now Davy turns round and smiles at him. The same mischievous smile he uses when he's done something wrong.

'I'll need your bank details.'

Tomasz frowns, trying to dismiss the idea that he probably knows them anyway.

'Ok, let me just go and check it out with Imelda.'

They're both smiling, but there's an awful lot more going on between them.

Tomasz puts his hand on the boy's shoulder and nods.

'Thanks . . .'

He has lots of other questions and worries but backs away and leaves the room.

On the way upstairs his head is full of questions. What will Imelda say? What if she says no? Does Amelia know her son can do this sort of thing? Is she okay with that?

What he doesn't see is the brightness of Davy's eyes as he resumes his investigations about what's going on in Ukraine. He's in touch with five young people over there. Two in Kyiv, two further east just recently relieved by Ukrainian forces and from yesterday a girl in Odessa, called Tania, who's been telling him she can see the dark clouds further east from her window and how her mother just cries all the time, because her father is out there somewhere fighting.

He looks out of the window across the valley, where the trees are beginning to go green.

It's difficult to imagine what it must be like to be there. All the images he's seen of Ukraine are flat vistas in every direction to the horizon. Lots of huge corn fields as far as you can see. Just one huge river called the Dnieper.

He shakes his head and then sees Yuri is wanting a contact.

Tomasz finds Imelda in the bedroom.

She's packing a case.

She's worked it out, maybe she overheard. She's always had that ability to shift from one place to another without making a sound.

He goes to stand in front of her.

'Are you okay with this?' he asks, knowing being direct is the only thing that works with her.

She nods but continues to fold and pack clothes into a case.

He sits on the edge of the bed and waits.

'I'm not coming with you,' she whispers.

He doesn't move.

She doesn't make eye contact as she folds and lays another dress into the case.

The room seems cold. The sun must have gone behind a cloud.

Now she looks at him.

'I don't want to stop you going and if you survive . . . we'll see . . .'

Neither of them speak and now she goes to stand by the window.

He stares at her silhouette, not knowing what to do. To say he wasn't expecting this is more shocking than her refusal to go with him.

But then he recalls how quiet she was whenever the war came up, often leaving the room or finding an excuse to do something else.

The signs were all there . . . he just hadn't recognised them.

She now turns to look at him, but with the sun behind her it's difficult to see her face.

He gets up and goes to her.

They embrace.

The usual passion ensues, but there's an awkwardness neither of them have felt before.

Now they're lying on the bed.

Her eyes are closed.

He traces the line of her cheek down to her neck.

She shivers.

He stares at the ceiling.

'Do you mean Harris?' he asks.

'My father's house, yes.'

'Okay, but can I take you there?'

She opens her eyes but then looks away.

'I've never been there, so I can't imagine what it's like,' he adds.

She looks back at him. Her eyes are hard, like she's trying to penetrate his mind.

He can't face such a gaze, so he looks away again.

It was probably only a few seconds, but it seems longer to him.

Her fingers touch his cheek.

He shudders.

'One day. One night,' she says.

He opens his eyes.

She's smiling.

*   *   *

URSULA

All this toing and froing is leaving me dizzy.

But now there seems to be a determination for action in the air.

Ellie has brought the girl's mother back and all the conversation is about her daughter.

I can't imagine being a haemophiliac. Having to be so careful what you eat or drink, watching out for every little scratch and worse still some quiet internal bleeding. Although Ziggy says it's rare in females and never as bad as it is for men.

I just overheard what Ziggy was telling that black detective about the possible connection to the Russian royal family. He's printed out a brief history of their terrible ending. Yet now he's suggesting one of them survived . . . and this girl might be descended from one of them.

As usual I go for a walk.

I'd like to have gone to be with Janet, but the nurses were stern and said the best thing for her was to be left alone for her body to fight for itself. I can't think there are many 'bodies' in the world more fiercely committed to living than Janet's.

Despite telling myself to stop thinking I'm always going to meet my hare, I can't help going along the path where I generally meet her, although since the last time I'm also looking out for the other two creatures as well.

Just when I'm thinking that none of them are about and have stopped to stare across the valley at the Steil house high on the opposite hillside, I can hear some rustling behind me.

I turn round.

Not the hare, but the crow stalking along the path pecking at this and that. It stops and cocks it head to one side as it gives me a stern look. Once again, I realise there's something wrong with one side of its face. Like it's wearing an eyepatch.

A glittery badge. Silver and blue with a red eye at the centre.

It's at this point it slowly dawns on me.

It's always seemed to me that the hare was like a 'what-do-you-call it', I looked it up . . . a 'wraith' . . . no, like a 'daemon', something only I can see. But the recent arrival of this crow and the frail dog makes me think they might be something else . . . or I'm going doolally.

Anyway, I've never tried to talk to them and often they disappear just after I realise they're there.

But today, it's not disappearing.

In fact, the crow is staring hard at me.

Then it squawks! So loud, I jump.

Then there's the hare the other side of the fence and out the corner of my eye I see the dog fading in and out to my left.

What do they want?

The crow squawks again.

Was that a word?

'Bucket?' I whisper.

The crow shakes it's feathers and jumps a few steps closer.

'Becket!'

I stare at it, then I run.

Back at the house, I get Ziggy to ring the convalescent home where Janet's been taken.

He's a little reticent, but maybe also a bit taken aback by my insistence.

The conversations are brief, but punctuated by long pauses, until eventually there's a longer response.

I'm fearing the worst, but eventually Ziggy's cuts the call.
I stare at him.
He looks stunned, but then shakes his head.
I can't bear this.
He seems to come to, stares back and me and then shakes his head.
'She's okay,' he whispers.
I can hardly breathe.
'Apparently, it was only because a nurse heard a noise, that she went into her room. Janet was half onto the floor, some of her drips had come lose and she was bleeding . . . but she's okay, they were able to resuscitate her and get her back on the bed.'
I know I'm staring with my mouth open but now the tears come.
Ziggy puts his arms round me and holds me. All I remember is the scent he was wearing as I sink to the floor.

Sometime later I am sitting with the obligatory mug of tea.
Calls have been made and updates received.
She's going to be okay, in fact, the fall has brought her back to consciousness.

But the really weird thing is that as the nurse went into the room there was a large bird, a crow she thinks, but a very big one, flapping at the window.
And guess what . . . she was adamant that it had a silver badge over its eye.
I know.
But who would believe her? Or me?

*   *   *

MARIA

It's not a big boat.
    But not a fishing boat.

More like someone's private yacht.

The two of us have been ushered up on to deck and told to sit on a polished wooden bench. We've both got handcuffs on and know jumping off would be suicidal.

The crew are all dressed in big jumpers or yellow waterproofs. They go about their business. It feels to her they know what they're doing and know the boat very well.

There's no-one ordering anyone about, but if she turns round and looks above, she can see what she thinks is the cabin, although the angle prevents her from seeing anyone.

From where they're sitting, they can see a skyline getting more and more distant, until it becomes just a line with a couple of smoke pillars rising straight into the sky.

She learnt to use maps and compasses when she was very young, going walking and climbing with her dad and then later school trips and climbing groups, so looking at the sun, she works out they're going steadily southeast.

Holland?

And then where?

Could be anywhere.

She shivers.

Two large anoraks are flopped down beside them.

They look up. A huge man gives them a lopsided smile and says something. She doesn't understand. Not French or German.

The other girl mutters something.

What language was that?

Are they speaking the same?

She frowns at her, but she's too busy getting the coat on.

After they've both struggled into the coats which are far too big for either of them, she snuggles back and pulls up the hood.

'What language was he speaking?' she asks.

The girl turns back to look at her from inside the hood. She's staring at her as though she's stupid.

'Ukrainian, of course,' she says.

* * *

ELENA MARY WALLACE 1958

She puts the phone down.

She's a grandmother.

She knows she should be happy, but . . .

Anyway, she's managed to persuade them to give him a Russian name, which she can tell Kenneth is not so keen on, and that his parents definitely don't like it.

So, he'll be called Kenneth Alexie McKinley.

She can't help but smile at that . . . although that triggers a deeper sadness. Thinking about her little brother, born to be . . . she can't even whisper it . . . not even . . .

But no tears come.

They dried up a long time ago.

CHAPTER ELEVEN

URSULA

Sometimes days and nights just float by and to be honest it's a long time since I could definitely tell you what day it is without thinking or having to look at a calendar.

As a secretary in a car sales office writing letters and composing other documents for men in suits, the date was always at the top of the page in front of me and on the 'tasteful' calendars on the walls.

But since I met Ziggy, time has become elastic.

And if you count my 'meetings' with weird creatures, space is getting unpredictable as well.

So how long ago did Janet get shot?

Two or three days?

She's much better, sitting up in bed and managing the occasional stagger to a chair. She'll be making life difficult for the nurses and constantly asking when she can get out.

Magda is now back at home, but under orders not to go anywhere near a horse.

Tomasz and Imelda have gone off to the Isle of Harris, which I had to look up on a map. You forget how strung out the UK is and how many islands it has. Even driving at his breakneck speed, it would have taken them half a day to get to the remote part of Harris where Imelda comes from. One and half hours on a ferry, which would be more than enough for me. The house is on the other side of the island just up from a beach. The view is next stop Canada, says Ziggy, nearly three thousand miles of sea, which is incomprehensible, especially as he tells me a lot of the island's population emigrated there two hundred years ago in boats a lot smaller than the ferries.

He also tells me that Ellie and her friend Mali have had a falling out and while Ellie's still at Louisa's, Mali has gone back to Edinburgh.

Meanwhile the two Edinburgh detectives have been told to stay put here at the moment until Magda is well enough to 'take over the reins again', which he thought was hilariously funny and couldn't stop repeating it. I eventually got the joke, but it's not that funny.

As far as I can tell there's not much other crime for them to deal with here and Walker can't stop going back to the house by the sea, as though he'll find some explanation for the girl's father's extraordinary Madame Tussaud exhibition.

So, I'm now cast in the nursing role. A first for me and like a lot of things I've got into since I met Ziggy, a 'steep learning curve' as my erstwhile boss used to call every problem he ever met, before he handed it to someone else to sort it.

And I have to admit, it doesn't really suit me. Ironically, I seem to have inherited my not-mother's attitude to other people's medical problems, which was largely 'buck up' and 'you're not dead yet' exhortations. I don't exactly say those phrases to Janet but changing her dressing is definitely not on my to do list. Fortunately, a no-nonsense nurse has now been detailed to do this on a daily basis, so that's a relief.

Other than that, everything has quietened down.

No appearances from any of my three stalkers when I go out for my daily walk.

But then, another one of my not-mother's many dictums was that 'it's always calm before a storm'.

*   *   *

Ellie is sitting on one of the old benches which are dotted along the banks of the Tweed, on the stretch which Fletch considers 'his walk'.

It's far too early for him anyway, as the sun is only just coming up above the tree line. Good job she's wrapped up in one of Louisa's fur coats.

But she's not really seeing the scenery.

Just restreaming the row with Mali.

It's not as if it's the first one they've ever had . . . arguing and disagreeing on almost everything has always been their way.

So, what was different about yesterday?

Ostensibly it was about going back to Edinburgh. Going to classes. Mali saying she needs the challenge of being able to argue cases, whilst Ellie is quite happy communicating with her professor via Skype and accepting her handwritten royal mail posted remarks on her essays – in what would have been called 'a beautiful hand' in Victorian days. Immaculate green copperplate ink swirls gently pointing out the errors which she'd found.

But . . . yet . . . there had been something else.

The way Mali wouldn't hold her gaze.

The shrugs.

The peremptory love making.

Was there someone else?

She'd asked, but only received a shake of the head.

Then yesterday.

It was the coldness in her eyes.

Was that Fletcher's heron?

Do birds recognise different people?

She watches as it glides serenely along just a few feet above the water, before doing that final upward lift and alighting ont the big log trapped above the rapids. A ruffle of feathers and then that imperious settling of the neck.

The cold breeze flutters against her face and she realises that she's crying.

Then she hears footsteps.

Fletch.

The incongruous overcoat. Not his.

The woolly hat. Definitely not his!

He stumps up to her and roughly barges his way on to the bench next to her.

She manages a smile, but then collapses onto his chest. His arm comes round her.

'You can never trust them,' he mutters, nodding at the heron, who is now readjusting a few feathers.

'You mean birds?' she whispers.

He shakes his head.

'Nah, you daft thing.'

She frowns.

He pulls away and looks her in the eyes. His still their distinctive green and blue, but the green becoming fainter every time she looks at them.

'Women,' he mutters.

Nothing more is said . . . although for some reason which eludes her this doesn't seem to include her.

They eventually get up and walk right down to the bend, where the path has to make the climb up to the top of the steep cliff as the river takes a sharp left through the gorge.

He stands looking across at the cliff side opposite.

She knows why he comes here.

Some rich villain. Someone Louisa knew. A long story, which ended with this man falling from a rusty old ladder onto a broken spike. No-one to help him. A slow and painful death . . . which Fletcher said was justifiable punishment for the evil he had done.

It's then Ellie asks her question.

The one she's been dying to ask someone for a long time.

'Do you dream every night?'

Fletcher is still back in time, standing in that underground chamber, skeletons and a deranged madman, the echoing of the gunshot reverberating along the corridors.

He looks at her.

'<u>Every</u> night?'

She nods.

He frowns.

'Well, if I do, I don't remember them. They always seem to drift away as I wake up . . . I think.'

She's staring beyond him.

'Mine don't . . . they linger.'

He wants to reach out and hug her, but he can't.

'They generally don't have anything to do with what I've been thinking about beforehand . . . like this morning.'

He waits, strangely aware of the bird song nearby.

'What do you know about the Jews in the concentration camps?' she asks.

Now he's totally confused and, yes, quite worried.

'I mean,' she continues, avoiding his eyes, 'what did they talk about? Did they know what was going to happen to them? '

Now he can't stop himself, he reaches out and pulls her towards him, putting his arms around her.

She lets him, but after a few moments she pushes him away.

He's expecting to see tears, but she's just shaking her head.

'I think it should make me weep, but actually I'm just curious . . .'

He doesn't know what to say.

But now she gives him a weak smile.

'The thing is . . . as I said, this happens every morning. I seem to wake up every day in a different story. Mostly nothing to do with what's happened the previous day. Nothing to do with what I'm studying. Nothing to do with something on the TV . . . it's the randomness that confuses me. . .'

He's expecting her to burst into tears, but she doesn't.

'The brain's an amazing thing . . . I suppose.'

He doesn't remember what happened next except they set off back to Louisa's house.

Neither of them talk about what she's just said and by the time they get back, he's just left puzzled, because she doesn't refer to it again and seems perfectly happy, stopping to watch two ducks squabbling about something.

But it worries him for the rest of the day.

*   *   *

Walker still has no message from Culshaw.

He goes back to the White house.

Gill is sitting at a table with the strange woman, who always looks away when he tries to catch her eye.

She doesn't this time.

But she doesn't say anything either.

So, he goes through to the even stranger computer man. Who as usual doesn't stop what he's doing, as though he hasn't heard him. Walker watches as his fingers flicker hither and thither, the images on the screens overlapping and changing at a bewildering speed.

But one of the screens stops on a photograph.

The Madame Tussaud's exhibition composed in that room at the big house on the cliff edge.

'You know who's missing, don't you?' mutters Ziggy.

Walker nods.

'Yeh, the daughter, Maria.'

'Exactly.'

'And you've done the family tree?'

'Yeh . . . which suggests the current missing suspect could be descended from one of the sisters or the boy.'

The photograph morphs into a map.

'But have you seen this?'

He has to go closer and would be the first to admit, geography was not one of his top subjects.

But then as he watches he sees a red line starting from somewhere in the middle of Russia with a long name he can't read. It dribbles all the way to what he recognises is the Black Sea, more to do with what's happening on the TV recently, than any prior knowledge.

The line stops and a name is highlighted. Odessa.

But before he can confirm this, the line dribbles on southwards but now at sea. Until it reaches Istanbul.

Then there's a different map and it's got a name.

'The Orient Express'.

A flick of a switch and the red line is from the place in Russia which he now sees is called Yekaterinburg all the way to Edinburgh.

He stares at the back of Ziggy's head, which is disconcerting in itself, as there seems to be a letter 'Z' shaved into his hair . . . although it's the wrong way round? What does that mean?

Ziggy turns round.

'The Odessa Express operated from 1878, only stopped by the war, so in 1919, if someone was taken from Ekaterinburg to Odessa, she could have got to Edinburgh in the early twenties.'

Walker stares at him.

'Are you serious?'

Ziggy shrugs.

'All the other pretenders were proved to be fraudsters, even Anna Anderson.'

Walker waits, he knows there's more.

'But what if the survivor didn't want to be found?'

Walker nods.

'Then she'd have a different name and be determined to get as far away as possible . . . and disappear.'

Walker shakes his head.

'But didn't they prove that all the family died?'

Ziggy makes a face.

'The rich always make themselves disappear when the going gets tough. Look at what's happening with the oligarchs now. One thing is certain if the war goes badly for Russia, Putin will be gone as well.'

Walker is still unconvinced.

Ziggy turns back to the screen.

A picture of a painting comes up, which Walker faintly recognises.

Ziggy turns round again.

'Ellie sent me this. It's the in Istanbul, which is hanging on the wall in the room where the old lady died . . . the painting's title says it's in Constantinople, because it didn't become Istanbul until 1930 and Ellie said there were old paintings of other cities in the house as well. One of them was the Eiffel Tower, Paris, another place on the route.'

Walker stares at him and shakes his head.

'But . . . what . . ?'

Ziggy smiles.

'The young woman would be a prize for either side . . . and a threat to whichever side doesn't have her.'

Walker stands up and leaves the room. He needs to clear his head.

Ziggy calls out after him.

'And guess who's setting off to Odessa in two days' time.'

But Walker's gone, doesn't hear him.

* * *

Tomasz is watching a seal.

It seems to be watching him, bobbing away only ten metres away. Just his forehead, round eyes, and whiskers. Or maybe he's a 'she'?

What is he/she thinking?

They must be used to seeing humans, even on this remote beach. Although, of course, as Imelda said, it's not that remote. The main road is only quarter of a mile away, beyond the dead artist's house, where they slept last night.

Imelda is far out where the river meets the sea, although right now it's the other way round, as the swell reaches a few yards further as he watches.

Beyond the river there's another beach, white sand curving to the headland, the one in all the photos. Out in the bay there's the island, sold a couple of years ago. How weird is that? Someone owning a whole island.

He shrugs and looks at the sand.

Not that many shells.

Imelda says that even in her own lifetime the number has dramatically diminished. Meaning the creatures who made them have too.

He sighs.

Makes his way slowly towards her.

Last night was his last night.

He's booked on the ferry at two.

Ullapool and then Inverness. Flight to Edinburgh, then onto Bucharest and the rest.

Is he really going through with this?

He stops and looks for the seal.

She's not there.

The next wave crashes heavily and wets his bare feet.

He watches as the sand sweeps up to his ankles.

Is he even capable?

He's spent the last few days practising and he'd never actually stopped. At least two practice sessions a week since he's been home. The targets in a field a good mile across the valley. Then, there were the more distant targets up on the hills.

He's forty-seven now. Too old for combat, but that assumes hand to hand stuff, which he's never been any good at anyway.

Will he be welcome?

The limited responses he's had seem positive, but that's on the internet. Face to face will be different.

He's been told he'll be met at the airport and taken to Odessa by car.

Then presumably further east.

Mariupol.

The images of the power plant.

The survivors still holed up.

His worst nightmare.

He looks for Imelda.

Can't see her?

It's early, not yet six. So, there's no-one else there either.

Where's she gone?

Then he remembers.
There's the beach round the corner.
He sets off.

Later they're back in the house. The woman who died. Her unfinished paintings still on their easels, others hanging on the walls.
Imelda's making breakfast.
The last supper?
He goes over to stand behind her, puts his hands around her waist and snuffles into her neck.

This all a memory as the plane powers up into the grey sky.
His face reflected in the window.
No tears on his cheek.
Just that cold, dead look that serial killers have behind their eyes.

* * *

MARIA

She comes awake with a jolt.
Where is she?
But then the heaving of the boat reminds her.
She sits up and bangs her head. A memory of a youth hostel. Her dad snoring.
And then she remembers. He's dead.
Lying there behind the montage of figures he must have assembled, which she now knows were representing the Russian royal family.
She shudders.

The boat does another huge lunge downwards and then up again.

She knows she never gets seasick, but then she's never been in a boat like this. It's not small but nothing like the channel crossing monsters.

She snuggles down again and turns on her side.

Across the cabin another pair of eyes stare back at her.

Is that a smile?

She sits up.

'What's your name?' she asks.

The girl frowns, but then shakes her head.

'Olivia.'

Maria stares at her.

Then the realisation of what's happened to her comes thundering back.

She bursts into tears.

The girl gets off her bunk and comes across the narrow gap between them and puts her hand on her shoulder.

'It's okay. Don't be afraid. They're not going to hurt you.'

Maria wipes her eyes on her sleeve and stares at her.

The girl smiles again and goes over to a little table where there's a coffee pot and a stove. She flicks the switch on and puts coffee into two mugs.

Maria thinks this is just like being in someone's flat, but obviously not.

As the pot starts to burble, the girl turns to stare at her. Then shakes her head.

'You really don't know who you are, do you?'

Maria can only frown.

The girl pours the hot water into the two mugs and then brings one of them towards her, but as she offers the cup, she makes a curtsy and whispers:

'Maria Nikolaevna.'

* * *

ELENA MARY WALLACE   MARCH 19TH 1950

She's standing alone in a churchyard.

It's a much bigger church than where she and John were married.

But this is where many of Kenneth's family are buried.

Elena will now be Mrs McKinley.

A huge gathering, she can hear laughing and cheering the other side of the church.

How should she feel about this?

Part of her is proud . . . but mainly she's sad.

John should have been here . . .

EIGHTEEN MONTHS LATER

AUGUST 2023

CHAPTER TWELVE

URSULA

I've never understood the ongoing fetish for running.

Yes, I know it's about keeping fit, but why does it have to become so obsessive? Keeping records on your phone, counting the number of minutes, the steps, the distance.

Me? I just go for a walk. Just the same two or three routes. Although now accompanied by the dog.

Dog? You might ask. Wasn't I one of those people who was afraid of them?

You're right, I was and I'm still afraid of most other people's dogs. You know the sort. People who let their dogs run free, saying 'he'll never hurt anyone' just before their dog is attacking mine.

It's not the big dogs, they don't seem to be bothered, it's the little terriers and weird mixed-up breeds.

I've got a cocker spaniel. He's a rescue dog. People who had him couldn't look after him after they'd all gone back to work after Covid, so he was left abandoned eight hours a day barking all the time, upsetting the neighbours.

So, there he was and now he's here.

It's like having a very attentive minder. Always watching for the possible movements that might indicate I'm even thinking of going for a walk. Follows me round the house as though he's worried that I might get lost and can't find the way outside.

Becket came with her friend John's dog, but he didn't last much longer than John did. Becket's a dangerous person to be around. Seems to attract terrible events and people.

But . . . I suppose . . . she's also reassuring, because anyone would think twice before coming anywhere near us.

Us being me, her and Ziggy . . . and my guardians.

I know.

Only I can see them, so they're probably not 'real' – just figments of my imagination. If you want to think that I don't mind.

So, Ziggy . . . aka Sigismund Hook, today dressed in yellow chiffon sitting in front of his bank of screens monitoring whatever he thinks the bad people don't want us to know about.

Not sure what he's into at the moment, but always keeping us abreast with what is actually happening in the war in Ukraine.

This morning he's been fairly quiet. No news.

But then he appears like a bedraggled fairy, but with a grin on his face.

'Guess who's just come home?'

Neither I nor Janet can guess, so we give him blank faces.

*   *   *

Eleanora de Camville is looking at herself in the mirror. Not in the bathroom, but the huge one in Louisa's hallway. She's wearing the full-length dress she bought from a proper couturière in that otherwise deserted village marketplace in France a couple of years ago. A sunny day, only one other customer before her.

Louisa and Fletcher have gone out. She'd declined to go with them.

'So . . .' she whispers. 'Shall you go to the ball?'

The degree result is finally sinking in.

A 'two one'.

She knows her tutor thought she was capable of a First, but the distractions of the last few years getting involved in all sorts of adventures – some of which nearly killed her, had curtailed the time for studies.

So, what now?

When her mother even looked like she was going to ask the question she'd given her the stoniest glare she could muster, which stopped anyone else thinking about it as well . . . even Louisa.

She snorted at the person in the mirror and flounced away into the library which she'd taken over as her study . . . now over a year ago.

All the books and papers about medieval France and England are now abandoned on a side table, whilst their places are taken up by her next obsession.

The Russian royal family.

She is waiting for the university to accept her MA proposal. It was bland enough, but good enough to hide what she was really going to do. The missing teenager and the house by the sea were going to be her real investigation.

She was going to persuade Fletch to take her back again as soon as he could. The girl's mother had given her the key on condition she kept her informed if she found out anything that might help her get her daughter back.

Now she's looking at the old family photograph next to the DIY Madame Tussaud's version, which the man who thought he was descended from them had created.

She smiled to herself and then burst out laughing.

She knew people, even Fletcher, thought that level of obsession was probably delusional.

But what if he was right. That one of the daughters, Maria, had escaped and managed to get to Scotland?

She looks at the family tree again, even though she knows it so well.

Elena <u>Maria</u> Markovitz died 1966 m (1931) John Wallace 1900-1944
/

Kenneth McKinley 1924 -1988 m (1950) Elena <u>Mary</u> Wallace 1930 - 2007

/

Kenneth <u>Alexie</u> McKinley 1958-2022 m (1990) Jennifer Leyton 1970 -

/

Elena <u>Maria</u> McKinley b 2004 –

She sighs.

'Not much use if we don't even know where she's gone,' she says aloud to herself.

'Talking to yerself,' says a gruff voice.

She swings round, eyes wide.

But it's just Fletch creeping up on her.

'Don't do that!' she shouts, but then she's laughing, until she realises, she's gripping Louisa's paperknife in her hand.

'Whoa!' mutters Fletcher, but he's grinning as well.

Knife left on the table, the three of them are sitting outside drinking the coffee Fletcher's just made.

'So how will you get access to any evidence,' Louisa asks.

Ellie makes a face. This is the reservation that her tutor has already pointed out.

'Well, actually there's quite a few people who I've already contacted - emigres, descendants of old families who escaped at the same time.'

Fletcher frowns.

'Aren't they worried about 'Poo-tin' finding out about them?'

Louisa shakes her head at his pronunciation.

'Well, I think he might have other worries right now,' she murmurs.

'Exactly,' says Ellie.

'Although . . .' Louisa says with a sly smile, 'there's someone who might have more up-to-date connections about what's going on in Russia right now.'

Ellie and Fletcher both frown at her.

'And he's recently been on the route you've got marked out on that map on your desk.'

Ellie stares at her.

'Who?'

* * *

Back in the Tweed valley, a taxi turns in the driveway of the house high up on the hillside and heads back to civilisation. Well, Edinburgh.

The figure left standing in the rain has a soldier's kitbag over his shoulder, but he's not looking at the big house behind him. Just taking in the view across the valley. The view that he'll never forget. Home.

A gaunt face, marred further by the black eyepatch over his right eye.

His stillness seems to have made all the other creatures go silent. No calling blackbird song, no chittering of the sparrows who live in the big oak tree. No dog hurtling towards him or horses neighing in the barn.

He turns to look at the house: it's many eyed windows not holding a face or two. But then he sees that there are no cars or Landrovers near the barn. Not telling them he was returning hasn't helped.

He turns to look at the view again.

Amelia's horses are in the field, next to the remains of the burnt-out house – a sad reminder of her dead husband's tenure.

He's still standing there when a landrover does make a late appearance.

It comes to a halt in a swirl of gravel.

The doors open and two people get out.

One immediately making her way as fast as she can towards him, the other standing watching.

Now he's in the clutches of his mother as she holds him so hard, he can hardly breathe. Kissing his face like she's giving him a wash. Tears now soaking his cheeks.

She stops, holds him away to see it's really him and then hugs him again and then pulling away again to rain a torrent of Polish expletives at him whilst she straightens his jacket and puts her fingers through his hair, but not going anywhere near the black patch over his eye.

All this is watched by the other figure standing, one hand on the jeep door, tears streaming down her face.

Now a dog is released from the landrover and defying his old arthritic bones gallops to his master and jumps and turns twirls of excitement around him.

Half an hour later they're all sitting in the sunshine on the terrace, glasses on the table and the second bottle of fizz resting ready in the ice bucket.

Neither Magda or his mother have asked him yet why and how he's back, both just so happy he's here.

There's a hesitant pause.

'I'm not going back,' he whispers.

The two women don't even glance at each other, but then he looks away, tears streaming down his face. Helena goes to put her arms around him.

The evening sun comes out from behind the clouds and blazes its dying light across the scene.

Later, after a hastily mustered banquet of Sunday's leftovers, they're sitting on the balcony in the cooling dusk, none of them venturing questions or answers although they're buzzing around in Magda and her mother's heads, whilst Tomasz has no intention of sharing anything that's happened over the last year and a half.

Even thinking 'only eighteen months' doesn't make sense somehow. Time out there was a difficult concept to grasp, memory both rejecting and then blaring out the horrors in vivid technicolour.

He shakes his head.

Hengist licks his hand.

And he realises he didn't flinch . . . and then the tears come.

It's only weeks later that he tells them the story.
How he lost his eye . . . and will never shoot again.

The first few weeks he'd just been in Odessa.
Not exactly a holiday.
The line fluctuated every day but was now a hundred fifty miles away.

When he'd gone there it was hopeless. No-one wanted him. Told him to go back. So, he doubled back and found another way. Not easy. Difficult to know who to trust, but eventually he found a group of ex-soldiers, an assortment of nationalities, who, when he demonstrated his marksmanship, decided to take him with them.

It was terrifying. Even for him.

Having to rely on their local knowledge and hoping they wouldn't betray him.

This worked for a long time. Especially when they were able to identify Russian commanders and where they might be.

It was like being back in Afghanistan.

But in the end, the daily sighting of individual heads or torsos bursting into bloody cabbages became too much even for him, so he said he'd have to leave.

This didn't go down well.

At first, they pleaded with him, but then it got nasty. Beatings and threats. Being left with no food in caves and burnt-out houses.

Taken from one place to another.

And then the worst thing. A couple of guys drunk and high on something came to get him. Told him what they were going to do and then poked his eye out with a gun barrel. He couldn't get the sound of his own screaming out of his head.

Then abandoned in a farmhouse near the frontline. No gun. No food or water.

Heavy shelling destroying what was left of the village, until he knew he had to try and get away.

The rest is a nightmare. Of staggering about in the darkness.

And then waking up in the hospital.

No memory of how he was rescued, although he was told he was lucky anyone found him. A group of soldiers on a recce, finding him huddled in the corner of a burnt-out house.

Taken back to Odessa and spending hours in the operating room as they fought the infection which would have taken his other eye.

All this a blur. Literally.

But eventually he could see again. Ironically the left eye he used to sight targets, but the other was gone.

The pain lessening but the memories filling his nightmares.

*   *   *

DI Walker sighs.

He's sitting in his 'office'.

A far bigger room than he's used to having, but that's because the Borders police don't have much of the higher echelons of power anymore.

In fact, the building's half empty anyway and feeling like it's not long for this world as a police headquarters.

The walls which might have been covered with boards back in the day just now only host a rather lonely photograph of the town. What date, Walker can't even guess.

There's no phone on the desk and no filing cabinets, just his laptop and an empty cup of coffee.

So, this is what's happened to the promotion, heralded as a breakthrough for 'people of colour' gaining positions of authority in Scotland. Instead, he's been shuffled off here to take over control in the Scottish Borders. Well, the eastern end. Where the western side starts, he doesn't know, somewhere up in the hills.

He looks at the to do list which has materialised on his desk. Who put it there or even who wrote it he's no idea, but even the cursory glance shows nothing 'to do'.

The only other news is that DS Gill has also been consigned to accompany him, which only confirms his view that this must be the dustbin. Three problems sorted.

There's a knock on the door.

Can't be Gill, she'd just come in without knocking.

He waits.

Another knock.

The door opens.

DS Gatti appears.

So not just blacks and troublemakers, foreigners as well. Walker gives him a questioning look.

'Er, sorry sir, we've had a message from the Highlands force.'

Walker has to smother a grin in case he might start laughing. He knows that it's a huge area and mostly empty, so other than poaching he can't imagine any other criminal activities.

Gatti ventures into the room holding out a paper.

Walker rolls his eyes.

'Just tell me,' he growls.

Gatti frowns.

'Well, apparently the woman who the girl who's been abducted was friends with has been arrested in Skye for possession and violent affray.'

Untying this knotty 'news update' Walker realises who he's referring to.

'Where's that?' he asks.

Gatti frowns.

'Er . . . well, it's in the Inner Hebrides.'

'Where?'

Another frown.

'Way up north . . . islands . . .' Gatti offers. He's never been there either.

'So . . .' Walker wonders, thinking does someone have to go there.

'Given her 'record' and possible involvement in the . . . case you were investigating . . . the waxworks . . . St Abbs . . . sir . . . they . . .'

'Bringing her back here?'
Gatti shrugs.
'I think so . . . sir.'
Walker stares at him.
Gatti waits.
'When?'
Gatti looks at the paper.
'About five,' he confirms.
This is the moment Gill arrives, pushing her way past Gatti.
'You heard the news,' she growls.
'About the girl?' asks Walker.
Gill frowns.
'What girl?'
'The waxworks guy's daughter.'
She frowns again.
'Oh, no, it's McAlister.'
'What?'
'He's dead! Shot by some dealer. Not sure about the situation, but it's been hushed up, I think.'
'So how do you know?'
She shrugs, trying not to grin and then looks away.
Walker looks at Gatti, who's trying hard not to be there.
'Er, thank you, sergeant,' he mutters and takes the paper from him.
Gatti backs out, not even glancing at Gill.

'So . . .' says Gill, but then Walker's phone chirps.
He stares at her as he picks it up and listens.
Gill goes to look out the window.
The call ends.

'Sorry,' says Walker. 'Looks like you've been chosen for Alice in Wonderland.'
Gill sighs, but then frowns.
'You as well?'
He nods.
She can't suppress the grin.

'Mad Hatter or Dormouse?'

MARIA

Maria looks out the window.
Just miles and miles of trees.
At the moment all is green, but she knows that's soon to change.
Will she still be here when they go orange and red, or will she be taken somewhere else?
She still really can't believe what's happening to her.
The horror show at the big house.
The weird hippies out on that island.
Then the kidnap at the station . . . is that woman they shot dead?
The boat.
The girl.

She looks at the piece of paper she's torn from one of the books.
Fifteen days now since she was kidnapped in Edinburgh.
Ten days in this chateau.
She's pretended that she doesn't know any French, so that she can listen in to the conversations between the staff, although they don't give much away, they're just looking after her and the house.
She knows they've been told that she has an illness that means she can't go anywhere without supervision, so even walking round the gardens she's followed by one of the men with a dog. Not nice dogs. Big Alsatians or mastiffs who growl at her.
Previously when she's been in France, she's visited places like this and used to like doing that, but not here.
She's pretty certain that this is just a stopover hiding place before they can take her further east.
To Russia.

Because she's the only living descendant of the Romanoffs.

She sighs.
Then shudders.

She dropped History in Year 9, preferring Geography, although not that bothered about that either. So, her knowledge of any history is only from seeing programmes on TV. Her knowledge of France is better, but she knows it's still very limited. Just beaches and hotels really. Although her mother was always dragging her to markets, where she would wander around, buying dresses far too young for her and then spend hours in bars and restaurants, letting young men try to flatter her.

Her father never came with them, even when they were still together. He would be off to the outer isles or the mountains.

Now her thoughts go back to her grandmother.
After all she was the reason for all of this.
If it's true.

A key rattles in the door.
One of the women who brings her meals enters with the latest offering. As it's France it's dinner, even though she generally doesn't eat much of it, because she's not hungry. Walking round the gardens for half an hour is hardly much exercise.

Today it's fish.

'Vous avez un visiteur,' the girl says with a smile, but it fades as she sees the glare this provokes.

She turns away and almost runs out.
'A visitor?' Maria murmurs to herself.

In the event it's a couple of hours later when the 'visiteur' arrives.

A tall woman, late forties maybe, elegant, and self-composed. She smiles and as she approaches, she drops her knee and bows her head.

Maria is getting used to this, but still feels pretty stupid, no intention of responding in whatever way might be appropriate in her captors' eyes.

'Votre Altesse, je suis honoré de vous rencontrer.'

Maria shakes her head.

The woman smiles and indicates the chair beside her.

'Je peux?'

Again, Maria frowns and makes out she doesn't understand.

The woman shakes her head, but the smile remains as she takes the seat and settles back in the chair.

'I know you understand French and speak it fairly well . . . a grade B I think in your last exams?'

Maria stares at her. It's true, but she's not going to play this game. She looks away.

'My name is Duchessa Natalia Orobchenko, my great grandmother was a friend of your great grandparents.'

Maria doesn't respond. Why are they doing this?

The woman lets the silence deepen.

'Why deny your inheritance?' the woman says softly in English.

Maria looks back at her.

The woman smiles back at her. She's either a good actress or she's somehow been deluded into believing these lies.

Maria stands up and walks to look out the window.

'Even if it was true, although I know it isn't, what use would I be?'

She turns to stare at the woman, who makes a face, but then smiles again.

Maria walks back towards her and sits facing her.

'My knowledge of Russian history comes from my father, who I now know was obsessed with this . . . this insane idea.'

The woman looks away.

'I'm afraid, my dear, that it's true.'

Maria shakes her head again.

'But what do you think my going to Russia would do?'

The woman smiles.

'We're not suggesting you do that . . . yet.'

Maria frowns.

'So . . ?'

The woman looks away.

'We have to be cleverer than that.'

Maria laughs, but the stern look the woman is now using silences that.

She waits.

The woman is still, staring at the window, but obviously thinking hard about what she says next.

Eventually she stands and goes towards the door.

She doesn't turn to face her but whispers some words that Maria can hardly hear . . . in Russian . . . and then she's gone.

'It's your destiny . . .' Maria translates to herself.

She goes back to the same window.

'Destiny?' She sort of knows what the word means, but . . . does anyone believe in that anymore. Like horoscopes? Pretend 'gypsies' holding your hand in a tent? It's all nonsense . . . isn't it?

She turns round. She wants to scream. This is making her go mad. She must find a way to escape.

As if the people holding her can see into her mind the door opens and two men come into the room.

Without a word they come over to her and dragging her by her arms they force her out of the room and down the stairs.

Down and down until there's no windows.

A door. They push her in and across the room.

The door clangs shut.

A key grates in the lock.

She stares about her.

A bed. A jug of water. A plastic cup.
A window high up. Too high to see out.
What time is it?
They took her watch when she was on the boat.

She drags the bed over to the window and stands on the headboard.
Just high enough to see the sky and the hills in the distance, but then there's a crunch and the headboard splinters and breaks spilling her onto the bed.
Catching her breath, she checks that she's not broken anything, but her hip hurts.
She sits on the floor with her back to the wall.
And shivers.
Looking round she sees there's no lamps and the only light comes through the high window and it's fading even as she looks.
She puts her head in her hands and weeps.

Just when she's thinking she'll be left in the dark, the key grates in the door again.
A man comes in and points at the bed.
She goes to sit down.

A different woman comes in. She has a brief conversation with the man. Her gestures and the harshness of her voice must have been to make him reluctantly leave them together, but the key grates in the lock again.
The woman comes and sits on the bed next to her.
She smiles.
'My name is Lydia,' she says, as though that might convince her that she's on her side.
Maria looks away.
The woman puts her hand on her arm. Maria brushes it off.
The woman waits.
Eventually Maria can't resist a sideways glance.

The woman is smiling, but still.

'Are you hungry?' she asks.

Maria shakes her head even though the thought of food makes her tummy rumble.

The woman pulls out a phone and speaks quickly . . . in French, Maria thinks, although it's with a strong accent.

The woman smiles but doesn't say anything else.

The door opens.

An older woman comes in with a tray of bread and cheese, an apple, some grapes and a glass of water. She gives Maria a strange look but doesn't smile.

When she's gone, the first woman nods at the food.

Maria looks away.

This impasse goes on for a few minutes, but then Maria's stomach rumbles and she reluctantly reaches for the water.

The woman watches, smiling.

Maria picks up the cheese.

This cat and mouse game goes on for some time.

Maria gradually devouring the food, while the woman just smiles.

'So . . ? she says, in English, 'what if I agreed to do what you want, what would I have to do?'

Lydia smiles and looks away.

'It's complicated,' she murmurs, 'The timing is very important, as is the place.'

Maria shakes her head.

'I think you're deluded. What do you think Putin will do? He'll just say it's a lie, a desperate act by the west to weaken his soldiers' resolve . . . and it seems like that to me.'

Lydia smiles again and then frowns.

'I agree a lot of people will think that, but they're not in touch with what many Russians are actually thinking – maybe not saying it yet, but the longer the war goes on . . .'

Maria shakes her head.

The woman looks away.

'We're already in touch with certain influential people, who are not rejecting the idea . . . in fact, they've asked for information, photographs of you.'

Maria stares at her.

'You're mad,' she whispers.

Lydia stands up. The smile has gone. She walks to the door.

'So was Stalin,' she rasps and knocks on the door.

It's swiftly opened, and she's gone.

Maria looks away, shakes her head, but then the tears roll down her cheeks.

ELENA MARIA WALLACE March 1942

She's standing at the window.
The paper in her hand.
She's read it three times now.
John is 'missing in action.'
She can hear 'their' daughter singing upstairs.
How can she tell her?
She's only eight years old.
Younger than she was when her father was . . .

CHAPTER THIRTEEN

URSULA

We've been invited to lunch to celebrate the prodigal's return.

None of us do 'lunch'.

Ziggy only eats when someone else puts it in front of him and even that doesn't always work, and the food goes cold and ends up for the birds.

Becket is much the same. A life spent on the run, hunting or being chased. Never time for lunch.

Me? I was brought up to think 'lunch' was something unchristian people did and bordered on the sin of greed.

And, therefore, none of us know what we 'ought' to wear.

So, Janet's in a green dress which was abandoned by some previous visitor. It's actually rather fetching, in an old-fashioned, upper-class way.

I had to ferret in some boxes I'd forgotten I had and found a skirt and blouse that I vaguely remember wearing when I was an office person.

Ziggy, however, has an extensive wardrobe of weird couture, mainly female, but today he's found a man's suit. A bit small for him and the trouser legs halfway up his legs. This being the only male attire, to clash with the blonde bob fringe, heavy makeup and shiny purple bootees.

Janet drives us along the lane to the bridge and doubles back to go up the hill. Rather sedately for her. Generally, her driving leaves me a juddering wreck after spending most of the time with my eyes shut and fingers clutching the car door handle. The final few hundred yards through the huge oak trees and then coming out beside the stables.

Getting out we're whinnied at by the two horses in the stable.

And then the old dog coming to see who we are.

Becket being the bravest and a natural dog fiddler greets him, but then he's sniffing around me wondering where my dog might be. I decided I'd leave him at home . . . now thinking 'home?'. How long has that been? And Ziggy neither bothers with dogs and they don't bother with him.

Then we're greeted by Magda and taken round to the terrace, where two bottles of champagne are basking in a silver bucket on the side table. Six garden chairs waiting.

Tomasz is standing looking out over the valley.

Helena, their mother is now coming towards us and we're all kissed in the Polish way whether we like it not. I don't . . . normally, but somehow this old lady makes it easy.

Tomasz now turns and comes to shake hands.

It's very difficult to not stare at someone with an eyepatch, but he carries it off like it's a fashion accessory. In fact, when I take another look, it does seem to have a jewel on it and a thin silver braid along the edge.

I realise he's smiling back at me, and I can feel my face glowing red.

'I know,' he says, with a laugh, 'but it's what I was given in the hospital in Odessa. That's all they had. Probably left by some Russian émigré, I suspect.'

My embarrassment was covered by the arrival of more guests. I hadn't thought that might happen, but now Louisa, Fletcher and Eleanor arrive, and I have to get through another bout of kisses.

However, I do find larger crowds allow me to gravitate to the edge and soon I've found a niche in the terrace wall where I can stare out over the valley.

Eating with other people has also always been difficult for me.

My mother regarded all mealtimes as something one had to get through as quick as possible so everything could be washed up and put back in their proper places as though eating was another sinful activity and at the very best only sustenance.

One thing that was the same, however, was that Helena insisted on saying grace . . . in Polish, and then in English, with a smile . . . and to my relief that was the last formality. The afternoon continued with friendly chat and laughter and I was not allowed to sit aside and just listen, which is my normal way of getting though events like this, because Helena was particularly insistent in asking for my opinion, even though I generally don't have one, never mind being able to share it.

Eating over, I helped Helena take away some of the debris and end up in the kitchen with her drying the pots, which surprised me as most people have dishwashers nowadays.

We did this in a companionable way, her chatting about the weather and the horses, but then I realised she was wiping her eyes with her sleeve.

A more forward person would have probably tried to comfort her, but I just pretended I hadn't noticed until she pulled out a large hankie and blew her nose.

She didn't turn to look at me but leant against the sink and sighed.

'You'd think a woman with my history would have got used to people coming and going . . . some never returning . . . at all.'

I froze. I'm no good at comforting people.

'He's promised he's not going back . . .' she murmured, but then did a strange laugh and turned to look at me.

I hadn't realised she had such blue eyes, like Tomasz . . . I couldn't look away, like she'd frozen me. Instead, she looked away through the window and sighed.

'But tomorrow he's off to Harris to try to find Imelda . . .'

Again, I didn't know what to do or say. Why was she telling me? Imelda was one of the weirdest people I've ever met.

'She didn't reply to any of his letters, and she hasn't a phone, so he doesn't even know if she's still there . . .'

I realise she's sobbing and then found myself putting my arms around her . . . something I've NEVER ever done in my life.

Thankfully no-one arrived at this moment, but anyway, she rubbed her eyes and laughed . . . and then she kissed me on the cheek!

The rest of the afternoon passed in a blur and then we're leaving, driving back down to our house by the river. I can't remember anything until I'm lying in my bed.

I touch my cheek.

When was the last time someone kissed me?

*   *   *

Arriving back from the coming home event, Ellie had gone straight to the library. She'd got very little from Tomasz about the war, but he was intrigued by her brief telling of the possibility of a surviving Tsarina ending up in a house in St Abbs.

He'd said he'd like to go and explore the house, but then he'd told her about going to find Imelda, so she would have to wait.

Now she's trying to find out more about Russian emigres after the Revolution.

The word she came across almost immediately was 'diaspora', which she had to look up. What then surprised her was the range of places the Russian upper classes escaped to . . . pretty well all over the world!

But many of them went via Constantinople, now Istanbul, and ended up in Paris, which had become the place to be after the First World War . . . even now there are a lot of descendants still living in France.

She finds herself down by the river.

Can't remember getting there.

How can she find someone who her captors definitely don't want to be found?

'But hang on, they DO want her to be FOUND!' she yelps and then realises Fletcher is a few yards away, stopped in his tracks and staring at her with a worried face.

She laughs.

'It's alright, I should have said 'Eureka', she giggles.

He's still looking worried.

She tells him what she's just realised.

He frowns.

'But how are you going to find them. I doubt there's a handy 'find a Russian émigré' guidebook.'

'No,' she says, 'but I bet there's any number of internet sites – there's plenty of stuff about Anna Anderson.'

'Who?'

'She was the woman who claimed to be Anastasia, Maria's sister.'

Fletcher vaguely remembers hearing about that.

'But wasn't she found out to be fraud?'

Ellie nods again, 'but Anastasia's body was found next to Maria's, although now it turns out the DNA is too degraded for both of them to confirm that.'

Fletcher puts a finger to his lips and they both watch as 'his' heron lifts off the tuft it was standing by and with one flap floats off downstream.

Neither of them had seen her, even though she wasn't hiding.

Ellie whispers.

'Hiding in plain sight . . .'

Back at the house, she's busy researching Russian emigre families in France. A big ask. Hundreds of them. How can she find where Maria has been taken?

Then it comes to her.

She rushes round to the sitting room. No-one there?

She finds Louisa in the conservatory tending to her 'dragon' plants.

'Isn't one of your card players a Russian lady?' she demands.

Louisa stops her spraying and turns to stare at her.

'You mean Sophia?'

'Yes, didn't her family escape from Russia after the revolution?'

Louisa stares at her and puts the spray tin down.
'Yes . . . but I wouldn't ask her to talk about it.'
Ellie frowns.
'Why not?'
Louisa laughs, but then shakes her head.
'Because she will go on and on forever. Nobody asks her anymore because we've all heard it a thousand times.'
'Would she talk to me about it?'
Louisa stares at her.
'You must be mad . . . but yes . . .'

So, half an hour later she's going round to see her, Fletcher driving Louisa's car.
'I ought to have a uniform,' he grumbles.
Ellie giggles.
'I bet Louisa's got one going musty in some cupboard.'
'Don't you dare,' he laughs, although he can't stop a racy encounter blossoming in his imagination.

It doesn't take long, and the first sighting was from across the river, but it's not the sort of house you'd expect an émigré Russian Countess to inhabit. No crusty old towers and hundreds of windows. Instead, a very modern building – almost science fiction.

They have to drive another couple of miles to the nearest bridge and then double back.

The outer wall is old, and the original gate house is still there, but they have to be buzzed through by an electronic voice, the huge metal gates silently opening. The trees are all densely planted evergreens, so it's only when they get to the end of the drive, they can see the house again.

Two men in black suits appear at the entrance. One of them points to the bottom of a set of concrete steps. Fletcher pulls in and while one of the men stands guard the other comes down to open Ellie's door.

They're escorted in and find themselves in empty corridors. No paintings or photographs. Just glossy brown wooden walls.

Then accompanied in a lift.

All this in silence.

No conversation. No eye contacts.

So, it's a relief to be ejected onto what Ellie thinks might be the second floor into a vast space, huge floor to roof windows and a good five metres away the tiny figure of Contessa Tatiana Dyachkova Vorontsova sitting in an ornate chair by a window. Only one table beside her, but it's covered with books and four or five more on the floor. Almost a copy of the old lady in the house by the sea but set in an abandoned warehouse.

She doesn't stand up, but gestures to them to go to her.

They're followed by one of the men and two elegant chairs are brought out from a door, which was hardly noticeable in the wall, and placed next to her.

She looks older than the last time Ellie saw her a few months ago at Louisa's. Ellie glances at Fletcher and is surprised to see him looking a bit overawed, she's never seen that before.

But the voice is that of someone younger.

She smiles and with a slight nod dismisses the shadows behind them.

'I'm sorry,' she says. 'They still think someone like that upstart peasant Putin would be bothered to try to eliminate me.'

Ellie's eyes go wide, and she can't resist looking behind her, but the Contessa is right – no-one in sight. Where to begin she wonders?

The Contessa smiles.

'You're the historian?' she asks.

Ellie nods, feeling a bit of a fraud.

'And you're the detective?'

This said to Fletcher who frowns.

'Retired,' he asserts.

The woman smiles.

'I doubt it, from what Louisa tells me.'

Ellie had to glance away at the look on Fletcher's face.

The space fills with silence.

'So, you're looking for a Romanov?' the old lady continues.

Ellie can still only nod, thinking that she's back at school wishing she'd done her homework and now bereft of excuses.

The woman shakes her head.

'And what on earth would you do with one?'

Again, Ellie is stymied, realising she's more excited by the chase than the outcome.

'They weren't actually that much use when they were alive: living in the past, whilst the future wiped them out,' the old lady continued.

She waited for a few seconds and then began to laugh. A giggle of a schoolgirl rather than a Contessa. Ellie glances at Fletcher, wondering if this old lady is demented, but he's just staring at her like he's been hypnotised.

But then she leans forward putting her stick out so she can bend towards them.

'I knew her, you know, my mother told me about her.'

'Did you ever go to see her? Ellie whispers.

'Once, years ago.'

'You mean at the house in St Abbs . . . the paper mill?'

Ellie's eyes go wide, but she nods.

The Contessa leans back and sighs.

'That's what killed them, thinking they were untouchable . . . like gods.'

Ellie glances at Fletcher, but he's still just staring at the old lady.

Then suddenly she laughs and presses a button on a remote on her chair arm.

'You look like you need a drink, mister detective,' she says to Fletcher, who can only nod.

Nothing more was said until the drinks cabinet is wheeled in, and they're all offered what they want from the huge selection.

The Contessa puts her glass down.

'It's no use living in the past,' she murmurs, 'unless you're looking for lessons . . . learn what not to do . . . not like the Romanovs.'

Ellie glances at Fletcher one more time, he raises his eyebrows.

'But it seems someone wants to resurrect them,' she begins.

'A girl my age, supposed to be the great granddaughter of Maria Romanoff, kidnapped recently and now disappeared, probably taken to Russia or somewhere else.'

The Contessa shakes her head.

'Whoever they are . . . and they could be anyone . . . Americans . . . they're just thinking they can cause Putin a problem.'

'Well, would it? asks Ellie.

The old lady shakes her head again.

'Of course not, they're deluded, whoever they are.'

Ellie stares at her. Fletcher knows that look. It would make anyone talk.

The old lady frowns, but eventually looks away.

Silence gathers and it has a huge space to fill . . . but eventually it becomes oppressive, and the old lady gives in. A tear slowly dribbles down her cheek.

She looks hard at Ellie.

'You don't understand . . . how could you?'

Fletcher watches Ellie. How did she become such an expert interrogator? None of his blood in her veins . . . and in any case not his style . . . the snake rather than the bear?

'You know why Elena lived like that, locked away in the past?'

Ellie waits; a thousand other questions kept at bay.

'Only fear,' comes the whisper.

Ellie still waits.

The old lady sits back in her chair and visibly sinks into a smaller wizened creature, trembling and then silently weeping.

Ellie leans forward and goes on her knees in front of her, reaching for her hands and holding them. Fletcher can't move, can't speak, just wants to know what Ellie would want him to do.

This lasts for a lifetime, but only a few moments in real time.

The old lady's head comes up and then she reaches up to push Ellie's hair back from her face . . . at which moment Fletcher sees she's crying as well.

The Contessa smiles.

'I'm sorry, but . . . you Engleesh . . . you've no idea.'

Ellie gives her a questioning smile.

The Contessa shakes her head.

'Even now, you're all blindly giving in to the rich, letting them fool you while they pile up the gold, hiding it away and building their underground bunkers . . . they know the apocalypse is coming . . . they're welcoming it . . . sick to death of being pilloried just because they're cleverer than the rest of you. Not just Putin, but everyone rich enough to know what's going to happen . . . in your lifetime, Elena.'

Ellie is startled by the adaption of her name, but tries to keep a straight face, not glancing at Fletcher.

She waits. Can't think of anything to say. Sits back in her chair. Waits.

The Contessa sighs and then looks up at her.

'I'm sorry, but . . .'

Fletcher feels the emptiness of the space between them, wanting to hold Ellie close, but knowing that won't work.

He waits.

'Well, maybe . . .' whispers Ellie, 'but actually this isn't about us, it's about a young woman my age who's been abducted by people who maybe want the world to end or just cause more chaos . . . the thing is I care more about people than politics.'

The old lady looks up, stares at her, then shudders.

Ellie wipes her tears away.

The silence was only for a few minutes, but again it felt longer to Fletcher.

Ellie just waits. Something tells her she might have touched a nerve.

The old lady looks like she's gone to sleep. Her eyes are shut.

Fletcher tries to catch Ellie's eye, but she's watching the old lady like a hawk.

And sure enough there's movement.

A wrinkled hand reaches out from her lap. Ellie takes it, realises there's something there. She allows it to be pressed firmly into her palm and her fingers folded over it.

The old lady sinks back and without opening her eyes, whispers something that Fletcher can't hear.

Ellie is still, but then stands up.

Fletcher realises that a figure has emerged from the wooden wall. A woman dressed as a nurse. She walks purposefully towards them.

'I think you will have to go now; the Contessa is tired and needs to rest.'

Minutes later Ellie's driving back across the bridge away from the house.

Fletcher realises he's been holding his breath.

Ellie pulls into a layby and turns the engine off, puts her head on the wheel . . . and bursts into tears.

*　　*　　*

Gill sighs.

Here she is driving Walker back to that creepy house on the cliff . . . again.

Whatever happened there is old stuff. Over a century ago.

And what would happen even if the old lady really was a 'Roman-off' or that her disappearing granddaughter has been spirited away by some weirdos trying to do . . . what? Another revolution? Dream on.

'I doubt you did any real history at school,' mutters Walker.

Gill glances across at him. He's slumped in his seat staring at his mobile. She gives that some thought.

'No, you're right, I dropped it when I was 14. Geography much more useful and you got to go on trips.'

He nods but continues to stare at his phone.

'You know the English had one?' he says, as though he can't believe it. 'Chopped the king's head off as well.'

She's vaguely heard about that.

'Sixteen forty-nine,' he confirms.

She waits, but he's flicking his screen.

'But we've still got one,' she asks.

'Uhuh, same name but number three.'

She wonders what else he's going to unearth, but he puts the phone away and stares out of the window.

Back in the house again, they go up to the room where the old lady used to sit.

He stands behind her chair looking out of the window.

'Have you got a compass?' he whispers.

Gill frowns, finds one on her phone and then realises he's doing the same thing.

'That's weird,' he murmurs.

She waits, thinking the whole damn place is weird.

But now he's pointing at the edge of the table. She frowns, what's he looking at? Until she sees what he's feeling with his finger – there's a slight cut on the edge and a faint line across the table from the chair going to it.

He stares out of the window.

'So, she wasn't just looking at the view or waiting for a boat to appear, she's looking much further away.'

Gill thinks Russia, but it's not that way, is it? France? Spain? Africa!!

Walker is now looking at the books, finds an old atlas. Fingers the pages until he finds a small-scale map of Europe. He then uses his phone to see where that line on the table takes him. East Anglia, then France, misses Paris, east of Lyon and then nowhere big until the Med, Nice?

'Like I said, a lot further away?' he murmurs.

He looks back out the window.

Gill stares at him, thinking 'drugs?' or 'wanting a holiday?'

But before she can ask after his mental health, they can hear people downstairs and she immediately knows who that will be. Ex-DI Fletcher and his nosy granddaughter. It's getting to be a conspiracy.

Sure enough Ellie's standing in the doorway, whilst they can hear the gasping for breath from the old detective coming up behind her.

'Fancy meeting you here,' says Ellie with a grin.

Fletcher was relieved to find a chair, but annoyed. When did his legs get so useless?

Five minutes later Ellie's staring at an atlas.

*   *   *

MARIA

She has decided to do as she's told and go along with their ridiculous ideas, in the hope she'll find a way to escape.

So now she's in a huge room with old photographs of the Russian Royal family in various poses. It occurs to her that these must have been some of the earliest photographs taken anywhere, but she has no idea when cameras were invented, although there's only one that's got any colour, but then realises it's just painted over.

A very small old lady comes to take measurements. Does that mean she will be decked out in modern versions of the photos?

She goes to look out the window, which she can see is on the first floor, although the gravelled pathway has steps down to a huge ornate garden, with small, cropped hedges and geometrical beds of flowers, mainly roses, stretching away to a wall and dropping down to another level with a lake and then trees with high mountains in the distance. Are they the Alps?

So, east of France?

She vaguely remembers a holiday when she was about five or six. A small village, a modern house with a pool. It was always really hot and the photos of her always wearing a hat.

Her heart does a beat.

Not just a hat.

A bracelet as well.

She glances behind her.

Then looks round the room, scanning for cameras.

There don't seem to be any unless they're disguised.

She turns to stare out the window again . . . and then brings her right arm in front of her body and feels for it on her wrist.

She looks down at it and twists it so she can see the light is on. Green now like a little jewel. She can't remember the last attack, must be months ago . . . yes last Christmas . . . probably brought on by the cocktail of drink and drugs she'd stupidly taken. Attack hardly the right word, just feeling woozy, hadn't been eating properly either. All Irena's fault.

So, has her mother told anyone about her condition?

Has she told them about the alert signal, which would warn her she was having an attack?

She fingers the button and presses the alarm.

The little light goes red, so it's working.

But does it work in France?

Would the signal go that far?

She presses it again.

It goes green.

She realises she's shaking, so she slips into the nearest chair and tries to calm down.

Surely, if they think she's who they say she's supposed to be, that they know about the Romanovs having haemophilia. Not bad for females, but certain conditions might bring it on.

They must know.

She frowns.

But do they know about her bracelet?

She resists the temptation to turn it on again.

What she needs is access to a computer . . . but how likely are they to let her do that?

* * *

ELENA MARIA WALLACE 1938

How can a person be so happy?

My husband has had his own surgery for two years now and our little girl will be five this year. I decided to call her Elena Mary, because . . . well, I still have nightmares. Men with guns and bayonets hacking at my sisters. Who just fly away like angels . . . but I'm in the back of a truck.

A woman, I can't remember her name, maybe Elena, trying to stop me bleeding.

Then it always goes dark . . . but I can still hear my sisters screaming.

But now John tells me there's going to be a war.

He tries to explain why.

About Hitler.

I don't really want to know.

I have nightmares.

CHAPTER FOURTEEN

Any thoughts of following up a line on a table are dashed for Walker and Gill by a call from Edinburgh telling them to get their arses over to a suspected murder further west.

Fletcher can't help himself asking where.

But Walker is fed up with being run ragged by these amateur sleuths. Only one glance at Ellie's bright eyes is enough.

'Police business, you're better off following up these fairy tales . . . and letting us do our job.'

With that he was off down the stairs leaving Gill momentarily uncertain where her curiosity lies, but then remembering who's actually paying her. So, she gives the staring eyes a shrug and sets off after him.

Walker is on the phone again, so Gill gets into the driving seat.

The call is brief, and he gets into the car.

'Where to?'

Walker sighs.

'It's that guy with the Rottweilers.'

Gill frowns.

'Kershaw?'

'He's dead . . . dogs eating him apparently.'

Gill pulls a face, thinking he deserved it, but then shuddering at the thought of it.

By the time they get there, the press have got wind, so there's a crowd at the gates.

Pulling up at the front door, a long way from the gates and through the trees, they see the forensic guys surrounding a body on the gravel, one of them kneeling taking photos. Gill's always wondered if they have nightmares dealing with dead bodies all the time, although when she asked, she just got a shrug and a grin.

This scene is particularly gruesome and she notices even Walker looks away after a quick look.

It's then she hears the wailing noise emanating from the house.

'The wife,' mutters one of the uniforms, looking glad he's out front.

Even before Walker can ask, the senior guy, who they've seen before, just shakes his head assuming they can see what's happened.

They go into the house.

From the outside the property is obviously old rich Victorian gothic style, but inside the walls are covered with a much wider selection of artwork, including some that look like Picasso's to Walker, although he's immediately asking himself what does he know?

The wife is pacing about in what he thinks might be a 'drawing room'? But that's only because it's not a kitchen or a bedroom.

A WPC is trying to persuade her to sit down but failing completely as the woman strides about wailing and screaming, which doesn't feel real, more like bad acting.

It takes all of Walker's patience to get her to at least stand still, while he tries to find out what's happened.

Gill leaves him to it and goes to find what's happened to the dogs.

'Taken away,' says one the PCs, 'going to be put down I think . . . they had to shoot one of them anyway, wouldn't leave the body alone.'

Just then a guy dressed in tweeds and boots appears.

'It's not their fault. Silly woman did na treat them right.'

'Who are you?' asks Gill.

'Robert Mackay,' he grumbles like she ought to know who he was.

'And . . ?

'Head gamekeeper.'

Gill frowns.

'So, aren't you responsible for the dogs?'

'Huh . . . the hunting dogs yes, but not her dogs.'

She could see that wasn't going to get her anywhere.

'Where were you, when this happened?'

'Back round at the stables. We heard three, maybe four shots, but weren't that bothered, she's allus shooting at things.'

'Things?'

'Anything. Shouldn't be allowed to have a gun. You lot have been told about her, but nothing has happened.'

'So, you think she shot her husband?'

He shrugs.

'Mebbe, they were allus arguing, shouting at each other.'

Gill stares at him, but then looks away.

'Was there anyone else here this morning?'

The man shrugs again.

'I keep out of their way when they start arguing . . . none of my business.'

Gill is disinclined to believe that, but the man was staring resolutely at her, so she turns away.

'We'll need to take statements from you and all the other staff . . . how many?'

The man grunts.

'I've got three men under me, two of them out in the forest. You'll have to talk to the cook; her staff come and go.'

Gill gave him a stern look.

'Well, get them back here soon as you can.'

The man shrugs again but turns on his heel towards the stables.

Gill smiles to herself. Just like her dad.

Back inside it's a bit quieter.

She finds Walker where she left him, the wife now sitting sobbing on a sofa, a younger woman with her arm around her.

Walker looks back at her.

She shakes her head.

He comes over.

'Apparently, a man called at the door. He went to meet him. Three shots fired. Car driving off.'

'Does anyone know who this man was?'

He makes a face.

'Young girl in the kitchen went to the door, didn't recognise him, asked his name. He said Mackay.'

'She went to tell Mr Kershaw, who told her he didn't know a Mackay, told her to go back and ask him what he wanted? So, she did.'

'And?'

'Kershaw was irritated but went to the door. She went back to the kitchen but then heard the shots.'

They both look out as the body is carried to a van.

'Anything from the wife?'

'Nada,' says Walker, 'although I'm not sure about the hysterics.'

She waits. Not a fan of female hysterics herself.

'However,' he continues, 'we do know someone who didn't like Mr Kershaw and does have access to guns.'

Gill stares at him.

'You mean Tomasz Steil?'

He shrugs.

'According to Mrs Kershaw, Steil threatened her husband after his sister was injured when his dogs attacked her horse.'

'But . . .' says Gill, 'doesn't he shoot people from miles away?'

Walker shrugs his shoulders.

'But that's in a war scenario, this was personal.'

* * *

The suspect doesn't know that he's just become one.

He's staring along a long empty beach.

The journey to get here always takes a long time by car and boat as he's not planning to go on any aeroplanes ever again.

He's been to the artist's house, no sign of her there, so can't think where she might be. He doesn't think she'd go to her father's house and in any case, he'd checked, she'd sold it.

He also knows that if she doesn't want to be found it will be almost impossible to find her.

'So . . .' he tells himself. "If you can't find someone, let them find you," which makes him smile, as he was told this mantra by an old Afghani warrior.

"Make a fire", "shoot your rifle into the air", were other things you wouldn't do if you wanted to stay hidden.

In any case it was getting late.

September was a strange month up here, the days roughly similar lengths day and night, but already turning towards the darkness that would eventually descend earlier and stay down longer as autumn progresses.

So, he began to gather sticks and pieces of flotsam. His rucksack was already nestling in the curve of a sand dune which would keep the wind at bay.

As someone who has spent nights outside in different darknesses lit by different stars, he was looking forward to revisiting the northern lights and the clarity of the sky right now was very promising.

Half an hour later, he's snuggled up by a little fire and eating his supper, while the birds flutter and dive into the high tide.

There's only been one other human on the beach, but way along the bay, throwing sticks for a dog, which had made him nostalgic for the days when Hengist was young.

Magda had phoned him to tell him about what had happened to Kershaw and that he was a suspect. This was followed by a couple of police calls which he didn't respond to, thinking they'll work it out, but now wondering if it was done deliberately to implicate him. Who would do that?

As usual for him, he slept lightly, waking two or three times to know that it was only night creatures creeping about.

But in the early morning light heralded by the call of peewits, he knew someone was nearby. Maybe because the rabbits and voles had gone quiet and there was a sense of movement away to his right along the empty sand.

And there she was.

Standing on a sand bed which was gradually rising from the ebbing tide.

Not looking his way, but as she often was in his dreams, staring out at the island . . . and beyond.

For a while he just watched her. Images of her closeup flashing through his brain, but then receding to just take in the reality of her actual presence.

Was she really that tall? Was she thinner than he remembered? How was her hair different?

And then he sees the dog.

All this was confirmed . . . and now, he was lying beside her on her bed. In a cottage just a few hundred yards from the beach.

The first sex was tentative from both participants, but the second . . . well! The third was necessarily gentle, but no less needed.

Now she's at the window, while he's trying to position himself comfortably.

'Does it still hurt,' she whispers without turning round.

The word 'still' indicating his 'eye' rather than the recent battle.

He sighs. Everyone asks him this question eventually and he's never sure whether they're meaning when it happened, which was the worst pain he's ever suffered or now, which is obviously far less painful, but it's always there. Sometimes a sudden piercing stab like being flash lighted or a grinding throbbing.

'Now and then, but getting better all the time,' he murmurs, which is what he wants rather than the truth.

There's another long silence, just the gentle shushing of the waves.

'Can I look at it,' she asks, turning to look at him.

He knows people are intrigued and must have horrific images in their minds, but she's the only person who's ever asked him.

He hesitates.

'Are you sure?'

She stares at him and then nods.

He stands up and goes towards her.

Two people standing at a window.

The silence gathers.

He reaches up and lifts the patch away.

She can't stop the gasp and closes her eyes.

He waits.

She turns her head away, but then opens her eyes and turns back to look at him, even though she's trembling.

Time slows down, but now she's reaching up to touch him. The blank hollow could have been worse, but it's still weird. He's spent a lot of time looking at it, especially when it was still healing.

'How is it different?' she murmurs.

Again, braver people like her ask this question and he now knows what to say.

'Loss of peripheral vision on that side and some difficulty with distances.'

She nods.

'So, you can't shoot anymore?'

He grins.

'That's why they did this eye . . . but they were wrong.'

She frowns.

'Don't worry, I'm not going to do it again, but it would be possible.'

This only gets a shake of her head.

They go for a walk along the length of the beach, finding shells and stopping to watch the seals or just standing holding each other.

The dog is called 'Cu-shithe' which she says is spoken as 'coo-shee', which can sound like a soft wind when said quietly or like a banshee screaming if she can't see her.

She's been wary of Tomasz, but when he calls her name quietly and holds out his hand, she comes over to lick it and lingers sniffing at the faint scent of Hengist.

He finds a stick left by the tide, sees the gleam in her eye and then she bursts into a furious rush to try and catch it before it lands. Only a few seconds then she's dropping it at his feet.

'That's you reeled in,' laughs Imelda, 'but be careful, she's a close relation to the 'Ban-shithe'!' This latter name pronounced in a long whisper and a serious look in her eyes.

Tomasz smiles and throws the stick into the waves again, but he knows what a Banshee is and remembers his father reading him the terrifying ghost stories when he was only very small.

Cushie isn't interested in any of that and is now barking at him to throw the stick again.

It's only as they get nearly halfway back that they see the police landrover and an officer waiting for them.

*   *   *

URSULA

Janet is having a sulk, which given that her standard behaviour is angry, means that bear with a sore head doesn't come near.

She was doing the washing up, usually my job, but then there's a crash and a bellow of expletives that would have made a 'navvy' flinch. Do 'navvies' still exist? Not that sure what it meant anyway.

Then the door slams and Ziggy comes out of his room, but then seeing nothing to worry about, goes back in.

So, I go and clean up the mess, put the broken stuff in the bin, including the shattered remains of my office mug which somehow or other had survived all this time. When was that? Three or four years ago? Or longer?

My mother would have regarded this as an omen. Generally. a severe message to be more careful . . . mugs don't grow on trees etcetera.

Apparently, Tomasz has gone to find Imelda? A relationship even I can see is pretty unpredictable. Somewhere in the 'Outer Isles', which I found on Janet's dog-eared road map. They're certainly 'outer', it takes four hours to get to Ullapool, two hours on a boat. She says Fletcher's been there but won't talk about it and that it made his eyes go scary.

Having put the kitchen shipshape again, I go out for my walk, part worrying whether I might find Janet storming along still in a rage.

As it happens, I don't see her and seem to have lost my ghostly companions.
I'm following my usual route where they generally accost me . . . but nothing?

The birds are still bustling about, chattering away and probably cursing me as usual . . . but no fading dog, or marble-eyed hare or eye-patched raven.

I stand still listening.

Nothing but a gentle breeze fluttering the early autumn leaves.

Have they abandoned me?
What might that mean?

I continue on, puzzling about them.

It's only then I realise Tomasz has lost the same eye as the raven and has an equally extravagant jewelled patch.

Was he the raven all along?

No, of course not, it was Carole, but then I start thinking how alike they are . . . angry, wilful and scary.

I'm now utterly confused and then there's Janet standing by the waterfall looking into the depths.

My heart in my mouth, I make my way towards her.

Then suddenly she puts her head back and yells the most enormously loud wail of frustration.

Birds fly up from everywhere and flap away in a riot of rushing and terror.

But then she opens her eyes and sees me.
Two frozen figures a few yards apart and then she bursts into laughter.

We arrive back at the house hand in hand.
Without even looking in on Ziggy, she takes me upstairs and . . . well, the door was shut behind me and . . .

*   *   *

Ellie is frustrated.

She thinks that the line on the old lady's table is the best clue they have to find where the girl has been taken. Even though the idea of finding a real descendant of the last Tsar wouldn't bother Putin.

No, it was more, or less, than that. She just loves the chase.

A female Indiana Jones?

That makes her giggle till she realises Fletcher's come into the room behind her.

'What are you up to?' he asks, realising he's been missing a bit of the excitement she generally seems to unearth.

She shakes her head.

'Come and look at this.'

He comes to stand beside her.

'Look at what Ziggy's sent me,' she says pointing at the screen.

He grabs the chair beside her and sits down.

All he can see is a map of Europe, but now she's zooming in towards the western side, showing the UK and France . . . and a line coming from the coast of Scotland to the middle of France.

'This is what Ziggy thinks might be where the old lady was looking towards . . . or worrying about?'

Now she zooms into where the line stops in France.

A bit closer and he can see a town called Epoisses and near it a little chateau sign.

He frowns.

'Why there?'

'Well . . . his theory is that Maria could have been taken on the Orient Express when it reopened in 1919.'

Fletcher frowns thinking that didn't take long, although he doesn't think he knows when the war actually stopped.

'So, what he did was follow the line on table to see if intersected with the railway route . . . and it does, in only one place . . . there.'

'But . . .' he manages to say.

'Yeh, my thought as well, but then Ziggy did some more digging and it turns out the chateau belongs to a rich American guy.'

'So, he's the person trying to . . .'

'No . . . he's never even been there. It's just an investment. He rents it out to whoever can afford it.'

Now Fletcher is getting really confused.

'But . . . so?'

'It's currently been rented by a firm based in Switzerland called 'Historic France.'

Now he's really flummoxed but can see the gleam in Ellie's eyes.

'And?' he asks, feeling like he can't take any more of this.

He puts his head in his hands and groans.

'Who are sub-renting it to a Madame Genevieve Sazonova.'

He peeps out from one eye.

'Who is Russian?'

'Yes, her family escaped from Russia after the revolution. She's the granddaughter.'

Fletcher shakes his head.

'But . . . that's . . .' but then can't think of a word to call it.

'Um . . . Ziggy thinks that's too easy and I agree. The people who've taken Maria would be a bit more secretive than that.'

Fletcher stands up and goes to the window.

'There is one thing . . .' he murmurs.

Ellie glances back at him.

'Did Maria's father know about the line on the table?'

She stares at him.

They're both thinking, trying to work it out.

'The table wasn't there in the room, was it?'

'So, who put it upstairs? Her father? Did he know?'

Ellie sighs.

But Fletcher can't help a grin coming.

'I don't think he did . . . because he wouldn't have put it away, upstairs . . . would he?'

Ellie nods.

'I think you're right, if he'd known he could have done what Ziggy did.'

Fletcher makes a face.

'Yes, but he could have put the chair away so no-one else could see it.'

Ellie frowns.

'Well, if they don't know about it either then . . . there's no reason for them to think we might know where they've taken her.'

But now Fletcher recognises the gleam in her eyes.

'Have you got an up-to-date passport? she asks.

He shakes his head, not that he has the slightest idea where his passport is, never mind if it's out of date or not, but the thought of charging off another the adventure with her? What will Louisa think or want to do and myriad other 'old gimmer questions'.

But she doesn't wait for an answer, just charges off shouting 'Louisa! Where are you!?'.

MARIA

She comes awake with a start, from a weird dream about being like Alice in Wonderland in a frantic race round a garden maze like the rose garden outside . . . but she was much smaller and the animals were huge. Not even sure what animals they were? Wolves? No, more like badgers?

Now she remembers they've put her in a huge bedroom, with a bed which has a canopy above and spindly poles holding it up.

She slips out of the heavy covers and goes over to the window.

It seems to be early, the remnants of a mist lying glistening on the hedges.

She tries the French window, but it's locked.

So is the other door.

She goes back to the window.

If they do really believe she's a descendant of the Romanovs, what are they going to try to do? She's already dismissed the idea that Putin would fall to his knees and beg forgiveness. More likely he'll just laugh at another pathetic Western attempt to undermine his authority.

There's a scraping at the door and it opens to reveal an older woman dressed as an old-fashioned servant carrying a tray, which she sets down on a side table. Then she curtsies and speaks to her in French.

'Bon matin, votre Altesse.'

Maria just glares at her and she retreats backwards trying to curtsey again, before blundering into the door as she exits.

But then there's the grating sound of the key being turned in the lock.

The coffee is disgusting. Really harsh and syrupy. She spits it out and then sees the splodge on the carpet, which she tries to eradicate, but realises she's just made a bigger stain. Momentarily embarrassed, but then realising she doesn't care, she picks up the jug and splashes the remains of the coffee all over the carpet and the grand settee.

Seeing what she's done, she can't help but giggle and looking down at the empty jug, her eyes shining, she picks it up and throws it at the French window.

Two of the panes are broken and she strides over and puts her hand through to release the handle, but it's still locked.

So now she looks round for something bigger to use.

An old-fashioned wooden chair with arms looks like a likely candidate and so she hoists it up and gives the French window a hefty wallop.

Glass and wooden splinters everywhere, but the lock still holds, so she hits it again.

'Banjo!' she shouts and then giggles at the memory of the girl at school who would always shout it like that.

Now she's outside picking her way through splinters. A bit difficult in the slippers they've given her.

Behind her she can hear an alarm wailing, but this just catapults her across the gravel and onwards down the garden.

Her greatest fear is dogs. Probably big dogs here, although she's never seen or heard any.

She gets to the end of the rose garden and hurries down the steps.

Looks left and right.

Still no sight or sound of anyone coming after her, she chooses right as she can see a dark line of trees a hundred yards away or so. It only takes a few steps through the grass for her slippers to be sodden, so she picks them up and sets off.

She's nearly there when she realises that what she thought were trees have now become men with guns. Three or four soldiers dressed in grey uniforms, which had helped their invisibility against the trees.

One of them now steps forward and puts out his hand.

'S'il vous plait, Altesse.'

She stops, looks right and left. Two other figures appear from her right. She looks back, where there is another one standing outside the broken window.

She realises it's hopeless.

Back in the house in another room with smaller windows, her feet have been washed and a pair of slippers are left on the floor.

A key rattles in the door and a tall woman she hasn't seen before comes in.

Irritatingly, even though she's tall and very severe looking, this new person curtsies and comes over towards her.

'Please sit down, Altesse.'

She obeys, more out of fear than obedience and in any case her feet are really stinging now.

The woman stares briefly at her then sits on a chair across from her.

'Please understand that there's no possibility of you escaping. There are over forty men guarding this property and beyond the wood there's an electrified fence which would have caused you a lot of pain.'

Maria stares at her.

'You're mad,' she whispers.

The woman smiles and gently shakes her head.

'No, Altesse, we are just very determined . . . and committed to your reinstatement to the authority you have been denied.'

Maria can only shake her head in disbelief.

Elena María 1925

The first few days in Edinburgh were really scary and she got very hungry, but then found herself in a huge market . . .

Which is why she ended up helping and then eventually getting a little stall of her own.

Her English was never good, but then it was with a Scottish accent anyway.

And then she met John, who was a student at the University, training to be a doctor.

And then she became Maria Elena Wallace.

That was the name on the marriage certificate after the wedding in St Giles and then there was a little boy called Kenneth, who would run wild around the cobbled streets like she did when she was his age.

And then she was happy.

Most of the time . . . except when she had nightmares . . . which slowly faded and became almost unbelievable.

CHAPTER FIFTEEN

Obviously, Tomasz had no choice but to go back to be interviewed by the police about the murder of Kershaw.

He tried to persuade DI Walker that he had a witness and that his journey could be verified by various other people en route at petrol stations and a hotel in Ullapool, but to no avail.

Then the next problem was persuading Imelda to go back with him. This was much harder but eventually she agreed with the agreement that he wouldn't get involved in any more adventures which would take him away.

Even as he was promising this, he knew that this would be harder to stick to, as he had heard that Ellie's investigation was shifting to France. This was on the phone so Imelda hadn't got wind of it yet.

So, the three of them drove back the following morning.

Cushie wasn't happy to be in the car for long periods, so the journey took longer than usual, even though Tomasz tried to drive at a speed neither she nor Imelda liked.

But now he was pulling up on the drive at the house.

He looks across at Imelda but she's looking out the window. Cushie is roving back and forth wanting to get out and explore a strange new place.

And now there's three figures coming out to greet them.

All three of them walking more slowly than they used to do. Hengist and Helena because of their age and Magda still recovering from the attack by Kershaw's dogs.

Imelda is reaching across the back seat to calm Cushie, but she's too excited.

So, they all tumble out.

A few minutes of mayhem ensue as the dogs investigate each other and the humans embrace each other. Even Imelda allowing this to happen although Magda feels it's like trying to hug a tree – her body is always so hard and stiff.

And then they don't have time to get indoors, because Walker and Gill arrive, so Tomasz has to answer their questions.

This doesn't take long and the police officers grudgingly disappear.

Now they're all on the terrace having lunch in the tentative sunshine.

No-one's talking about either the return of Imelda or the disappearance of Maria.

Instead, they're all enjoying the floor show being provided by Cushie leading an eager but much slower Hengist in a race round the garden.

So, Helena frowns when Tomasz gets a call.

Seeing it's Ellie, he can't resist answering and walks away to the front of the terrace.

'Guess what?' she says, without a 'hello, how are you?'.

Tomasz sighs but can't ignore the excitement in her voice. And predictably, she doesn't give him time to answer anyway.

'We think we've got a lead,' she gushes. 'Is your passport up to date?'

Before he can think about it, he answers 'yes' and then looking over at the assembled listeners, who are all staring at him like the Grand Inquisition.

'We think the girl might have been taken to a place in France, just west of Dijon.'

Dijon is not a place he's been, so that's no help.

'Southeast of Paris, on the route of the Orient Express.'

Now he's intrigued. Can't help himself.

He can hear Ellie's breathing, knowing she wants him to go with her.

'Ah,' he says, 'that is intriguing . . . but we've just got back from Lewis, middle of lunch . . . can I get back to you?'

He can almost feel her frustration, but she only says: 'Okay . . . can we talk later this afternoon?'

'Yeh, sure, give me an hour or so.'

'Okay – see you at three,' she affirms and cuts the call.

He sighs and then makes his way back to the table, all eyes on him.

Magda is the first to speak.

'Is that the police again?' she demands.

'No,' he replies, 'just Ellie.'

Again, all the eyes are on him, all of them suspiciously.

He shrugs.

'You know what she's like when she's on the hunt.'

This just enhances the looks of apprehension.

He makes a face.

'To be honest I could do with a rest from adventures just now.'

This is met with even more suspicion, so he just shrugs again and says he'll go and get some more wine.

*   *   *

Ellie glares at the phone, but then flounces off to find Fletcher.

He's nowhere to be seen and then she remembers they've gone into town. Can't remember what for, but it probably means he'll be sitting in a café somewhere while Louisa sneers her way through all the dress shops and then comes home without buying anything, complaining that she's not ready yet to be attired in such dowdy remnants.

So, she calls Ziggy.

Who answers immediately.

'I've been researching this woman, Sazonova,' he answers without any questions or why she might be calling.

'What do you know?'

'Not a lot. She's very secretive . . . and I mean hardly anything.'

'Really?'

'Well, it means that she's got massive protection online or no footprint at all, which is virtually impossible.'

'So, she's using a pseudonym?'

'Uhuh, maybe more than one.'

Ellie thinks about this.

'But there must be details about the house and who owns it, pays the bills etcetera.'

'Ah yes, but that's all in the name of the company who own the house and they're just as secretive.'

'What about aerial surveillance,' she asks.

'Get you,' he laughs, but then grunts 'no coverage.'

'How is that possible?'

'Two ways. One, that it's a French government property, which I doubt or . . .'

She waits.

'Or?' she whispers into the silence.

Which goes on for more than few minutes. She can hear his breathing and the clicketing of keyboards and snatches of music.

'Aha,' he whispers, but then a sharp intake of breath.

'Oops . . .'

Then silence.

She waits again.

A few snatches of computer noise.

Then nothing.

What can this mean?

The thought that this involves people who can hide like this from someone as computer savvy as Ziggy is beyond Ellie's imagination . . . but definitely scary.

She waits another few minutes and then stops the call. Ziggy will get back to her when he knows something . . . but nevertheless it's puzzling? Worrying?

As someone who lived in France for a few years and had numerous holidays as a child, her French is quite good and Louisa's library has numerous books about France collected by her and her husband, so she decides to do some investigation of her own, thinking no-one can see what she's doing in such a non-digital manner – which makes her laugh.

As it happens, Louisa seems to have visited that area quite a few times, judging the number of books about it. She's marked various places and hotels where she'd stayed near Epoisses like 'Semur-en-Auxois' and even 'Avallon', which surprises Ellie as she thought it was just an invented Arthurian place. And then checks to see that the Arthurian version is only one L? So . . . is there a connection?

'But that doesn't tell us why they've got a place there?' she says out loud and then jumps when she realises Louisa's sneaked up on her and is looking over her shoulder.

'Aha,' she laughs, 'checking up on my romantic Dijonnaise dalliances, are we?'

Ellie's eyes go wide.

'Dalliances?' she asks turning round to look up at her.

Louisa shakes her head and sighs.

'I wasn't always an old witch, you know,' she whispers, 'Juliette and I often sneaked off for a couple of weeks when both our husbands were far away in Singapore or some other overcrowded metropolis.'

Ellie frowns but then remembers who she's talking about – a woman who always comes to Louisa's bridge parties. Not exactly a beauty anymore and the glossy black hair is definitely not her own.

'So . . . you know it really well?' she asks.

'Yes . . . but it's, what, ten years ago since we last went there and well before Michael.'

The 'Michael' arrives just in time to hear his name.

'Not me, guvnor!' he says, in his best Cockney voice.

'Damn right, it wasn't,' laughs Louisa.

Now he's intrigued.

'So which toyboy are we referring to?' he asks before he thinks, which means he gets the icy stare it deserves.

'I shouldn't go there, Michael, if I were you,' says Louisa.

He adopts the 'bad boy in trouble' pose, but then they're all laughing.

'So,' he asks, 'what have you found?'

Ellie shrugs.

'Nothing much . . . even Ziggy's struggling to find anything . . . and I think he's just transgressed someone's protection and is still covering his tracks.'

Fletcher and Louisa know that means nothing to either of them so they just shake their heads.

'Anyway,' says Louisa,' Michael's about to go and make us all a lovely lunch and I have flowers to attend to.'

With this, she sashays off.

Fletcher grins but hesitates.

'I mean it, be careful, who knows which villains are involved in all of this, not to mention government geeks and such.'

Ellie stares at him.

'Maybe, it might be safer to go 'a pied', she whispers.

His eyes go big and he glances after the departed Louisa.

'Are you serious?' he whispers back.

'Well, Ziggy has already sent me a link to ferries from Hull.'

'What? But . . .'

URSULA

Well.
Suffice to say that was a surprise!
But I have to say utter bliss.
I think I'm in love!
And I think she loves me . . . although she hasn't said the words . . . yet?
Afterwards when she'd gone for a shower, I tried to remember the last time I had sex! And who with?

Anyway, who cares?
So? What now?
I'm not worried about Ziggy. His morals can be summed up as 'if you can do it, why don't you?'
And unbelievably the first sex I've ever had with a woman! Although I don't think it was a new experience for Janet. She obviously knew what to do and where to go! But I know she's had

sex with numerous men, probably including Ziggy and Fletcher . . . and maybe Tomasz? Maybe Imelda?

I shake my head and get out of bed . . . taking the sheets with me.

Just then she arrives back naked towelling her hair, which wasn't the best seductive approach, but it worked for us.

And now we're lying on the carpet, both of us gasping for breath . . . which is when Ziggy decides to make an entrance.

For once in his life he's momentarily stuck for words, but then laughs and shakes his head.

'Well,' he smirks. 'Can anyone join in?'

What happens next, I'll leave to your imagination, but, although I was certainly the only one of the three of us who hadn't had multiple sex couplings, this didn't stop us doing things which I'd only read in books and some that I didn't know were even possible.

What I could do afterwards was to make us all a feast to celebrate our Bacchanalian debauchery.

So, we are all lounging in a soporific manner when Janet's phone rings at the same time as there is a signal from Ziggy's room.

It's Ellie.

Janet nods at Ziggy, so he goes back to his room and wakes up numerous machines, as he listens to their conversation through his headphones.

Janet's eyes go big and she stands up to adopt her favourite way of having a phone conversation stalking about.

Ziggy is now clattering away on various screens.

So . . . as usual I do the washing up.

But half-way through I find myself standing there, hands in the basin washing a glass, when I stop and think.

My life has changed so many times but I think this seems to be the best thing that's ever happened to me . . . and then I realise I'm weeping into the washing up.

* * *

Walker is having a sulk.

Partly because he's still annoyed about being posted to this nowhere wilderness and now having to deal with the murder of a man most people seem to think deserved it.

It didn't help that Culshaw said he'd got other people investigating Edinburgh suspects, so that only left a few names to follow up, including at the top of the list Tomasz Steil, which had quickly hit a dead end, because he was way up north somewhere on some 'outer isle' as Gill called it.

As this seemed to summon his sergeant, he gives her a glare.

She shrugs.

'Nada.'

'Every other possible suspect accounted for . . . I'm afraid . . . so my money is on the wife.'

He has to admit that the overflowing histrionics were a bit suspicious, but he hadn't the stomach to go and interview her again.

'She's the one who will benefit the most,' Gill adds, but without much conviction.

Walker shrugs.

'What about the guy who was supposed to be in charge of the dogs?'

'I told you, he was in Peebles at the time.'

He sighs, she did.

'So . . . what we've got is a man killed and eaten by his own dogs, who was privately disliked by everyone, including his wife probably, despite the tears . . .'

Neither of them can think of anything more to say.

At this moment his phone interrupts and Walker has to repeat all that to Superintendent McGregor, who is not best pleased to have high ranking politicians and other worthies wanting answers.

'Well, you'll have to start digging again, Inspector,' and he cuts the call.

Walker didn't need to relay this conversation to Gill, but she did ask if they would be getting reinforcements, which made Walker laugh and suggest they go for a drink.

So, they were in the bar when the call came.

'Is that DI Walker?'

'Yes, who's asking?'

'BGH.'

'Who?'

'General hospital in Melrose.'

'Oh . . . OK?'

'This a bit awkward, but we have to inform you we have no record of having the body of the woman you asked about some time ago. 'Elena Mary Wallace nee Markovitch' you told us, who died in 2005?'

Walker is speechless for a few seconds, while giving Gill a frown.

'What? Who?' But then realising who the woman he's talking about.

'You mean the mother of Kenneth McKinley?'

There's a pause and in intake of breath.

'I'm afraid so.'

'The doctor?'

Another laboured pause.

'Yes.'

Walker shakes his head at Gill, who is now very intrigued.

'But how? Why?'

Another pause.

'Well, it is most irregular, but apparently he was allowed to take the body from the mortuary.'

'How?'

'As far as I can see, it was an agreement between the person in charge and McKinley, that as a pathologist, he would be able to deal with the internment or disposal himself.'

'Where?'

'There's no information about that in the records.'

Again, Walker can't believe this.

'But who permitted that?'

'An administrator in the hospital called Monks. David Monks.'

'So, is he still working there?'

Another pause.

'I'm afraid not, he retired shortly after that and then died two years ago. It's only now we uncovered the information in his files which were going to be deleted.'

'Well, don't,' rasps Walker. 'Can you send them to me?'

There's a long pause.

'I'd rather not . . . you can see that this would be difficult for the hospital.'

Walker sighs.

'Well, don't delete them, I'll have to ask my superiors . . . but have you any idea how or what he would have done with the body?'

Again, a long pause, sounds like he's having a conversation with someone else.

'Hello . . . we think at the very least he would need a big freezer and access to the chemicals to keep the body from putrefying, or an oven, but that would have been unlikely because of the fumes, assuming he was doing it in the house in St Abbs.'

'So, a big freezer?'

There's a short pause.

'I think it has to be that.'

Walker can't think of any more questions at the moment, so he ends the call.

Gill waits, wanting to hear the rest of the story, but she can see he's digesting what he's just been told.

This takes a good two minutes and then he tells her.

Gill shakes her head.

'Well, that's not just weird, and can't have been legal . . . could it?'

She's only been to one funeral when she was sixteen. Her grandmother. She hardly knew her and really didn't want to be there.

They're rather stumped for what to do next.
'So how do we find out where his mother and grandmother are buried?'
Gill shrugs.
'In the garden?'
Walker sighs, knowing full well the difficulties of persuading anyone to dig for dead bodies.
So, he starts looking through the list of funeral directors in the vicinity, not having much hope for success.
And that's what happens. No-one knows anything about either McKinley's mother or grandmother's burial arrangements. His father is buried in his family graveyard in Edinburgh, whilst his grandfather was killed in the war – body never found.
'So, it's only the women,' he says out loud.
Gill gives him a frown.
He stares out of the window.
'What's so special about them?'

* * *

MARIA

Her feet are still hurting the next morning, but a young woman, not much older than her, who she hasn't seen before appears and asks if she can have a look at them.
At first, she doesn't understand, because her accent is very strong, but then she catches 'pauvre pieds', so she carefully pulls her slippers off, but wincing more at how her feet look, rather than the pain.
The girl is very gentle and then goes to get some 'eau chaude'.

It's a bit odd, but actually quite soothing to have your feet gently washed, especially when they're so scratched and sore. It stings at first but the girl is careful and whispers words she doesn't understand, but sound nice.

Then the girl brings some food, which she wolfs down and asks for more, which makes the girl smile.

Now she's waiting to see what else they've got in mind. What's all this 'Altesse' business mean? She tries to remember if there were any clues back at the big house on the cliff.

All the paintings were either of gardens or old Victorian type gatherings of people she now supposes may have been her ancestors. Men in white uniforms and women with long hair and huge dresses.

Like her grandmother . . . sitting in her chair . . . looking out of the window. She always thought that she was just looking at the view . . . but what if she was looking further than that.

She looks round to see if there are any maps. None on the walls, so she carefully limps over to one of the bookcases.

And realises there are only old books. Some in French which she can just about read, although there are words she doesn't know, but mostly in another language, which is weird. Some of the letters were like English, like B, M, H, p, c, T, X, but the rest were like maths signs or hieroglyphics.

'So, is it Russian?' she whispers to herself, but then frowns because all the people here speak French or English.

Then she finds an English French dictionary and looks up 'Altesse' to find it's a wine grape . . . or 'Highness'.

Which is confusing?

Why are they calling her that?

The little foreign history she knows is that the French royal family and a lot of other aristocrats were all killed in the revolution – 1790s, she thinks.

But then what happened to the Russian royal family?

Only a vague idea that they were all killed by the communists during the first world war.

She limps back to the bookcases.

And eventually finds photographs of the Russian royal family. Hundreds of them. One boy and lots of sisters all looking older than him. And who's that man with the long hair and a huge cross on his chest?

She realises she's seen them before.

Not just in history books . . . but in the attic in her grandmother's house. Not on the walls but hidden away up in one of the attic rooms.

She stops looking and limps over to the window.
What does all this mean?

'ELENA MARIA MARKOVITCH' 1921

She doesn't remember much about the chateau. She was ill most of the time. Even when it was sunny.

She had French lessons, but she wasn't very good at other languages, not like her sister Ana.

At some point Elena disappeared. They said she wasn't well and had been taken to hospital . . . but later one of the women told her that she had died and they'd buried her in the woods.

And remembering her made her cry.

But that was nothing to where she eventually ended up . . . which still made her shake her head.

How did she do it?

Why hadn't they come after her?

She shivers.

Another long journey and then a boat.

The station in London.

It was really crowded. She'd never been surrounded by so many people, all pushing and shoving. The men who had taken her from the chateau weren't used to it either, muttering to each other and getting looks from people in the crowd.

Then one man shouted at them, and then another.

She was terrified and then they were fighting.

She didn't mean to escape, it was more that she was abandoned, as her guards were carried away in the struggle.

She only wanted to be away from all that shouting and fighting.

And then there was the train.

An open door.

A woman helped her up, smiling at her.

She made her way down the carriage and eventually found a seat.

She'd no idea where this train might be going and she only spoke a few words in English.

And then the train set off, slowly at first, but then gathering speed.

Still no sign of her guards.

She knew that people had to pay to go on trains and that she hadn't any money, so when she saw the man coming slowly down the aisle, she got up and went further along the opposite way, until she came to a carriage which was full of luggage, where she crawled in and found a little hidey-hole.

She'd no idea how long the journey took, but slept quite a lot of the time, barely realising the three or four stops there were on the way.

It was dark when they arrived and she looked out of the little window to see a sign saying 'Edinburgh Waverley'.

It was fairly easy to get off while the men were getting the luggage out and she scuttled along the platform till she could see everyone going out through an open gate,
so she just followed.

And when anyone asked her, she said she was called Elena, Elena Maria 'Markovitch', which was the name of one of the doctors who tried to help her brother.

CHAPTER SIXTEEN

URSULA

I'm awake before dawn.

Realising this I try to turn over to find there's a body in the way.

I flinch but then remember it's Becket – I mean Janet!

And then the whirlwind swirls back into my head!

The fact that she's lying there, warm and breathing proves it!

I try to stay still, but I'm trembling so much I know I'll wake her up . . . which might . . . I can hardly breathe in the excitement of what then might happen.

But she's fast asleep, not a muscle stirring, no eyelids fluttering.

I manage to turn without waking her up.

Her face is calm, no sign of the angry stare or the mischievous sneer, and now I can see a faint scar on her cheek. I've no idea when or how she got that, but suspect the retaliation would have been swift, violent and life threatening to whoever dared to do it.

Carefully, I slowly creep out from under the bedclothes, find my dressing gown and slippers, whilst realising she has neither of those items. Are they somewhere else or more likely she doesn't have them anyway?

I open the door and creep out.

Old bladder relieved, I go to the kitchen.

Even Ziggy's not awake yet, no sound emanating from his room.

A few minutes later I'm staring out of the window, as the kettle starts to rumble.

Is this really happening?

Me and Janet Becket?

'Chalk and cheese' comes to mind, which makes me snigger. She's definitely the hardest cheese ever, whilst I'm the softest chalk.

My reverie is broken by the sound of computers waking up and Ziggy doing his exercises, which means he's hanging from the circus acrobat pole in the doorway and doing body contortions which defy gravity.

So, I put his coffee on. Another life-threatening activity he engages in, far too many times a day.

When I take it to him a few minutes later, I'm surprised to see that he's only got one screen working and that it's covered with the sort of dense script, which in my limited experience with computers compared to him, can only mean serious hacking or recovering crash scenarios.

But then he sighs and his hands flutter across other keyboards and the machines respond like a gaggle of geese crossing overhead and then a fairground lighting up.

I put his coffee on the only designated space he's made.

For once he glances at me and grins.

'Ground control to Major Tom,' he sings.

Even I know that's David Bowie, but I can't imagine how I could have heard it.

'When was that?' I ask.

'March 1969.'

I try to calculate.

'Fifty-four years ago,' he tells me.

I decide not to say I was in secondary school by then and certainly not at home.

Back in the kitchen I stare out of the window.

'What a long time to wait for love?' I'm thinking . . . then screaming because two strong arms have lifted me off my feet.

The same two arms which carry me back to the bedroom, throw me on the bed and slam the door.

Later Ziggy informs us that his contacts in Russia tell him the anti-Putin groups are getting a bit excited but trying to keep quiet – calm before the storm. However, some of the eastern European countries like Slovenia are leaning towards Russia in the conflict with Ukraine. I can't get my head round these manoeuvrings so just nod at him.

On the other hand, Janet is getting restless, as though she senses conflict, which means going for a long run, a series of exercises which would have put me in hospital and then gun practice . . . which is all very worrying . . . but also, a bit exciting?

* * *

Ellie has persuaded Fletcher to drive her back to the house on the cliff. Again.

He tells her she probably won't be allowed in and that he's not up to climbing over fences anymore. Ellie ignores this and has dressed herself in old jeans and anorak, anticipating the climb over the fence, which may have been mended.

But what she hadn't expected is finding Walker and 'Gromit' to be there before them. She tells herself not to call Gill that in case she says it to her face.

Fletcher pulls up and points at the car.

'Too late, I think, Miss Sherlock, the rozzers have beaten you to it.'

Ellie frowns at him, 'rozzers', shakes her head, gets out of the car and strides over to DI Walker who's staring at her.

'What can I do for you, Miss . . ?'

'Ellie,' she says. "Well met by moonlight.'

Walker knows that's Shakespeare but has no idea which play and it's a dull morning anyway.

'I think there's the likelihood that there might be a photograph or a painting of a French chateau, where the girl who's been kidnapped might be being held,' says Ellie, without pausing.

He stares at her.

'Why on earth would they do that?'

'Well, first because it's not in the UK and secondly because that's where her great grandmother was taken after the revolution while the rest of her family were murdered.'

'What?'

Ellie sighs.

'Can I show you something?'

He shakes his head, but now she's showing him a family tree on her phone.

'Yes, I've seen that, but why do you think she'll be in France?'

Ellie sighs again.

'You know the table by the window?'

He frowns.

'You mean the one where the old lady sat?'

'Yeh, we checked that the faint line on the edge intersects the route of the Orient Express in only one place in France. A town called Epoisses . . . near Dijon.'

He stares at her.

'Orient Express?'

'Istanbul to London – reinstated in 1919 after the First World War.'

'So, you think . . . that's where they've taken her?'

Ellie shrugs, thinking she doesn't want to let them take over.

'It's just a possibility . . . a long shot.'

Walker laughs, but then sighs.

'You've no idea, miss, how that would go down with my superiors. They're far more worried about a murder over near Peebles than chasing long dead hares in France.'

Ellie is half pleased to hear that, but still wanting to go into the house again, although now not wanting to tell him what she's looking for, but then she gets inspiration.

'Um, okay, but can I go in for a few minutes, I think I left my scarf the last time.'

Walker makes a face.

It's at this point Fletcher has managed to get out of the car and ambled over to them.

'If it helps, I can go with her to make sure she doesn't touch anything,' he offers benignly.

But then Gill is holding out her phone.

'Pathologist for you, sir,' she says.

Walker sighs and takes the phone, but then gives it back to her.

'Take these two into the house and watch they don't move or take anything. I'll phone the pathologist myself.'

Gill frowns and relays this to the caller.

Then she tells them to follow her, nodding at the uniform on guard at the gate.

Inside, Ellie decides not to tell her about the chateau, but goes from one room to another, quickly scanning the paintings. Fortunately, most of them are of local places or flowers, but then in the room the old lady sat, there are two possibles. One is definitely a chateau with a lake and the other an early photograph of a large group of people on the steps in front of an arched doorway.

'Hey, these would be good for my latest assignment.'

She smiles at Gill, who frowns, but shrugs as Ellie takes a couple of pictures with her phone, before going up closer to see if there's any description.

There isn't . . . but then she realises it's been blanked out, which is annoying, although then she thinks about why that might have been done.

'That's strange,' she says to Gill, who isn't really interested but comes to look more closely.

'You're right,' she says, thinking 'so what', but then realises Ellie's disappeared.

* * *

Imelda comes out of a dream.

Not a nightmare.

But weird.

Something to do with a forest . . .well lots of trees . . . not really a comfortable place for her . . . she prefers the wide openness of the Hebrides.

Not being chased or anything scary . . . just a sense of unease . . . as though something's there, but not visible, something or someone watching her.

She then realises Tomasz isn't there, which is unusual. He generally wakes her up . . . which makes her worry.

So, she slips out of the bed and finds her clothes.

Down to an empty house.

Not ever wearing a watch means she 's adept at figuring out the time by the sun. Not showing yet, so must be before six.

She opens the balcony window and immediately shuts it again against the cold blustery wind. The fluttering leaves and waving branches should have warned her.

Finding her anorak, she tries again.

Not visible on the terraces, so more likely he's gone to the stables.

She's right, but too late. Tomasz has gone and then she realises Magda isn't around either.

She shrugs and makes her way back to the warmth of the kitchen . . . it's not as if it's unusual for him to go for a morning ride and she never accompanies him.

Opening the door, she finds Helena at the cooker making her porridge.

She turns and smiles.

'He's been gone over an hour,' she confirms.

Imelda frowns.

'He's gone to the Kershaw's.'

Imelda shakes her head.

'I know,' says Helena, 'I told him not to, but he said he wasn't going to cause any trouble, just wanted to ask Clarissa some questions.'

Imelda sighs and turns away.

'Do you want some breakfast,' says Helena softly.

Imelda turns to her and eventually nods, but then Helena steps across and puts her arms around her. This produces the usual stiffening, but surprisingly it eventually softens and the two of them embrace properly for the first time.

Nothing is said afterwards and the two of them are still at the table drinking a second cup of tea, when Tomasz arrives back.

His immediate frown at seeing these two sitting together quickly disappears and he smiles.

'Aha,' he murmurs, 'when my back is turned.'

The two women both smile.

Helena goes to heat up the porridge, while Imelda stays at the table.

He goes over to kiss and then hug her.

'So, what did you find out?' she asks.

He shrugs.

'Not a lot.'

'Was she still weeping and wailing?' asks Helena.

He grins.

'Not anymore, she's spoken to the solicitor, she's going to be a very rich woman indeed.'

Helena shrugs.

'Well, that won't last very long, will it? The way she drinks.'

Tomasz shakes his head.

'You never know . . . maybe drinking was the only way she could manage to stay with him.'

He tucks into the porridge.

'So, what about his contacts with the Russians?' asks Helena.

Tomasz frowns at her.

'How do you know about that?'

Helena comes back to table with two cups of tea for her and Imelda.

'Tomasz,' she shakes her head. 'Have you forgotten? I can smell them a mile off! You know as well as I do, he was involved in some sort of money laundering with them.'

Again, he frowns.

'Maybe . . . but who?'

'You mean which side?'

He laughs.

'You mean the official or the clandestine.'

'Both probably,' she rasps back, her eyes glittering with hatred.

Imelda is stunned by this rapid exchange.

The other two realise this and immediately the atmosphere changes. Helena picks up Tomasz's empty bowl and takes it to the sink. He shrugs at Imelda.

'My mother has 'issues' with the Russians,' he grins, but then catches the stiffening of his mother's shoulders. 'She can never forgive them for what they did in the War.'

'And afterwards,' comes the grim response.

Imelda waits. Her upbringing never had any arguments like this. Long silences were her father's way of dealing with any kind of problem.

But then the standoff is broken by the phone ringing.

It's Ellie.

*   *   *

An hour later Tomasz and Imelda arrive at Louisa's.

Ellie hustles them in and takes them through to the sitting room where they find Fletcher, Louisa, and a lady she's not seen before.

Louisa takes charge and introduces them to her friend.

'I think you've met Juliette before . . . last Easter?'

Ellie isn't sure, although she has a good memory for faces, so smiles as though she does remember.

'Hi, how are you, I hope Louisa hasn't bullied you on my behalf.'

Juliette smiles.

'Of course not, who could ever refuse an invitation from her?'

This produces a series of fleeting glances and eyebrow raising, but Tomasz doesn't hold back as he strides across and kisses her on both cheeks as though he's already gone to France. Imelda gives her a curt nod, which everyone knows is the best one could expect from her.

Introductions over, Louisa suggests that Ellie should ask Juliette about Epoisses.

It turns out that her family came from there and she still has many relatives living in the area.

'So, you know this chateau?' asks Ellie showing her a picture on her phone.

Juliette gives the photo a quick glance.

'Why, yes, of course, it's very famous in the region, I've taken numerous friends there . . . but not you, Louisa?' she asks.

Louisa smiles sweetly, which makes Ellie frown.

'No, we didn't get to go, because on both occasions it was closed, I think.'

Juliette laughs, breaking through the faux polite repartee.

'No, not at all, we were far too busy partying to bother about old chateaux full of Americans with their bloody cameras and dreadful children.'

Louisa pretends to be astounded, but then bursts out laughing as well.

'Anyway,' Juliette continues, 'your missing girl couldn't be held captive there. No-one lives there, just a few gardeners and estate workers . . . and they don't live in the chateau. It's only in the summer that it's open for visitors.

Ellie can only say: 'Oh, but . . .'

Juliette shakes her head.

'No trust me, it's not possible to hide someone there, all the full-time workers are locals.'

Ellie makes a disappointed face.

'However,' interjects Louisa wanting to claim back the story, 'there is another smaller chateau which might be a possible place for your missing girl to be held.'

Ellie focuses back onto Juliette, who now goes to the table where Louisa's ancient laptop is waiting.

'Come and look, these photos are old, black and white, probably taken in the fifties, which is the last time it was inhabited, although before the war there were people there.'

Ellie and Fletcher look at the old photos, mostly without any people.

'So . . . 'murmurs Ellie thinking aloud, 'could there be people living there without anyone knowing?'

Juliette frowns

'Well, it's surrounded by huge woods, much more than the big chateau and a lot of wild forest, which is even more diffcult '

Ellie stares at her, sensing she has more to tell.

Juliette shakes her head and smiles.

'Louisa told me you're 'a bit of a ferret' when you're hunting a story . . . especially old ones!'

Ellie tries to look offended but can't maintain it for a long before giggling and shaking her head at Louisa, who's trying to put on a 'what me?' face.

This makes everyone start laughing . . . apart from Fletcher . . . and Imelda.

'So,' he says, 'is there someone living there?'

Now Juliette isn't smiling.

'There is, but my friend, who lives in Epoisses, says it's very 'hush hush', like it might be government people.'

Ellie frowns.

'Apparently there's electrified fencing about fifty metres into the trees and dogs. Big dogs.'

Everyone gives this some thought, until Fletcher is the first to speak.

'Well, that counts me out . . . I'm allergic to big dogs.'

Everyone laughs, but the serious looks soon return.
Eleanor frowns again.
'So . . . wouldn't the local council know?'
Juliette makes a face.

'According to my friend they're a bunch of fascists, who would like the idea of 'secret military operations' in their midst. Makes them feel important.'

No-one can think how to respond to that.

'Good heavens!' says Louisa in her best 'ladyship' voice. 'Michael where's the drinks, this is beginning to feel like that terrible Michael Caine film.'

Instead of his awful grovelling Manuel impression, he frowns and disappears, wondering which film she means.

There are a few minutes of awkward conversation, while Louisa invites everyone to find a seat, sending Ellie out to her abandoned 'workroom' to get a couple more.

She finds this strangely sad, seeing the library returned to a dead space, no tables covered by her notes and books . . . but it does occur to her to find a map of the area they're talking about.

Successful, she returns and holds it up.

Card table retrieved and assembled, she finds the right section and refolds it so they can all see it.

Juliette quickly finds the chateau, which is indeed surrounded by a substantial forested area. And they can all see that it's well away from any main roads.

'Well,' says Fletcher into the silence, 'I don't fancy the chances of anyone getting in there.'

He daren't look across at Ellie, who he knows will be already figuring out how.

But no, she is shaking her head as well.

'So, we give up, do we,' says Tomasz softly.
All eyes turn to him, to see his are very bright.
Louisa stares at him.
'You're not thinking of a 'mission impossible', are you?'
Ellie stares at him as well, her eyes now glistening with excitement.

'Well,' murmurs Tomasz, 'I might know a few guys who could do something like this.'

Imelda's face has turned to stone.

'Not me,' he adds, looking at her.

She looks away.

'It was never my role, and forests aren't places I could operate in anyway.'

'Well . . .' says Louisa, hoping this conversation doesn't get any darker.

'Let me make a few calls,' he mumbles.

* * *

MARIA

She realises she's been standing at the window for a long time.

Not that there's much to see.

The square flower beds and the manicured avenues disappearing into the distance and beyond that just trees. Oak and beech she thinks but that's just the first line, because beyond them there are just fir trees, tightly packed together, which she knows will mean it would be very dark and difficult to get through and then she'd soon be lost.

And then there are the guards.

She's seen them marching about. Not like ceremonial soldiers. They're dressed in dark uniforms, which would make them difficult to see in the forest.

Is all this for her?

Just to stop her escaping?

Or stopping people getting in?

Who would that be?

Who even knows where she is?

What do they want?

Now she realises she's crying.

Just like her mother, which jolts her back . . . because that was what she hated about her, always crying when her father shouted at her . . . although she doesn't think he ever hit her.

What does she know? Why did he shout at her?

But then she finds a tissue and wipes her face.

She tells herself not to give up . . . and then an idea comes to her . . . well, if they think she's so important, why not act like that, play the part?

This makes her giggle.

And then there's a key rattling in the door.

She sits up and stiffens her back.

If they want a princess, they can have one . . . and they'd better do as they're told!

This comes as a bit of a surprise to the woman who comes in holding a heavy full-length dress and a sewing basket.

She hesitates and then curtsies.

Maria looks at her with as much disdain as she can muster without giggling.

'What do you want?' she asks.

The woman is obviously shocked by this transformation and frowns.

'Forgive me, Altesse, I've been sent to fit this dress, if you will allow me.'

Despite feeling a complete fraud, Maria gives her an evil sneer.

'Well, get on with it woman. I'm tired of wearing these peasant rags.'

Again, she can hardly stop herself from laughing, but then that slight shake of the head her drama teacher used to give when students were being silly comes into her mind. So, she copies it.

The woman tries not to fuss and helps her into the dress.

It's only just a bit too small.

'I can let this out, Altesse . . . and it will fit perfectly.'

'Well, stop dallying and get on with it,' rasps Marie, thinking Miss Thompson would be shaking her head again.

The woman helps her out of the dress with trembling fingers then flusters her way out of the room.

Marie waits a few moments and then bursts out laughing.

But then she thinks what can she do about this?

If she's going to escape, she needs some help.

She tries to recall all the people she's seen. Obviously not the strict looking woman who told her off for breaking the windows. But then the 'servants' like this one with the dress would be probably too scared to help her. The same with the soldiers.

'Well, 'she says out loud, testing her 'Altesse' voice, 'we'll just have to see, won't we.'

MARIYA 1920

Her sister Ana was often ill and she would look after her. Read her stories and tell her all about what everyone else was doing.

And now Elena was always trying to comfort her and make her smile, but day followed day.

Walks in the gardens. Not ever in th the trees, where there were men with huge dogs, that barked and kept wanting to escape their leashes.

Being urged to keep playing the piano, which she hated, because she was no good at it.

Then Elena became ill.

Not like Ana, but days and weeks feeling weak and wanting to sleep.

They insisted she take all sorts of pills and evil tasting potions, but none of them seemed to work, until she thought they were poisoning her, so she would hide them or spit them out when they weren't looking.

This went on for ever and she thought she would die.

But then one night she was woken up in the dark.

Two men saying she had to come quickly.

They waited impatiently until she'd dressed and then hurried her out of the room and into another where they opened a cupboard which led to an underground tunnel.

Which was so scary.

They had torches but they made a lot of smoke and made her cough.

But eventually they were climbing out into a room in a smaller house and then into a carriage and whisked away.

It was only then she asked where 'Elena' was and they just looked away.

CHAPTER SEVENTEEN

Imelda shrugs.

She doesn't want to go to see the grieving wife. She's certainly going to be drunk. Imelda gave up drinking a year ago. Weirdly, because of Tomasz. When he left for Ukraine and she stayed at the painter's house, she hardly saw anyone, so no reason to drink.

In the end just as he's about to drive away, she opens the passenger door and climbs in.

Tomasz only glances at her, doesn't smile and says nothing.

It's only when he's down the hill, that he looks her way to check the oncoming traffic and smiles.

She ignores him.

And says nothing until they get there.

Tomasz pulls up in the driveway and waits for the dogs to appear.

Not a sign, so he opens the door and steps down.

Then there is a dog.
But only one.
A small spaniel.
Who only barks apologetically, while his tail gives away his friendliness.

The front door opens and Clarissa appears.

She stands there waiting. No evidence of the usual sassy drunkenness, just an apologetic smile.

Tomasz frowns back at Imelda who shrugs but makes no move to get out of the car.

So, he gets out and goes over to the waiting woman.

They go inside.

Imelda stares at the hills, her face giving nothing away.

Inside the house, which is unexpectantly neat and tidy, Clarissa takes him through to the kitchen.

'Coffee?' she asks.

He nods, still wary that there might be a sudden rush of snarling dogs.

'I gave them away,' she says. 'I hated the bloody things, but I didn't think they needed to be put down.'

Tomasz shrugs.

No more is said until they're sitting in the conservatory, which is surprisingly resplendent with huge flowering plants he doesn't recognise.

They sit there in silence for quite some time.

'I didn't know much of what he was up to,' she says quietly.

Tomasz waits.

'But from how much he had in his various bank accounts, some of which the police have closed while they investigate them, it looks like he was dealing with some seriously bad people.'

She looks away, but Tomasz just waits again.

She sighs and then turns to look at him.

'I was getting more and more worried . . . some of the people who came here . . . well, they were generally polite, but . . .'

Tomasz sighs and reaches out a hand.

She starts to cry.

The little dog comes to lick her hand.

She picks it up and puts it in on her lap.

Tomasz waits, thinking 'give her time'.

She sighs.

'I don't know where to start.'

He shrugs.

'It doesn't matter. Most people think they should start at the beginning and then find out they didn't realise where that was . . .

often way back from where they started . . . so just start anywhere.'

She smiles . . . and he realises there's a nice person in there somewhere.

She looks away.

'He was never violent with me or hurt me, you know, just ignored me most of the time, unless it was a public situation, when he would do the 'big yin', contacts everywhere, knows important people, a generous patron of the arts and charities etcetera . . .'

Tomasz nods, to indicate he knew all that.

She looks away, finds a handkerchief, and wipes her eyes.

'But recently . . . he was worried about something. Wouldn't say . . . 'Just a sticky situation' and 'it'll sort itself out'.

Tomasz frowns.

She shrugs.

'I assumed it was some dodgy deal gone wrong . . .'

She looks straight at him.

'I knew nothing . . . and now I'll never know.'

Tomasz expects her to cry now, but no . . . maybe she's done that already?

He hesitates.

Maybe she really doesn't know anything.

She gets up and pours herself another coffee. Tomasz shakes his head.

He's thinking.

'This might seem like a . . . an odd question . . . but what nationality were his most recent guests?'

She frowns, then looks away trying to remember and then shrugs.

'Well, Germans, French, Americans . . .'

He waits, not wanting to put words in her mouth.

She frowns.

'Mind you, the last gathering . . . there were Russians, I think, although I don't know how any deals with them would work.'

Tomasz waits.

'They don't live in Russia . . . and I don't think they were happy with Putin, from what I heard.'

Tomasz smiles.

'So where do they live?'

She shakes her head.

'No idea . . . don't they just live on yachts? The ones who were at the last gathering had flown from Glasgow I think, two huge helicopters set down in the middle of the back field.'

'How many of them?'

She smiled.

'Well, if you count all the bodyguards, there must have been about fifteen of them, women too, very beautiful . . . but only three men who seemed to matter.'

Tomasz tries to keep calm.

'Did the police know about this?'

She laughed, a cynical laugh.

'They were here as well. Not in uniforms. High ranking people I suspect, but I'd never seen them before. I heard them all being introduced, although by then I was past bothering . . . I was sent to bed shortly after their arrival.'

'Sent?'

'Ay, I didna care . . . it's what usually happened.'

Tomasz hesitates, not sure what to ask next.

But she shakes her head.

'They were all gone in the morning . . . well, afternoon by the time I got up.'

Ten minutes later he's back in the Landrover, staring out of the window.

Imelda hasn't spoken, no questions.

As usual.

He sighs.

'Are you ever bothered about other people,' he asks.

He waits, trying not to explode.

Just at the moment he would have done, she sighs.

'I care about you . . .'

He stares at her.

'And your mother and sister . . .'

He can't help but smile.

At which point Cushie puts her chin on her shoulder.

They both laugh.

                            *   *   *

Gill is fed up.

Walker has insisted she accompany him back to the big house again.

'What are we looking for?' only enlists a frown as he gets out of the car.

She waits five minutes, wondering what she should do and then reluctantly follows him indoors.

Finds him sitting in the old lady's seat staring out of the window.

She stands behind him.

'You know the girl and her . . . whatever he is, have this daft idea that the woman was pining for somewhere in France?'

Walker sighs.

She waits.

'There's no way we're going to France, is there?' she asks.

He frowns.

'Well . . . I do have some leave to take.'

She can't help but laugh.

But then there's voices downstairs and people running up.

Before they can even think who it might be, three guys come hurtling into the room. Guns out, shouting.

Five minutes later, apologies grudgingly accepted, they're escorted back to their car.

The captain, public school accent, repeats the instruction to keep away and 'let them do their job', whatever that means?

So now they're heading back to Kelso.

It's only when Walker gets back in the car after refuelling that he shows her the letter.

'Where did you get that?'

'Where do you always hide letters?'

She's thinking she hasn't ever done that. Who gets letters anyway, nowadays?

'It was in the bookcase near the old woman's chair . . . I just reached out to the nearest shelf and there it was between the books.'

She takes the letter out of its envelope to see that it's written in gobbledygook, lots of maths symbols and a few ordinary letters.

He sighs.

'It's Russian . . . the second word is 'Maria' . . . her name.'

Gill looks again.

The first two letters are 'M' and 'A', but then there's a 'p' followed by a backward N and an R.

She frowns.

He takes the letter back and starts the engine.

'There's a guy I know back in Liverpool who speaks Russian. I'm going to scan it and send it to him.'

An hour later he gets the email back, which isn't exactly that enlightening.

'Just one friend to another,' he sighs. 'The weather and their dogs.'

But then he realises the guy hasn't translated the address. He copies it and sends it.

The answer comes back, with a link.

'It's been for sale for years. Uninhabited. In France.'

Walker reads the details, then finds it on a map online.

He shows it to Gill, who sighs. She's never been to France and doesn't want to go now.

'What are you going to do?' she asks.

He shrugs.

'Better let someone else do it, I suppose. No chance you and I get to go.'

'Thank God for that,' she whispers under her breath, as he goes to pass on the information to someone else . . . probably that gang who kicked them out of the house.

*   *   *

But at Louisa's, bags are being packed.

At first Louisa said: 'no way, France at this time of the year will be filled with red faced Brits'. But then as she listened and watched the frantic packing, she realised she didn't want to be left on her own, so she changed her mind.

'Someone's got to be able to speak to the natives,' she announced and told Fletcher to bring her suitcases down.

He, of course, touched a non-existent forelock and hobbled off, to come down five minutes later huffing and puffing with two enormous cases.

'We're not going to live there,' he gasped.

Louisa ignored him and gave him a stash of maps she'd taken off the shelf.

Inevitably he managed to drop them and couldn't stop giggling when they fought back as he tried to get them into a bag.

Ellie only had the one rucksack and could only giggle with him.

Then her phone burbles.
'Hi,' says Tomasz.
Ellie frowns.
'Are you ok?'
'Er . . . yeh . . . we went to see Clarissa, this morning.'
'Clarissa?'
'Kershaw's wife.'
'Yeh, how was she?'
'Better, I think . . . she's got rid of the dogs. Well, apart from a small one.'
Another pause.
'We're going to France,' she says.
'Why? Where?'

'Well . . . er . . . a bit difficult to explain, but we think we might know where Marie might be held kidnapped.'
'Marie?'
'The missing girl?'
'Yeh.'
She can hear him breathing.
'Do you want to come?'
Another pause.
'Maybe . . . when are you going?'
'Overnight crossing Newcastle to Antwerp.'
'Er . . . maybe I'll fly, send me the details.'
'Okay.'
No reply and then the call is cut.
Ellie looks at the phone.
'Problem?' asks Fletcher.
Ellie frowns, as she taps in the link for Tomasz.
'Um . . . not sure . . . it's Tomasz . . . says he's going to come as well.'
Fletcher grins.
'Well, that's good, armed reinforcements.'
Louisa frowns.
'I hope it doesn't come to that.'
Ellie shrugs.
'Who knows?'
Fletcher and Louisa exchange glances.
Who indeed?

URSULA

My idyll is over.
 Janet gets a call.
 I know immediately it's 'to arms.'
 The way she walks about, going from one room to another, which makes my head spin, sometimes for no reason, but then she'll find something.

A rucksack . . . she's never been seen with a 'handbag' . . . an anorak from a cupboard where I'd put it, because she just leaves things where she takes them off . . . and then a gun, which she did actually put in a drawer herself.

Now she's hunting for something else, under tables, behind doors, until I figure out, she's looking for shoes.

I find her walking boots and a pair of trainers.

But then she finishes the call.

Looks around until she sees me.

Then strides towards me and gives me her version of a bear hug, which is more like being crushed by a bear . . . if a very sleek thin one.

Then she holds me at arm's length and sighs.

'That was Fletcher, they think they know where the girl might be held captive. Somewhere in France. Ferry to Antwerp.'

I don't know what my face is doing, but my heart is pumping.

She frowns.

'Do you want to come?'

I can't move, can't speak.

But then I see Ziggy waving a passport in his hand.

'Go pack your bag,' he orders, 'I'll be ok, someone has to man the fort.'

How did he . . . know where my passport was? Is it still legal? When did I last use it?

The next few hours are a whirlwind of car chases and last-minute running for the plane, but we make it.

Now we're taking off and my heart is in my mouth.

As soon as we're airborne and everyone's putting their mobiles back on, Janet's furiously texting.

I look down to see the land disappearing and the grey sea lying like a huge bedspread, flecked with white stars, but then we go upwards again and are enveloped in clouds.

I close my eyes and listen to the reassuring engine noise and the chatter of people who probably do this all the time.

Janet's still on her phone, but now sighing and leaning back.

She turns towards me and gives me a peck on the cheek.

'Ziggy's fixed us up with a vehicle at the airport, so we'll be catching up with Fletcher and Ellie . . . oh, and, apparently Louisa as well.'

I just shake my head and look out the window.

'What has that girl done now that is causing such a whirlwind.'

* * *

Gill is dissolutely flicking through travel brochures. Greece or Spain being her preferred destinations, although unfortunately that's also the preference of lots of English 'holiday makers' at this time of year, which is enough to put anyone off.

She throws them in the bin, just as Walker comes through the door.

It's immediately obvious he's planning something, as he flutters the papers on his desk and then stacks them all together and puts them in a drawer.

Then he goes to stand by the window.

'Have you got leave as well,' he murmurs.

Gill frowns.

'Yeh. Why?"

Without turning round, he whispers: 'do you want to go somewhere with me?'

She stares at him in disbelief, but then it clicks.

'You want to follow that girl?'

He turns round, a fierce grimace on his face.

'I don't like 'our' case being hijacked by a bunch of hyped-up military bastards,' he rasps.

Gill waits to see if there's anymore, but he just goes and sits behind his desk and stares at her.

'Well . . .' she whispers, 'what are you thinking of doing?'

He continues to stare at her for few seconds then looks down at his hands.

'You know that retired detective and his lady friend are on a plane as we speak . . . no doubt with that young woman who's always poking her nose into other people's business.'

Gill nods, still worrying how this might be seen by their superiors . . . but then they haven't supported them, have they? They've been sent to this backwater, because their 'methods' are deemed 'reprehensible' . . . even though they've both got long lists of successful results.

She sighs.

'So, you're suggesting we go and join them?'

He shakes his head.

'No, but we could follow them and see what they find.'

Gill frowns.

'But what then?'

He gets up and goes back to the window.

She waits.

'If what the young woman, Ellie, I think she's called, is right, then they're going into a potentially very dangerous situation.'

Gill frowns.

'Do you really believe all that stuff about the Russian royal family?'

He turns round.

'The girl's father did . . . and look what happened to him.'

Gill's thinking 'exactly! Why does he want to take on people like that? With no back-up?' So, she just stares at him.

He turns away, goes back to the window.

She doesn't know what to say.

'Okay,' he whispers. 'Forget it, you go and have a holiday.'

She waits. His shoulders drop and he leans on the window ledge, head down.

'Well . . .' she says quietly, 'I've never been to France, before . . .'

He turns round.

An hour later they're on the way to the airport.

MARIA

The next day the dress is brought back and fitted.

She lets this happen without any resistance, even walking back and forth for the girl and the woman to admire her.

But then she asks if she can speak to the other lady, the Duchessa.

The woman frowns.

'I'll ask,' she says, but then quickly leaves.

It's much later in the day that the woman arrives.

She comes in without knocking, accompanied by another young woman who is carrying a tray of biscuits and a box of chocolates.

'Would you like something to drink,' asks the Duchessa.

Maria nods.

'I'd love a cup of coffee,' she asks, trying to be subservient.

The young woman nods, curtsies and leaves the room.

The Duchessa smiles at her and sits down opposite her. But then stares at her with a severe expression.

'So have you come to terms with your situation?'

Maria stares back at her.

'You must forgive me,' she begins, but then falters, as though she's upset.

The woman waits, her hard eyes not giving any encouragement.

'Well,' she continues, 'you've got to admit . . . it's a bit difficult to accept what you're telling me . . .'

Again, the woman's gaze doesn't falter.

'My father . . . well, I thought he was mad.'

The Duchessa allows herself a fleeting smile, but then continues to stare at her.

'Do you know what he did?'

She nods.

'Unfortunately . . . your father was correct about his inheritance, but, well, very naïve about how the current administration in Moscow would feel about it and that they had been monitoring his every move since he was a child.'

Maria looks away.

'So, you had him killed?'

The Duchessa shakes her head.

'Not us . . . you still haven't grasped who the real enemy is . . . that upstart apparatchik, Putin.'

Maria is thinking 'well we can all agree on that,' but just gives her a frown, wondering what she might say next.

She waits . . . but the woman is looking out the window . . . although not at the view, she surmises.

It's a long wait, but eventually the Duchessa looks back at her. No sign of any tears, but the voice is softer.

'I don't expect he ever confided in you?'

Maria can confirm that without lying, so she shakes her head. He did rant on about 'history', but she never listened.

Again, there's a long pause, which was disquieting, because the Duchessa just stared at her, so she looked away.

'Your grandmother was a very beautiful lady,' she whispered, like she was in church.

Maria looks back at her, to see tears running down her cheeks. She brushes them away and shakes herself, before standing up.

'But there's no time for sorrow or 'what might have been', we live in the present and your time has come.'

With that she backs away, curtsies, and swishes out of the room.

Maria stares after her.

Shakes her head.

Doesn't know whether to cry or laugh.

The woman must be insane to think that presenting her as the Czarina of All Russia would stand up for five minutes in the real world. Putin would just laugh.

She walks over to the window.

What would Zelensky think? Maybe he might see it as a possible way to divide Russian opinion, she knew there was resistance to the war, but still, it would be highly unlikely it would make a difference.

But more worryingly, she would be a target if her claim was publicly announced. Is this why they're measuring her up for some fancy Czarina gowns?

She shakes her head.

Madness.

MARIYA 1920

They didn't get to Paris.

The train stopped in the middle of the night.

It was very dark.

She was woken up and pushed and shoved along to the door.

It wasn't in a station.

So, there was a huge drop to the ground. Then she could feel the cold wind.

Had she been taken back to Russia?

Two men roughly helped her down a steep slope and then there was a van.

They pushed her in and closed the doors.

They didn't set off straight away and she heard the train slowly pulling away making a terrible noise and a lot of smoke, which got into the van and made her cough.

Then there was a long drive.

First on bumpy roads and then better ones.

Finally, they pulled up and she could hear gruff voices and then a shout.

Not Russian, maybe French.

Then a huge screeching and metal dragging, which she thought were big gates.

Then another drive.

Until it stopped again.

She could hear people talking, some in Russian and others in French.

The van doors opened and she was dragged out and marched in through a great door and along a corridor to a room, shoved inside and left alone.

The only good thing was that there was a great fire burning in a massive fireplace.

She was so exhausted she fell asleep.

CHAPTER EIGHTEEN

URSULA

I hate flying.

I hate airports. All the hustle and bustle and then people like me standing, looking around, lost.

Janet, obviously, the complete opposite. Always knowing where she's going, forcing her way through the scrimmage, annoyed by and annoying other people.

I follow, like the Queen, sailing sedately along the avenue she's created, telling myself not to apologise for her disappearing figure.

Sometimes she remembers that I'm following and waits, trying not to be too impatient.

I suppose after the incident at the station In Edinburgh she's become even more on edge, searching the crowd for any possible attackers.

Anyway, I arrive safely, if a little bit out of breath after the steps and then Janet is grabbing my arm next to the second seats from the doorway.

She puts my bag on the rack and pushes me into the window seat, as other people are trying to pass her. She sits down and mutters curses about other people, airline staff and the rest of the world I suspect.

But then she sighs and relaxes . . . and manages a smile.

But for me the fear hasn't started.

I can't believe that this giant structure full of what, a hundred people, is going to rush down a runway and then launch itself into the air.

But it does!

Not that I see anything. My eyes tightly closed until that voice tells us we can release our seat belts.

Janet smiles . . . and then five minutes later she's asleep! How can she do that?

I don't go to sleep at all.
I also don't partake in any food or drink, thinking it wouldn't stay down five seconds, especially as we're soon being told we're descending.
I always think it's like there's a big giant out there letting the plane down through a string on his fingers. Not smoothly or gently, but malicious sudden drops to frighten the tiny passengers.

Now for the worst bit.
The way the whole world drops out of the sky. Then the funny noises, which hopefully means there's plenty of wheels.
And finally, we 'hit' the runway.
You can't possibly call it 'landing' – when it's much more like 'thumping' the tarmac and then the braking, like some boy on a bike showing off.
At last, the torture stops.
Janet wakes up!
The next hour is a whirlwind of pushing and shoving, me trying to keep her in sight, until our bags are retrieved off the trolley and stuffed into the boot of a hire car.
Thankfully we stop at the first service station and go into the café, where she orders coffees and croissants in fluent French.
It's only then she calms down.
'I hate flying,' she mutters and then looks at me.
'Are you okay?' she asks.
I just stare at her, until she comes round and hugs me.
And to my relief she doesn't like the autoroutes either, so we're soon on country lanes and then pulling into a small hotel in the middle of a little village.
She gets out and reaches for our bags.

'Come on, you'll like Davide and Stephanie. I booked us in for evening meal as well.'

*   *   *

Imelda is used to flying, but the little planes going back and forth to Lewis are nothing like the giants that fly south from Edinburgh.

Even worse is the jostling throng that carries everyone this way and that as the mixture of confident long-term aviators and the less experienced holidaymakers gaggling about like a bunch of lost flamingos looking for their offspring is not the best example of human behaviour.

Tomasz being one of the former and her the latter means that eventually he takes her by the hand and guides her through the throng.

So, soon, they're sitting not too far from the front of the giant plane, he insists she has the window seat.

'I'll probably be asleep by the time we get airborne,' he says, which Imelda can't imagine herself ever doing.

So, flying alone isn't too bad, because he's not asking how she feels every five minutes, which she could only describe as holding her breath for ever.

Anyway, the lack of chatter means she eventually calms down and can manage to look down through the window and is surprised to see they're already over the water and can see land below. She's never resolved the conundrum of whether to crash into the sea is better or worse than hitting the ground.

CDG is another nightmare, but miraculously Tomasz has navigated the hire car out onto the motorway and then quickly leaving it for a much more sedate main road.

So, he stops in the first small town and orders breakfast and coffees. Well, pastries!

'What is this?' she asks, looking at what looks like a large flaky turd.

A '*qwason*',' he mumbles, mouth full of flakes.

She shrugs but takes a bite.

Not unpleasant, but why would you want to eat pastry for breakfast . . . don't the French eat porridge?' She doesn't ask and drinks the coffee, which is very strong and bitter, even with hot milk.

The café seems to be full of locals, many of them solitary, reading papers or on their mobiles.

Soon they're back in the car and driving along long straight roads, she hadn't imagined that France would be so flat.

And as usual she goes to sleep.

She wakes with a lurch and realises they're in a small village square.

Tomasz is stretching his back and then smiles at her.

'Avez-vous faim?'

She frowns.

'Lunch,' he explains, gesturing round the square where there seem to be restaurants on every side.

She nods.

'You choose,' he says.

She looks from one to another and then shakes her head.

'So . . .' he grins, takes her arm, and sets off to the one which seems the busiest to her. Must be at least ten tables outside under an awning, although he takes her indoors and they are offered a table in a corner.

She looks at a menu but can't see anything she understands, so passes it back to him.

A smiling waitress approaches and Tomasz smiles back.

They then have a conversation, which could be him chatting her up, the amount of smiling she does and then laughing. But somehow, he's told her what they want without asking Imelda.

So, she waits.

Looking round there are men in suits, women in dresses and she realises it's quite warm and takes her anorak off.

Tomasz smiles and pours her some water.

'I love France,' he murmurs, 'the food, the pace of life . . . look at all these people, they're eating 'plat du jour', probably taking an hour or more. In the UK, people have a sandwich or don't take a break at all.'

Imelda frowns, thinking 'pla de jure'?

Then his phone's burbling.

It's not a long conversation, from his side anyway.

'That was Ellie,' he says, 'poor lamb, having to come the long way on the slow boat to Amsterdam – but now at least they're on the road, Louisa driving at her usual terrifying speed. She thinks they'll get to Epoisses for dinner.'

Imelda has no idea of how far away Amsterdam might be, but she has only once sat in a car driven by Louisa and never wants to repeat the experience, so she just shakes her head at him.

So, sitting in a café waiting for food to arrive seems a much better option and so she manages a smile at Tomasz who grins back . . . his lascivious look. So, she shakes her head, but can't stop a smirk taking over.

* * *

Ellie has managed to stop gripping the side of the seat as Louisa sweeps along in the outside lane. At least she's concentrating and not talking. Fletcher has gone to sleep. How can he do that?

Being on the boat was sedateness itself compared to this.

She's not having to navigate because Louisa says she knows the way to Epoisses having done it quite a few times before.

And this includes an evening meal in a place just off the autoroute, where she is welcomed with lots of hugging and kissing which Fletcher and Ellie have to weather as well.

Fletcher being still resolutely non-French speaking even though he's spent numerous holidays with Ellie's extended family, including the nightmare murders of Tata and Tonton which eventually led to the horrific slaughter in the grounds of Dryburgh Abbey, which is still a mystery . . . that Ellie survived it.

He glances across at her now, to find her eyes glued to him. He knows one of her many gifts is somehow knowing what people are thinking.

He shakes his head, but she gives him a haunted look, which make him reach across the table to squeeze her hand. She shakes her head and wipes her eye, before managing a smile.

He takes this to mean say nothing, so he doesn't and tries to key back into the other people's conversation, which he'd have trouble keeping up with anyway.

Later in bed, which he knew would be a chaste experience, he mumbles something about old nightmares, which at least elicits a hug, although he knows Ellie is alone in bed and might not have that comfort.

As it happens, she's talking to her mother, Grace, as she always does if she goes to France, especially if it's near where the nightmares began. Epoisses being much further north than the Dordogne means she's not too bad and realises she's not spoken to her for some time.

*   *   *

Unlike the people they're following, the two detectives have never flown together before, so it's a bit of surprise to find that neither of them is frightened nor bothered about the activity at all. If anything, they both find it boring.

Equally they're both happy driving on the wrong side of the road. So, Gill suggests he drives the first two hours and then she'll have a go.

They've decided that they'll find somewhere to stay a few miles away from Epoisses as they don't think they'll be welcome, in fact they both know it's bordering on stalking.

MARIA

As if yesterday wasn't bizarre enough, this morning was like being forced to go back in time.

The first thing was being woken up and dressed in a ridiculously outsized ballroom gown even before she's had any breakfast, but then taken through into what is probably regarded as the 'breakfast room', where she finds a collection of people she hasn't seen before, didn't realise there was so many of them. This is compounded by them all getting up from their chairs and bowing and curtsying.

Then she is taken to a table which is a step above all the rest, where there are only two chairs, one huge one for her and the other, slightly smaller, for the Duchessa, who offers her a hand and helps into the chair, as if she might stumble if she isn't accompanied.

Then the whole room is clapping as if walking to a table and sitting down is an Olympic challenge and she's won.

So now they're all chattering away, looking occasionally at her and daring to smile at her. At first this just makes her frown at them, but then sees it as a game and gives some of them a smile and others a puzzled look . . . although the inclination to make a funny face she decides might be a step too far.

But she soon tires of this and concentrates on getting something to eat . . . which is easier said than done.

Some of the things put in front of her like one dish which she thinks might be herring, but other things aren't recognisable as food to her and even if she risks a taste of them, she still can't identify what they might be. So, in the event she's left wishing she could have a bowl of cornflakes.

Most of the people near her are speaking in either French or Russian, but just too far away to only catch the odd word or two which doesn't really inform her what they're talking about.

The Duchessa isn't in a talkative mood, after asking her if she slept well and wondered if she'd like to go a for a walk later.

Maria nods at this enthusiastically, but then wonders if the whole of the room will accompany them.

This is in fact what happens.

At the end of some allotted time, the Duchessa stands up and everyone else does as well.

Looking up at her, Maria wonders if she should also stand yet and seeing a slight widening of her eyes, thinks that's the signal, so she gets to her feet, which is ridiculously accompanied by a lengthy round of applause, which she inadvertently stops, by raising her hand.

But then she realises they're all staring at her, smiling, as if they're waiting for something else.

She can't think of anything to say or do, so frowns at the Duchessa, who smiles back and then announces that her Imperial Majesty will be taking a walk in the gardens later this morning.

'Her Imperial Majesty'!? Will be taking a walk? Like a dog? In these clothes?

In the event, it's more like a rock star giving a hoard of photographers an opportunity to take hundreds of photos . . . except no-one has a camera unless someone is taking them from the chateau with a telescopic lens or maybe from the forest which surrounds the whole building and gardens.

The Duchessa makes it feel like she's being allowed to go where she wants, but every time she veers towards the trees, she gently directs her back. The idea of running anywhere in this huge dress would be ridiculous anyway.

So, she strolls back and forth, which has the effect of meeting different people who give way and show off their ability to bow and curtsey.

The whole exercise seems utterly pointless to her, so she turns back towards the chateau and picks up some speed. The Duchessa keeps up with her until, giggling to herself, Maria picks up her skirt and runs towards the steps which go back up to the terrace.

At the top she stops and swings round to see the Duchessa frowning up at her, like she's a naughty girl, but then manages to smile before carefully stepping up to stand next to her.

She turns to look back at the crowd of . . . Maria supposes they're 'courtiers' . . . and says something in Russian and then turning to her and smiles. The 'courtiers' burst into a prolonged applause and a few cheers from the men.

Maria just stares at them.

Are they really Russian 'emigres' who believe in all this tosh? Or are they actors being paid to play the part?

At which point, the Duchessa comes close and says: 'Just wave, turn round and go back into the dining room.'

Maria looks at her and senses the steel in this command, so she does as she's told, resisting the urge to turn and give the crowd a twirl like a movie star.

Inside, there are only 'men in black' with dead eyes, so she stands and waits.

A couple of them close the French windows and then stand in front of them.

The Duchessa has walked a few further steps and now turns round.

Maria can see sense that she's seething, but she seems to get control of herself.

She waits.

The Duchessa comes towards her and clears her throat, but then again gritting her teeth, before she speaks.

'I would advise you not to . . . behave foolishly . . . these people are not actors trying to make you feel important . . .' Again, she stops and her eyes burn into hers. 'They want to believe in you . . . that you are indeed the Czarina they have waited for . . . for three whole generations, so give them the respect they deserve.'

Maria's inner voice wants to say 'Or what? like the teenager she is, but the more mature part of her suspects that would be dangerous, so she settles for a sterner look.

The Duchessa waits sensing this might be an important moment.

Maria looks away.

'What proof have you got?' she eventually whispers and then in a stronger voice says, 'I am a history student after all and you'll have to do better than dress me up and tell those people what they want to hear and see.'

At first the Duchessa seems to be struggling with an angry response, but then she turns away and walks to the closed windows.

Maria doesn't see the signal, but the guards quietly disperse leaving only a couple either side of the windows outside, which looks like the final image of this 'shoot', she supposes.

The Duchessa turns to face her, silhouetted against the light.

If this is meant to frighten Maria, it's so melodramatic she nearly giggles, but she composes herself and looks round for a chair. Seeing none she turns back and stares back at the silhouette.

'I'm prepared to listen to what evidence you have, but can we stop playing with the embarrassing 'film noir' routines, because I can't take them seriously.'

The Duchessa doesn't respond until her mouth turns into a sneer.

'How's your Russian, little history student?'

'Svobodno govoryu, poprobuy menya.'

This evinces big eyes and then a smile.

'Very good, but we'll have to work on the accent.'

Maria shrugs.

* * *

MARIYA 1920

They're on another train, but it's going faster than before.

She's in a carriage all on her own, but people come in with food and drink.

She has more clothes now and has a small washing cupboard with soap and clean towels.

There is one girl, called Aline who seems to have been told to look after her, but she doesn't say much and although she can speak Russian, she has such a terrible accent that it's often difficult to understand what she's saying.

And now she's saying: 'we go Franche next day'.

Does she mean France?

Why?

How have we got here?

She remembers the teacher who tried to tell them about European history and geography, but he was hopeless and her sisters just teased him all the time.

She knows the capital is Paris, which is supposed to be very beautiful and full of writers and artists.

Is that where they're going?

She asks the girl what the date is and she says it's le six Mars, dix neuf, dix neuf - which means she's been away from her family for two years now.

But this only makes her miserable as she can't remember what happened to them and when she tried to remember it makes her frightened that it was something terrible.

Are they still alive?

Something tells her that they're not . . . which makes her cry.

CHAPTER NINETEEN

Imelda slept better in the car than the hotel bed. Being on that plane which she thought was driven by a mischievous child, the number of bumps it took to get from whatever stratosphere they came down from and then hitting the runway twice before staying down . . . and then huge revving of the brakes, which caught the eager beavers who were already standing up to fall down, taking their luggage with them.

Tomasz couldn't help grinning as they were berated by one of the flight stewards. The blonde one he couldn't take his eyes off.

So, then it took ages to actually get off the plane, through customs and get the car.

And now she wakes up again to find they've stopped in the middle of nowhere and Tomasz has disappeared.

No, she can see him walking up a long driveway towards huge gates set in a high wall which extends into the distance both ways.

She gets out of the car and stretches her back.

What is he doing?

He's now reached the gates and seems to be looking through.

But then she can see a couple of guards talking to him.

Too far away to hear anything.

Now he's walking back.

It takes a good few minutes, before he arrives and then she can see the disguise he's wearing, which makes her shake her head.

Her sunglasses, the Hawaiian shirt and his old soldier cap.

He turns round and looks back at the gateway.

No sign of the soldiers.

'Well, they were polite, but just told me to go away, as it's a private residence . . . I asked who lived there, but that made them a lot more aggressive. None of my business.'

'Do you think this is the place?' she asks.

He nods.

'So . . .' she murmurs, 'how on earth can we rescue her from there?'

Tomasz shakes his head.

'No idea . . . yet.'

He reaches into the car and finds his binoculars and trains them on the gateway, then travels both directions along the walls.

It becomes obvious the guards have binoculars too, because the gates open long enough for a jeep to come out and race towards them.

Tomasz tells her to get back into the car.

She only just manages it before the jeep pulls up in a cloud of gravel.

Three armed men get out and surround them, automatic guns raised.

A further officer steps down and walks up to Tomasz.

He gets very close.

'You were told this residence is private, what are you doing?'

Tomasz adopts an apologetic manner, which she knows is not his best role.

'Excusez-nous,' he says, in bad French. 'It's just I was surprised to see it, as it's not in our guidebook.'

The man stares at him.

'That's because it's a 'private' residence.'

'Well, sorry,' mumbles Tomasz.

The man shakes his head.

'Get in your car and go away. If I see you again, I'll contact the local gendarmerie and they will arrest you . . . or maybe we might accidentally shoot you!'

The last option said with a smile.

Tomasz manages a frown, but then shrugs and gets into the car.

The soldiers are still holding their guns in an aggressive manner, while Tomasz makes a show of incompetent reversing and turning, before he can drive slowly away back to the main road, where he hesitates before turning left to go back to Epoisses.

It's only when he pulls up in the town centre that Imelda can relax with a sigh.

'You're mad,' she mutters.

'Probably . . . but that's told us what we're up against.'

They both sit there for a few more moments, until he points through the window.

'Isn't that Janet Becket?'

Imelda stares at the woman standing in front of a bar across the road. As can be expected she's looking totally cool in her shades, black t-shirt and black shorts.

Tomasz gets out of the car and waves at her.
She stares at him and then waves back.

Imelda reluctantly gets out of the car and follows Tomasz across to her.

Kisses exchanged they go inside to find Ursula sitting at a table with an empty cup of coffee, reading something on her mobile.

More kisses, like they've all turned French, before drinks are ordered and arrive.

URSULA

Having spent the last few years living in a valley hidden from the rest of the world, the easy going way both Becket and Tomasz greet each other as if they live here, chattering away in French like natives, is as usual intimidating, but then there's Imelda.

She's more like me.

Shy . . . no; more like sullen. Doesn't do small talk. Not sure why she's here.

So, I give her a smile while the other two prattle on about the traffic, the French etcetera.

I ask if she wants a drink.

She manages a smile back.

'Coffee?'

'Not black,' she murmurs.

I go inside the bar and order four coffees, two white and two 'noir'.

The woman says she'll bring them out, if I understand it right, but then she nods.

I go back to Imelda, who is staring across the square. It's late morning, but there's still some shade on this side.

I sit down and smile at her.

'You speak French?' she asks.

I shrug.

'Enough, I think, to survive.'

She smiles sadly, but then the other two come in and sit with us and the coffee arrives.

'So . . .' says Tomasz, looking at Becket,' how do you think we can get in there?'

She shrugs.

'Parachutes?'

Tomasz laughs.

'Not me . . . too many bad experiences doing that, although the ground in Afghanistan is harder than here.'

'At night?'

Again, he shrugs.

'Nah, I think we need something more 'left field'.'

Becket nods, she but hasn't got any idea about that.

So, the four of us are sitting there, just watching the world go by . . . like you do on holiday?

*   *   *

Ellie has persuaded Louisa to drive a bit slower, pointing out the traffic camera before the next village.

Fletcher thinks that's a good chance to stop and have another coffee. So, they pull up outside the last one in the village. How can small places like this manage to make any profit she wonders? They'd passed two others looking permanently closed. And the one they've stopped at has only one old man sitting outside with his eyes shut, empty cup and glass on the table.

They go inside, Louisa doesn't like sitting in full sun, unless she's in her conservatory.

Ellie's brought the road map and opens it up on the table.

'It's only another hour or so,' she murmurs, then picks up her mobile and calls Becket.

The conversation is as usual brief.

'They're already there,' she confirms, 'Imelda and Ursula as well.'

'Ursula?' asks Fletcher with a frown.

Ellie shrugs.

'Chalk and cheese,' murmurs Louisa.

Ellie's now looking at photos that Tomasz has sent.

She shows them to Fletcher.

'Hum,' he says. 'Fort Knox . . . how are we going to get in there?'

Ellie frowns.

'Tomasz is checking out helicopters.'

Fletcher laughs.

'You won't get me in one of those?'

Louisa meanwhile has been on the phone with Juliette, who's kindly told them they can stay at her house.

She knows about the key, which is with the neighbour, but has forgotten the woman's name.

So now she's on the phone to her, switching effortlessly into her posh French voice, which makes Ellie giggle, because her own French was learnt from Tonton and Tata . . . which makes her sad.

Conversation over, Louisa stands up and sets off for the car, leaving Fletcher to struggle to pay the bill, so Ellie helps him out.

Louisa checks her map and estimates another hour, but seeing the look on Ellie's face, sighs and says: 'alright an hour and a half'.

In the event it's nearly two hours, because of roadworks.

So, it's nearly aperitif time when she sweeps up and parks outside the café where the other four musketeers are lounging outside in the sun.

To the embarrassment of Ursula and Imelda there is an extended English version of French greetings, which only makes the locals shake their heads and smile.

Drinks are ordered and then dinner booked for seven.

Much later, some of them have gone to bed, leaving only Tomasz, Ellie, Becket and Fletcher sitting outside on the verandah, assorted drinks and coffees to hand.

They watch the sun go down in silence and then wait for someone to begin.

Inevitably, it's Becket who can't stand silences.

'Force isn't an option . . . from what Tomasz has told us.'

This is met with shrugs and acceptance.

'So . . . any ideas?'

*   *   *

Given the limited French between them, Gill and Walker still find it reasonably easy to acquire a vehicle at the airport and, because Gill is such 'a planning freak' according to both her mother and now Walker, a road map, they're soon on their way.

They also both agree about not paying for motorways, so as soon as they can leave, they head south on an ordinary main road.

Gill waits for about an hour of this before saying they've to stop in the next place and get something to eat or she will be turning cannibal, so Walker grins and swerves across in front of a huge lorry to get off the main road and heads towards somewhere they didn't catch the name of.

It turns out to be a small town, not busy and they're able to park in a half-empty carpark just off a square where Gill spotted an open café.

Fried breakfast not on offer, they settle for a coffee and croissants, although Gill has to ask for extra after wolfing the first two and muttering about 'how do the French survive on these?'.

Now they're looking at the road map and again choosing the non-motorway option, which seems to get them there for about five pm.

Gill's driving in a surprisingly less aggressive mode than Walker, who tells himself to chill and watch the scenery, which to be honest isn't that exciting. Huge fields to the horizon are not his idea of countryside views.

This continues until after signs for a place called Sens, she takes that road and pulls up in the centre of town, where they're early for lunchtime.

Food eaten they sit watching the world go slowly by.

'I think France might be alright,' murmurs Gill.

Walker frowns.

'In what way?'

'Well, nobody's rushing about. Most people seem to be having a lengthy break . . . not like we never get . . . lucky if we can grab a sandwich or a coffee.'

He can't disagree.

'But what do you think about this idea that this girl might be a granddaughter of the last Romanoffs,' he asks.

'You mean 'great granddaughter."

He nods.

'Well,' she murmurs. 'Despite the fact that she's a student . . . I think she might believe it . . . but the person who definitely thinks it's true is that annoying young lady with the ex-detective in tow.'

Walker sighs his agreement.

It takes another two hours until they pull up in a baking hot square in the middle of a place called Semur-en-Auxois having quickly bypassed the centre of Epoisses a few miles back.

Unintentionally Gill has parked in front of a hotel, so they go in and settle for a double room as they don't have any singles. This is okay because it actually has a double and a single bed.

Gill needs a shower, so he goes down to sit in the bar.

So, when she does come down 'in a dress', he does a double take.

'Alright,' she snaps, 'yes, it's a dress.'

Recovering, he stands up and signals to the young woman behind the counter, who's grinning at him.

Deciding to eat here as well, they reserve a table for seven and then set off to explore the town.

Which doesn't take long.

So, they end up in another bar and settle down to watch the townsfolk carrying on their desultory business. No-one rushing, lots of them stopping to chat.

'I could do with this pace of life,' murmurs Walker.

Gill snorts.

'No, you wouldn't, you'd get bored after a couple of days.'

He shrugs and sighs.

Then she's taking a map out of her bag.

It has a blue cover and she tells him it's the local area, then refolds it so they can look at the area round Epoisses.

They saw the big chateau as they passed through, but the one they're looking for is further north outside the town.

'Completely surrounded by forest, I think,' she murmurs, pointing at the green area. 'Fir trees,' she adds pointing at the Xmas tree symbols.

He sighs.

'Well, that looks like we won't be welcome to have a look round.'

Gill then produces a small book, which she acquired in the shop she went to while he was still in the shower.

'There's a few photos and a bit of history, but it says it's privately owned and not open to visitors.'

He has a look, but going round old buildings has never been on his to do holiday lists.

She sits back in her seat and frowns.

The square in front of them is nearly empty, only a few folk walking about, mainly locals on their way home presumably.

'How do we get into a place like that without backup?'

Walker shrugs again.

'Subterfuge,' he murmurs.

Gill stares at him. Where did that word come from?

* * *

Ellie can't sleep.

Three o'clock in the morning.

There's something she's forgotten. Something important?

How can they get into the chateau?

They don't even know for certain that the girl is there.

But it comes to her.

The bracelet!

She throws the bedclothes aside.

Finds her phone.

Calls Ziggy.

Who of course is wide awake and answers in seconds.

'Bon soir,' he mutters.

'The girl's bracelet, can you find it?'

There's a pause.

'You mean a signal?'

'Yes.'

There's another pause, but the inevitable sound of typing.

'Theoretically, yes, but . . .'

'But what?'

'Well, firstly, she would have to be wearing it . . . then is it turned on, I mean live . . . and is the battery still working?'

Ellie frowns.

'I've no idea . . . about any of that.'

She's stumped.

'What about the mother?' he mutters.

Ellie realises she's pacing the small bedroom.

'Yeh, right, but . . . I don't know her number or any other contact.'

There's a pause.

'I've got it. I'll call her.'

'Now?' says Ellie, looking at her watch again.

'Um,' says Ziggy, 'maybe not, but you never know, she's quite likely to be having sleepless nights wondering about her daughter. Give me a moment I'll try.'

Ellie is pacing the room. Stands at the window, looking down on the square beneath her. The streetlights are still on but there's a slight pink tinge over to the left-hand side.

'No answer . . . so I left a message,' he mutters. 'I'll let you know.'

The line goes dead.

Ellie gets back into the bed . . . but she knows she'll not go back to sleep.

MARIA

She's in her grandmother's house again.

The walls are very close, rustling, even though she's trying really hard not to touch them.

Sometimes it seems like whispering.

She can't make out what they're saying.

Who are they?

They seem to think she knows them, but she doesn't, can't imagine who they could be?

And then she comes to a corner.

She peeps round.

Was that someone there, just disappearing round the next corner?

She can't go any faster because she doesn't want the walls to fall in on her, because when she looks up, she can't see a ceiling, paper just disappearing into the darkness.

But there is light in here.

Not a bright light and there's no sign of any light bulbs or windows . . . just a grey light, which makes the air look fuzzy.

She comes to another corner.
Waits.
Then quickly looks round.
Was that someone?
Just a slight figure disappearing?
She calls out.
'Hello?'
But her voice sounds fuzzy . . .
and there's no answer except a slight echoing . . . 'ello . . .lo . . . lo. . . oh . . .

She stops.
What if she pushed at the walls?
Could she get through?
She gets her arm up and puts her hand into the paper.
It crumbles in her fingers and the paper above quickly fills the gap . . .
And even though it's soft it gradually seems to be congealing on her hand like glue setting.
She pulls it out and there's a gasp from the wall . . . which actually sounds like an angry noise!
She's so scared she backs away, stumbles and falls forwards, knocking both sides which now softly start to fall on top of her.
She's gasping for breath, her mouth and nose getting clogged up with fluffy paper.
She can't cry out!
The weight of the paper is now getting heavier, trying to crush her!
She fights back . . .
     and bursts out into a room,
      a dark room
         dark wooden walls
     empty?

But then a figure appears
A woman
        dressed like a nurse?
No, a waitress?
She's reaching out to her.
Calling her name
Maria . . . Maria . . . MARIA!

She's awake.

She's hanging onto the girl's arm - she's staring at her – terrified.

Maria lets her go and the girl stumbles backwards onto the floor. Then she backs away towards the wall, crying and staring.

Another person appears. A man. He grabs her and pushes her to the wall and holds her there.

He shouts something to the girl, who's getting up.

It's not English, but she does recognise the name:

'Duchessa'

MARIYA & ELENA 1918

Is that the sea?

Seabirds calling.

She can hear voices, not speaking Russian. Realises it's Turkish.

Odessa??

She knows where it is on a map, but it's not in Russia.

She knew a boy, a servant, who said he was from Odessa and said it was the most beautiful place in the world.

Most days they are allowed a short time walking in a courtyard. It has walls so high they can't even see any other buildings outside, but they could hear the noise of people shouting and animals braying and birds calling.

Crows appear on the walls and sometimes drop down to see what they can find.

The servants change each day except one.

A small thin man who looks at her sternly.

Today he asked how she was feeling. She wanted to say 'frightened', but she said she was hungry, so he brought her some oranges.

Then she asked where they were, he just smiled.

'At least we're safe,' he whispered and then looked over his shoulder as if someone would punish him for saying that.

Later, back in their room, one bed, one chair and a small window high up, she wondered who might want to punish him?

Now it was getting dark and she sighed, hoping she wouldn't have another nightmare again tonight.

Then she remembers what happened to her sisters and weeps.

CHAPTER TWENTY

Magda arrives back from her early morning ride to find two police cars on the drive.

Fearing the worst, she quickly gets down from her horse and runs to the kitchen doorway to find her mother chattering away with four, no five policemen, who are assembled around the kitchen table. Two of them are in plain clothes the rest uniformed, hats on the table.

Helena is pouring a cup of tea, having already served three of them, but now stops to welcome her daughter back.

'Ah, there you are, Magda. I'm afraid they've come for me at last!' and grins.

The uniformed officers can't stop embarrassed smiles at that but the two plain clothes officers remain stony-faced.

One of them now stands up and show his warrant card.

'We're here to talk to your brother, Detective Inspector,' he says. 'I'm DI Forester.'

Magda frowns.

'What's he's supposed to have done now?' she asks, without smiling.

Forester doesn't smile either.

'Can you tell me where he is?'

She hesitates. The police officer in her head at odds with the sister.

'I'm not sure about that, he left home yesterday.'

Forester waits. She can feel the tension.

'Could you be more specific . . . Inspector?' he asks, which she thinks he's using her rank to urge her to come clean.

'Well . . .' she says, turning away. 'I'm afraid he didn't say where he was going exactly, but I think he's gone abroad.'

Forester gives her a stern look.

'Well . . . France I think, as I said he didn't say where.'

Forester clears his throat, aware that the other officers are watching him.

'Am I right in thinking that he went to visit Mrs Clarissa Kershaw recently?'

She frowns, Tomasz said she was okay, only one small dog.

'Yes,' she says softly. 'Why, what's happened?'

Forster hesitates.

'I understand your brother didn't get on with the Kershaws?'

Magda frowns again.

'Well, Kershaw himself, not at all, he was a boor and a bully . . . but I don't think he dislikes Clarissa . . . everyone felt sorry for her.'

Forester hesitates again.

'Everyone?'

'Well . . . she isn't particularly 'liked' . . . more that we all feel sorry for her.'

Forester waits.

'Why, what's happened?' she asks.

He clears his throat.

'She was found dead earlier this morning.'

'Dead?'

He nods.

'Murdered.'

Magda shakes her head.

'When?'

He shrugs.

'Not sure yet, but probably more than twenty-four hours ago. She was found by a woman who cleans for her.'

Magda shakes her head and looks round for a chair to sit on.

Forester waits a few moments, then sits as well.

'The thing is, another member of her staff says your brother visited her two days ago?'

She frowns at him, then shakes her head.

'How?' she whispers.

He hesitates, not wanting to be too specific.

'Blunt trauma, repeated blows with as yet an unidentified weapon . . .'

Magda shakes her head, knowing that's 'police speak' when they don't want to reveal the probable weapon.

She gives him a stern look.

'Well, that puts my brother out of the frame . . . as I'm sure you know he has a row of medals for long distance kills in Afghanistan and elsewhere . . . but what you might not know he is unbelievably squeamish about the sight of blood . . . and more likely to run away than hurt someone physically. . .'

Forester holds her gaze until she looks away.

'As I said, we do have a witness who says he and his friend visited her about the time the pathologist estimates she was killed.'

Magda is shaking her head and now Helena speaks.

'I think you've got the wrong man, Inspector, my son wouldn't have done that.'

Forester sighs and looks from one to the other.

'But you must understand that we need to speak to him?'

Magda nods.

'Of course, but he's not the sort of person to tell you where he's going and has often gone off without telling anyone.'

Again, Forester hesitates.

'Can you give me his mobile number?'

Magda hesitates.

'Well, yes, but don't expect him to answer it, he doesn't really like them and often forgets to power it up . . . and unlikely to have acquired a French connection.'

Forester frowns yet again, not really able to believe that, but decides not to challenge her . . . just now.

He stands up and produces his card.

'If he does contact you, please tell him to get in touch as soon as possible.'

The other four officers stand up and find their way to the door, looking awkward and then they're gone.

Magda stands looking at her mother who now starts to cry.

She puts her arm round her and whispers: 'this is a set-up, mama, you know Tomasz wouldn't do anything like.'

Helena pushes her away and gets out her handkerchief to blow her nose nd then cries out: 'Why can't he keep out of trouble?!'

Magda shakes her head and then they're both laughing.

Helena finds her phone which was hiding on the window ledge.

'Stupid English, thinking old ladies don't have phones!'

Magda can only shake her head.

And as usual Tomasz answers almost immediately, which means Helena lets out a stream of Polish expletives, which always makes Magda blush. Then she pauses for breath and tells him what's happened, but then says not to tell her where he is, because 'someone could be listening'.

Tomasz must have agreed with this because the call is ended.

Magda puts her arms round her.

They both have a cry, then pull apart.

'Wait a minute,' says Magda and goes upstairs to her room and returns with a different phone.

Helena frowns.

'Won't they still know it's ringing from here?'

Magda grins at her.

'I'm not ringing him.'

Helena shakes her head; she's always suspicious of unexpected phone calls . . . or knocks on the door as well.

'Hi,' says Magda.

She listens.

'I see . . . that's awful . . . poor woman.'

Listens again.

'Who?'

Pause.

'Well, that's quite a scary . . . unit.'

She listens some more and then closes the call.

Helena is staring at her in frustration.

'Well?' she demands.

Magda takes a breath and then relays everything that Ziggy has just told her.

* * *

Tomasz sighs.

The others have been chatting but now look to see what the call was about.

He tells them about the police visit and then what Ziggy has found out about what happened to Clarissa.

Most of them don't know her, but Imelda eyes go wide.

'Poor woman,' mutters Tomasz, but he's puzzled.

'Why would someone want to kill her? She was sozzled most of the time and would have no idea what Kershaw was up to?'

Fletcher pulls a face.

'Well, if they were after anything that might incriminate them, they would need to be certain that there's nothing there, so . . .'

Tomasz stares at him angrily and then looks away.

But Fletcher is used to people not wanting to accept the truth.

'So, more reason for us to see what is so important here.'

Tomasz eventually nods.

'I suppose so, but I don't think it's going to be easy to get into that place and the hired thugs have got very twitchy fingers.'

While this conversation has been going on a waitress was clearing the table behind them.

'Je connais un moyen d'entrer,' she whispers.

They all turn to look at her, although only Ellie and Tomasz understand what she's just said.

'Vous parlez anglais?' she whispers.

The girl shrugs.

'A little.'

It turns out that her friend used to work there for the previous owners, but then they died and the chateau had remained empty for a few years, until it was bought last winter.

'Do you know who they are?' asks Ellie.

The girl shakes her head.

'Personne d'ici n'y travaille.'

Ellie looks round at the attentive audience, wondering what else she can ask the girl, who's looking over her shoulder towards the café owner.

'Je dois . . .' she whispers and takes the glasses she's collected and goes back inside.

The others stare at Ellie.

She shrugs and relays what the girl told her, that 'no-one local works there,' . . . but not what the girl said about 'a way in'.

'Well, that fits in with the heavy mob on the front gate,' murmurs Tomasz.

Becket shrugs.

'So . . . we give up?'

It's then that her phone burbles. She answers with a frown not recognising the number.

She listens, her eyes go wide, she listens some more, then the call ends. Six pairs of eyes stare at her. Even Imelda's.

Becket can't help but grin.

'Secret tunnels!' she whispers.

That just makes them all frown.

'Apparently,' she says, 'Ziggy says the chateau was built in the fifteenth century, when tunnels were a 'must have extra' and they're still there because they were used in the second world war by the resistance.'

This doesn't meet with the excitement she was expecting, as at least three people are shaking their heads. Although for some reason Ellie is looking after the waitress.

'That's all very well,' says Fletcher, 'but you'd have to know where the exits and entrances are . . . and presumably the current occupants know this as well.'

Becket speaks again to Ziggy, but he can't confirm or deny that.

But then Ellie gets up and goes inside the restaurant.

The others share glances and frowns, although she's always following leads others don't see.

Inside she asks the girl where the toilets are and takes the opportunity to give her one of the cards Ziggy made for her and whispers 'appel moi.'

Back outside a few minutes later she her phone vibrates.

'J'ai finirai a dix-huit heures, vous me trouverai à Café des Acacias.'

*   *   *

It's mid-morning when Gill and Walker set off to find what she has decided to call the 'Disperados' – as she says they're either auld gimmers or weirdos led on by a very annoying young woman, who can't keep her nose out of police business.

Walker can only smile at that, considering the barely official way Gill goes about 'police business', especially when it's definitely not official and certainly illegal in France.

In the event this proves very easy as they spot them gathered together outside a café in the main square.

Inevitably it is the 'annoying young woman', who sees them first and points at them as they stroll across the road.

This meeting could have been awkward, but Walker puts up his hands and laughs.

'It's a fair cop,' he says. 'Guilty as charged.'

The other party are puzzled by this.

'We're on holiday, taken off the case, sent packing, so we thought we'd do a bit of independent investigation as the brass aren't exactly pleased with our 'working procedures'.

This leaves the other party still confused.

'But you've no authority here,' says Fletcher.

'Correct . . . neither have you,' Gill murmurs.

So, allegiances confirmed, Fletcher suggests they get a couple of chairs and join them. This still gets a few frowns from Ellie and Tomasz, but they both shrug at each other and accept it.

Whilst they're waiting for another round of drinks and coffees, the conversation is stilted. The weather and the locals.

But drinks appear and each party wonders who's going to kick off the real conversation.

Inevitably it's Ellie.

'So, what do you know?'

Walker grins at her.

'Probably less than you . . . but I think the main question is what are the people, who have kidnapped Maria McKinley, going to do next?'

Ellie stares at him, thinking what he might know that they don't. So, she smiles.

'What do you think?'

Walker stares back at her.

'Have you found the chateau she's probably been taken to?'

Ellie glances at Tomasz, who gives her the slightest nod.

'Yeh, but it's heavily guarded and surrounded by impenetrable evergreen forest and electric fences.'

Gill frowns.

'Is that legal . . . here?

Tomasz laughs, but then his face is serious.

'Just like anywhere else . . . there are places like that all over the UK as well, whether its legal or not.'

Walker shrugs, thinking that's probably true. He's not had much experience of mansions and castles, but he's been on quite a few pointless raids of gangsters' properties only to find birds and valuables had flown.

No-one speaks for some time. Lots of looks and glances.

A waitress appears and asks if more drinks are required. Even though it's the holiday period, her boss probably wanting to capitalise on such a big party.

She goes back in with a lengthy list and silence reigns.

Inevitably it's Ellie who begins again. Patience never one of her virtues.

'Well, apparently there are hidden tunnels.'

Gill and Walker both stare at her, whilst her party share glances fearing she's really up for that.

'That counts me out,' says Gill. 'I don't even do wardrobes.'

This gets a few shrugs and sighs from everyone else.

There's then a long silence . . . only interrupted by the arrival of two waitresses with their drinks.

Again, it's Ellie who restarts the conversation.
'Well, personally, I'm up for tunnels . . . but not on my own.'
Fletcher is the first to demur.
'Not me, I'm afraid, too many bad experiences, thank you.'
This quickly followed by Louisa, who can't abide the creatures that hide in them, Ursula who just shakes her head, and Imelda is very stone faced.'
'So,' asks Gill, 'that's . . .' and she counts them off getting nods from Becket, Tomasz and eventually Walker.

But then Ellie shakes her head.
'It's no use unless the waitress tells us how to get into them, where the entrances are.'
'Where is she?' asks Gill looking towards the café.
'Ellie shrugs.
'I'm meeting her in another bar at six thirty.'

This rather deflates the tension and there are a few sighs and slumping shoulders.
'So has anybody done a recce,' asks Walker.
Tomasz can't help grinning.
'Well, I wouldn't call it 'covert'.'
Walker frowns.
Tomasz laughs.
'You know the US general in the 'Dirty Dozen'?'
Walker makes a face, recalling a fat guy driving into battle with a cigar in his mouth, but he nods.
Tomasz shrugs.
'Didn't go down well . . . but it did confirm that they're seriously trigger happy and not bothered about the law.'

Again, this stalls the tension . . . and as no-one else offers any other suggestions, Fletcher catches the eye of the waitress and another round of drinks are ordered and everyone reverts to people watching as the square is getting more crowded.

* * *

Ellie has asked Tomasz to accompany her to meet up with the waitress, who's called Stephanie.

She arrives late and is a bit wary.

Tomasz gives her his best smile, but she glances at Ellie.

Ellie sees this and laughs.

'Don't worry,' she says, 'he might have only one eye, but he's still one of the best long-distance marksmen in the world.'

Stephanie frowns at him, but he just shrugs.

'But that won't help in the tunnels,' she murmurs.

Tomasz's French is good enough to understand that and nods.

Ellie worries this isn't going very well, so asks if she can tell her where the tunnel begins.

She nods and produces a piece of folded paper, unwraps it and flattens it on the table.

Ellie can't help glancing at Tomasz who is frowning at it.

It's very simple. It appears to begin in a small house outside the fence a long way from the main entrance and trails fairly directly to the big house.

'Une ecurie', she whispers, pointing at a square u-shaped building separate from the main house.

'A stable,' translates Ellie, 'pour les chevaux?'

The girl nods.

'Is the little house occupied?' asks Tomasz, pointing at the cottage where the tunnel begins.

Ellie translates.

The girl shakes her head.

'C'est barricade.'

Ellie thinks that means 'boarded up'.

The girl then stands up.

'I go now,' she mutters and hurries away.

Tomasz and Ellie go back to the others and tell them what they know.
Which isn't greeted with much enthusiasm.
So, Ellie asks Louisa to drive her round to see the boarded-up house and Fletcher agrees to go with them.
The rest of them are at a loss to know what to do, so they go off for a look round the town.

MARIA

Maria is lying in bed wide awake.
Last night's nightmare is still too strong a memory to allow her to sleep.
She did sleep for a few hours but suspects it was drug induced, because she didn't dream.
She's always dreamed . . . every night since she can remember, not often nightmares, but when she does have one it's generally the paper corridors and rooms . . . which she knows is because of her grandmother's house.
She was only three when she died, but the paper walls were still there until her mother insisted that they had to go as they were a fire hazard, one of the many rows between her parents. She thinks she was about eight. She recalls the time the nightmare was real, when she was playing hide and seek by herself, whilst her father was somewhere else in the house. One of the towers did fall on her and was so heavy she had difficulty getting out from under them and her father didn't hear her, until she'd rescued herself.
He made her promise not to tell her mother, but she did.

Now a woman has brought her some breakfast, which she wolfs down and still feels empty.
The woman has put her clothes on the chair next to the bed, so she gets up and dresses . . . even though they're

ridiculous. Like somebody in a pantomime . . . more like an ugly sister than Cinderella.

She's standing looking out of the window, which she knows is locked, when there's a knock at the door and a woman comes in and curtsies.

A tall, thin woman with her black hair pulled back into a tight bun.

'Dobroye utro' she says, 'my name is Aline Litvinsky and I've been asked to help you with your Russian.'

Maria frowns.

The woman indicates the chair by the table.

'Shall we sit here?' she asks and brings another chair from the other side.

Without waiting to see whether Maria is going to do this, she sits down and pulls a couple of books out of her bag.

'I understand that you might know a few words, because your father spoke Russian . . .' she murmurs.

Maria stares at her. She reminds her of Miss Gibson at secondary school, all efficient and well meaning, but utterly incapable of handling a bunch of teenagers. Maybe she might be a weak link, someone who she might get information from.

So, she makes a face and reluctantly sits down opposite her.

The next half hour is one of the most boring times she's suffered in her lifetime, although she knows she's never been a good student, because most of the time they're telling you stuff that you already know or could find out about on your mobile anyway – like now, as she knows her Russian is fluent, thanks to her father who started teaching when she was only four.

And the Russian this woman is getting her to speak is nothing like he taught her . . . and gradually she realises she's using a sort of posh version of the language. This becomes more apparent when she starts to correct her pronunciation.

The lesson goes on for ever, but she detects that the haughty attitude is covering something less confident.

'So where in Russia do you come from, miss,' she asks in clumsy Russian.

The woman frowns.

'Well, my family come from Kazan, but I became a translator, so I've lived elsewhere in Russia and other countries.'

'So, why have you come here?' Maria asks, risking a direct question.

The woman stares at her. Is that fear in her eyes?

Maria reaches out with her hand.

The woman looks away.

'It's an honour to be asked,' she whispers, looking back at her.

'An honour?' says Maria, trying not to laugh or sneer.

'Well . . . of course,' the woman says, trying to be strong.

Maria stares hard at her and then reaches out and squeezes her hand.

'So, you believe that I am who these 'people' think I am?'

Aline can't hold her gaze and looks away.

'Do you?'

Maria holds her hand until she looks back at her.

'Of course,' she whispers.

Maria shakes her head.

'What evidence have you seen?'

Aline frowns.

'Your family tree, you're the great granddaughter of Grand Duchess Maria.'

Maria shakes her head.

'Yes, my father believed that and the Russians killed him.'

She sees this is news to her by the frown and the shake of her head.

'It's true, probably the same people who captured me and smuggled me into to France.'

Aline looks away, but then stands up and starts to gather up her things.

Maria reaches for her hand again.

'They're lying to you . . . maybe they're Ukrainians wanting to cause a problem for Putin.'

Aline stops and frowns at her.

'Why do you think that?'

'Well, he wouldn't be pleased, would he? He wouldn't want their murders being dragged up again . . . even if it was his ancestors who were part of the revolution?'

Aline shakes her head.

'You don't understand . . .'

Maria smiles at her and reaches out with her hand.

'Well, you're right about that . . . I can't see how it would help anyone for me to be . . . what?'

She struggles to find the right word.

'Proclaimed?'

Aline stares at her . . . and then bursts into tears.

* * *

MARIYA & ELENA 1918

The train?

She knows it's a train.

She can hear the rattling of the carriages and the clinks when they pass over where two pieces of track meet.

The only window was a small opening high on the side of the carriage, but it was only a few inches wide, enough to refresh the air, but too high to see out.

It must be daytime because there was light coming in, but she can't tell even whether it's fine or raining.

Not cold so not Siberia.

But where are they going?

She tries to shift her position and cries out from the agonising pain striking up from her side and leg.

Then she realises Elena is staring back at her from the other side of the carriage.

Then she remembers . . . the horror of the soldiers slashing at them with their bayonets, the stench of their drink, their eyes blazing with excitement . . .

Elena scrambles over on hands and knees and puts her arms round her.

Eventually, she stops crying and wipes her face.

'We must change clothes,' whispers Elena.

'Why?'

Elena shakes her head.

'You must – you're the only survivor.'

Maria stares at her.

'We're safe with the people on this train, most of them don't know who you are.'

Maria can't help sobbing again.

'And we'll take each other's names . . . you'll be Elena and I'll be Maria.'

Maria frowns, but then nods her understanding.

'Where are we going?'

Elena looks away.

'Anywhere.'

CHAPTER TWENTYONE

URSULA

All this planning makes my head hurt.

Not just because it's so complicated, but because I seem to be the only one who's scared stiff by what's being planned.

Mind you, I noticed that Imelda has her blank face on, which is often a prelude to her disappearing. In all the hustle and bustle Tomasz seems to have forgotten about her and that's not good.

Equally Louisa is quieter than usual, which in some ways is even more surprising. It wouldn't surprise me if she disappears as well.

So, when Tomasz has gathered everyone together in their bedroom, Imelda sits by the window . . . like she just might fly away.

The others have brought some extra chairs while Ellie is on the floor with maps and diagrams laid out ready.

Tomasz brings the meeting to order.

I've never been good at meetings, even though as a secretary I sat through plenty, generally the person who was asked to keep notes and produce a record of who said what, which then went to the manager who deleted lots of stuff he didn't like and then I'd retype it, which was what he wanted them to do in the first place.

This meeting wasn't like that.

Tomasz was good at getting everyone to have a chance to say something even though Imelda just frowned and shook her head.

In the event she got a job, which she seemed to be up for, as the driver for the tunnel team, who will be Tomasz, Becket, Gill and, of course, Ellie who speaks the best French. Thinking about it, this is a pretty fearsome bunch . . . but then Imelda puts her hand up.

Tomasz was the most surprised but asked her what she wanted.

She didn't speak immediately and when she did her voice was so soft, I could hardly hear her.

She said she had an alternative suggestion.

Tomasz nodded.

She looked straight at him.

'How about you cause a distraction instead, while the others go in the tunnel?'

Tomasz frowned.

'What do you mean?'

'Well, as far as we know the only guards are at the main gates, unless there are any other gates?'

Tomasz shrugged and frowned again.

Everyone else is glancing at each other.

'Classic attack procedure,' murmured Becket staring at Tomasz, 'sounds like a military tactic to me.'

Everyone waited.

Tomasz stared back at Becket and then looked round the whole group . . . until the frown disappeared and he laughed, then hugged Imelda, which I imagine is a very scarce event, but she just smiled at us over his shoulder.

Ellie said she'd go straight away to the waitress and ask if she knew about any other gates and whether they were guarded like the main one.

So, the meeting broke up, Fletcher and Louisa going to get a round of drinks.

But this only took ten minutes or so and Ellie came bustling back to say that all the other entrances were closed with huge metal gates which the waitress says she's never seen open.

Tomasz brought the meeting back to order again and agreed to provide a distraction while the others would get in through the boarded-up house.

But again, there was a hand up.

This time it was Gill.

'Sorry to be difficult, but what if the little house is rigged up with alarms or booby traps?'

Everyone's enthusiasm was once more deflated.

Again, Ellie was sent to talk to the waitress.

But, also yet again, she returned with a smile.

'Apparently not,' she said. 'Her younger brother and his mates have been in and found the tunnel, but they were too scared to go any further.'

'So, that's what the plan is . . .'

But then there was another part to it.

What if they get through the tunnel and come out in the stables, how will they know which way to get into the main house and where would they be keeping Maria?

'Ta-dah,' cries Ellie and turns her laptop for everyone to see.

It took some time for everyone to figure out what they were looking at, but gradually realise they are ghostly black and white photographs of various rooms and then a trio of floor plans – including 'les ecuries', horses and riders as well.

It turns out that one of her professors, retired now, whose hobby is collecting plans and photos of castles and grand houses all over Europe. It took him some time until he found it in an old compendium of French Chateaux. He reckons they were taken before the First World War, because the accompanying photos of the family and their servants are the same vintage as the photos of the Russian royal family.

And guess what, it was later owned by a rich Russian family who fled the revolution.

'So do they still own it?' asked Tomasz.

'She shakes her head.

'No, they're all dead . . . Max can't find out who owns it now.'

My head was spinning by now so I said I was going to have a lie down. Partly down to too much wine I expect, so I slept through to the events that happened that afternoon.

* * *

The tunnel team, Walker replacing Tomasz, set off first.

Tomasz was going to set up and wait for a signal from Fletcher and Louisa, who would go to the gates and pretend they were lost, so they could gauge the number of guards.

The tunnel team would wait for the signal from Tomasz, who would already be in position by one of the trees at the entrance to the driveway, after Fletcher and Louisa had returned safely, before entering the little house.

Imelda was backup for Tomasz because there wasn't much cover for him at the entrance.

This all took half an hour, even though Ellie confirmed that they'd got into the little house, easier than they thought, as they were able to get in the same way as the young lads.

Which is why they didn't hear the message to abort.

Tomasz is starting to think something is wrong when Louisa and Fletcher were coming back a lot faster than they went.

Their car pulls up.

Fletcher stumbles out, white faced.

'They're all dead!' he gasps.

Tomasz stares at him.

'Who?'

'The . . . guards,' he splutters. 'Riddled with bullets.'

Tomasz can't take it in.

'But . . . all of them?'

It's then he notices Louisa, hands gripping the wheel.

He tells Fletcher to look after Louisa and gets on the mobile to tell Ellie.

No reply!?

At which point the French version of the 'Keystone cops' arrive.

Three Citroens and a riot van complete with mothballs.

Tomasz quickly realises that this isn't a moment for either heroics or stories so tells Imelda to get out of the car and put her hands up. Fletcher is also doing the same, but Louisa was still immobile in the driving seat.

This causes the police to be a bit over the top, until Fletcher tells them he'd help her out, because she is in shock.

Uncertainly and with lots of guns trained on them, they allow this, but then the couple are pushed roughly into the van.

Then the same happens to Tomasz and Imelda . . . although his gun causes a lot of excitement and is very carefully put in the inspector's car.

Then they were driven away with screaming alarms back to the station.

The detachment left carefully approach the gates and find the bodies.

The inspector coming up in the rear trying to direct the operation, but this becomes unnecessary when they realise that they are all dummies.

He orders them to search the guardhouse, they discover a young woman who is hiding, whimpering, in a cupboard.

She is in a such a state of shock they can't get any sense from her, so they put her in the captain's car and the driver told to take her to hospital.

By now the captain has called for reinforcements and the sirens could be soon heard wailing in the distance.

It was only then that the officers could allow themselves to look at each other and shrug their shoulders.

*   *   *

Ellie's tunnel gang have no idea about what has happened at the gates. They are too busy scuttling along the tunnel.

They are all having to move bent double because it was built for dwarves. Now and then, there are rock falls and collapsed roofs, but they are all passable by crawling, even though that is a bit scary.

They are able to make sure they can get back the same way, because Gill had brought her climbing ropes, but she is eventually coiling out the third one, when Becket who is at the front whispers to be quiet.

At first, they can't hear anything, but then there is unmistakeable sound of someone coming towards them.

Becket directs them to take as much cover as they can, which is almost impossible, other than flattening themselves against the walls or the occasional post.

And then she tells them to turn off their torches, leaving just her with her mobile on.

The sounds get closer and then there is the flickering of a torch.

*   *   *

MARIA

After the tears neither of them could speak.

Maria had eventually put her arms round the girl and waited until she stopped shivering.

But then neither of them can think what to say or do.

Now Maria is standing at the window.

Aline eventually stops sniffing.

'Well, I suppose I'd better go,' she whispers.

Maria shrugs, but then stiffens and then backs away from the window . . . and now they can both hear the sounds of gunfire and screams.

Maria comes further back into the room.

Aline is terrified.

'They're fighting each other,' Maria whispers.

Aline shakes her head.

Maria is looking round the room . . . for a weapon? Somewhere to hide?

Nothing like a weapon, of course, but then she spies the cupboard by the side of the fireplace.

She hasn't looked in it before, but now she opens the door to see empty shelves.

It might seem pointless, but she knocks the shelves out and places them behind the settee.

'Come on,' she whispers, and stepping inside, beckons Aline to join her.

She hesitates until there's the sound of shooting outside the room, then runs to join her. They hunker down and pull the doors shut.

Only just in time.

They hear the door burst open. Heavy steps and shouting.

Then really loud gunfire, shouts and screams and thudding of bodies.

Silence.

One voice, speaks quietly, but harsh.

Russian?

They can't see each other and are now trying not to move or hardly breathe.

The voice now loud and angry, ordering the others to 'find them'.

Other orders are given and the rustling of bodies leaving the room eventually stops and the two girls are left trembling in disbelief that they're still alive.

But even though they think no one's there they daren't move, until Maria tries to move away from whatever is sticking into her back.

In doing this there's an audible click and she falls backwards into space.

She doesn't fall far and realises she's lying on a stone surface which disappears into further darkness.

She switches the light on her bracelet.

It's not very bright and they can't see much further, but it's obviously some kind of hiding place. She vaguely remembers her daffy History teacher, Miss Wilson, wittering on about priest holes, which was far more interesting than her usual boring delivery.

She points the light further in and they can see it isn't a very big space, and not high enough to stand up in. Other than that, there's nothing there.

She shuffles in as quietly as she can, reaches up to find that the roof will only allow her to crouch.

But then her foot bumps into to something on the floor.

She feels for it and finds a heavy metal ring, covered in dust and mouse droppings.

She shines her bracelet at it and fingers the dust away.

It's stiff and obviously not used for a long time, but eventually with Aline's help they pull it out and then manage to gradually lift up the slab hoping this might be a way out.

What they find is a set of steps going downwards.

First Maria and then Aline crawl down the cold wooden steps into the darkness.

The bracelet torch can barely light the next step so they can't see how deep it's going to be.

Then Maria whispers to her.

'My room is on the first floor, yeh?'

Aline nods and then whispers 'yes, but . . .'

Maria shines the light at her.

'But what?'

'The kitchens are in the old cellars underground.'

Maria sighs, thinking that's where they'll come out.

But no.

They keep going down until Aline thinks they must be lower than that.

And now they've reached the bottom.
The steps end.
Another door.

Really old.
Maria tries the handle.
It turns but it doesn't open.

She grunts with frustration.
There's a keyhole.
But no key.
She shines the light around and back up the steps.
'Where could it be?' she grumbles.
Aline's face is just blank, beyond frightened.
Maria tells herself to stop and think, like her dad taught her. She used to find his mind games rather tedious and not as hard as he thought they were.
So where have they put the key?
She fingers along the top of the door jamb and then the walls either side . . . nothing, so that must mean?
She fingers the slabs on the floor. Nothing.
So, she turns and looks back along the tunnel, which is supported by hefty wooden posts.
She goes to the first one and fingers along the top and the sides. Then the second one.
And feels the metal hiding in a hollow.
Retrieves it and gives it a kiss, which isn't a good idea, getting ages old dust in her mouth.
Spitting it out she can't help but giggle, which only makes Aline stare at her like she's mad.
But . . . the door opens and the bracelet light shows a tunnel going into the darkness.

Maria shivers, but carries on, thinking where on earth might this come out.
In the middle of the forest?

It seems like for ever, but probably only half an hour or so, when they hear noises.
Maria turns the light off.
She listens.

Voices?

They're whispering.

Can't make out what they're saying, but then she realises they're speaking English, not Russian or French?

Who could they be?

She takes a deep breath and whispers back.

'Hello?'

It's only then she realises Aline isn't behind her anymore.

MASHA

Is that my mother calling?

Where is she?

Where am I?

A carriage?

Rough voices. Not soldiers?

Not <u>those</u> soldiers.

Where is she?

Where's Elena?

Then the pain comes again and she faints – dropping through a veil of blood . . .

AFTERWORDS

URSULA

As usual I missed most of the excitement.
I woke up when I heard voices in the next room. Took my time getting dressed and eventually found them all sitting downstairs in the café as it was raining heavily outside.
The conversation dwindled to a silence as they all turned to look at me as though they'd forgotten who I was, which is not the first time that's happened to me.
'Where to start . . .' muttered Becket, which made Fletcher cough.
'Er . . . you do remember we've signed government documents to not say anything to anybody about what . . . happened.'
I looked from one to the other.
A few sad smiles, a couple of shrugs and Louisa giving me that stare that you don't want in your direction.
I don't know what to do or say.
Fletcher gets up and offers me a chair.
I sit down.
He asks me what I'd like to drink and I ask for a cup of tea, then remember we're in France, so I suggest a milky coffee.

Ziggy hadn't followed much of it either, apart from police cars rushing about and the panic of lots of calls.
The whole event then became ushered into highly secret channels, which even he found difficult to penetrate or follow.
Nothing in the press anywhere, never mind the French . . . and silence from the Russians, not even a dismissive sneer or two?

When we got back home Ziggy was able to show us a few awful images of the carnage in that big house. Bodies everywhere, blood all over the carpets and the walls.

He'd found this on a Russian émigré channel, but then that was taken down as well after a few hours and later he thinks it was a staged event . . . that they weren't real bodies.

He'd also done some extensive research into the murders of the Romanov royal family, including the lengthy investigation into Anna Anderson's claim to be Princess Anastasia, which concluded that she was an imposter. He couldn't find anything about Maria, so he reluctantly gave up looking.

Tomasz and Imelda's homecoming was difficult. Amelia's son had been spoken to by some detectives, who weren't local, about accessing sensitive information from government sites. Amelia was furious, blaming Tomasz and Ziggy and everyone else for encouraging him to join in with their 'stupid spy games'.

So, Magda was more than relieved to be told she could go back to work.

Walker and Gill were reassigned back to Edinburgh, but in separate teams . . . although they were seen together in a restaurant behaving more than just friendly.

Louisa kept saying to anyone who would listen, that she was too old for all of this 'detectoring', whilst Fletcher could be seen nearly every day talking to his heron. What they discussed no-one knows.

My relationship with Janet seems to be continuing, although I do find sex every day becoming a bit of a marathon . . . not that I'm complaining, just wishing it had happened earlier in my life.

Ziggy is disappointed . . . no, disbelieving, that he can't find anything about what happened at the chateau on any wavelength or any government sites anywhere in the world!

Maria was finally reunited with her mother, although they haven't communicated with anyone else since . . . Ziggy says they will probably be given different names and life histories and end up somewhere else, hopefully where no-one can ever find them.

He also mutters that he now thinks the whole business, including the set up in the chateau was all smoke and mirrors and definitely not real.

When I eventually asked why, he just frowned and then smiled.

'There are more things in heaven and earth, Horatio, than are dreamt of in your philosophy.'

And I know where that quote comes from, because I was made to read 'Hamlet' in the sixth form . . . but it still doesn't help . . . just confirms that even clever people often don't have any more of a clue than the rest of us . . . they just don't want to admit it.

* * *

A long beach, waves rippling further and further up the sand.
The winter sun just touching the horizon, washing the sea and the sky in rose and mauve.

Two figures.

One slowly walking along in the ripples, shoes in her hand.

The other, standing looking out to sea, his shoes still on his feet, now filling with sandy water.

His face, minus the eye patch, the shadow hiding the wound.

He reaches up to touch it.

Only the other eye can weep now.

POSTSCRIPT

There have been numerous investigations and thousands of pages written about the demise of the Russian royal family.

The dismissal of the claims by Anna Anderson are well documented and recent discoveries included the exhumation of
Anastasia's and Maria's bodies
. . . but they were too degraded to be scientifically confirmed . . .
so . . .